Krissi was born in Yorkshire and now lives in Dorset on the Isle of Purbeck with her husband, Bob. After spending the last 20 years in the world of estate agency, she is now retired. So, with the family grown up, she is free to spend her time indulging in her love of walking, gardening, volunteering and, at last, her passion for writing.

For my daughter, Lisa, and step-daughter, Alison, who together are a constant inspiration and support to me.

Krissi Morris

WHEN SPARKS FLY

Mary

Enjoy

Krissi Morris

AUSTIN MACAULEY PUBLISHERS™

LONDON · CAMBRIDGE · NEW YORK · SHARJAH

A CIP catalogue record for this title is available from the British Library.

ISBN 9781528983044 (Paperback)
ISBN 9781528983051 (ePub e-book)

www.austinmacauley.com

First Published (2020)
Austin Macauley Publishers Ltd
25 Canada Square
Canary Wharf
London
E14 5LQ

Writing for me, like many, began as a hobby: writing short stories that soon became an obsession. I am thrilled with this—my second novel. Special thanks to my husband, Bob, who patiently listens and encourages me. Thanks again to Clair Bossons, for her proofreading skills and advice.

Chapter 1

Molly gently squeezed her mother's arm as they stood staring into the open grave, watching as the coffin slowly slipped down with its shining brass plate declaring that her father was inside, gone forever. The vicar droning on 'ashes to ashes', she wanted to scream 'that's my dad in there'. The vicar, who should have retired years ago, had condensed her dad's life into ten minutes of platitudes. He was more than that. Her throat constricted with pain as she swallowed her grief, it wasn't as though they were close, in fact, Molly could hardly remember much about him, as he was always out in the fields when she woke up in the morning and often she was in bed when he came in at night. She still felt an aching loss, wishing that she had known him better. Her mother had whisked him away to live in Spain as soon as he was too ill to work and had to give up the farm. Her mother never really wanted to just be a farmer's wife, preferring to keep her part-time job in the village at the hairdresser's.

She shuddered as a cold wind rushed around her legs, bringing her back to the hole in the ground, to reality.

She dropped a long-stemmed white rose onto the coffin. It had to be white as her dad was; forever a fiercely strong Yorkshire man. She whispered 'Goodbye'. The other mourners followed a gentle *thud* as each rose fell onto the coffin, a tangled mix of colour and thoughts.

The small group of mourners glanced awkwardly at each other, itching to leave and find somewhere warmer. An occasional sniff broke the silence but the birds were singing their hearts out. Molly instinctively looked up just as the sun broke through. She smiled, hoping that it was her father looking down on them, but knowing it could not be. She shivered as the weak sun attempted to warm her, failing miserably. April can be warm and sunny, but today the cold crisp air matched her mood. The daffodils already drooping as the primroses smiled and the bluebells began to push forth, their scent filling the air. Her sister, Stella, caught her eye, indicating that they should leave. Molly obliged.

***

"I've made up my mind," said Sandra, turning to look at her two daughters. Not one for patience, she would often make announcements that stunned everyone around her, making her unpredictable. Like the time before Molly was born when Sandra had wanted to leave Yorkshire and move to Dorset, regardless of what Dad wanted. To Molly's dismay, Sandra was not the warmest of mothers.

"About what?" they declared in unison. Molly and Stella glanced at each other and back to Sandra, wondering what revelation she had for them now. They were used to her sudden declarations, often bizarre, but totally 'her'. The Aga gently warmed the big old farmhouse kitchen, polite conversation buzzed around the room, with Rex hiding in his basket trying to avoid feet. His tongue sloshed around his lips and he gulped at the sight and smells of all that food, but he remained curled up protectively in his bed.

"Come on, Mum, you can't just say that and leave us hanging." Molly, fearing the worst, crouched down next to her mum stroking her hand, wondering what was coming their way this time. Their mother was not known for being realistic and did things on a whim far too often; like her sudden decision to move to Spain. Rex ventured out of his corner and slid his nose onto her lap. She ruffled his ears absentmindedly and Rex gave an appreciative lick.

"It's a bit soon to make any decisions, don't you think?" she asked, tentatively looking up at Stella and rolling her eyes.

Sandra pulled out a handkerchief, dabbing her cheeks and sniffing. Molly had seen this tactic so many times, she relaxed, turning her attention to Alistair. They had held a surprise wedding the previous autumn on Studland beach and Jessica was born a few months later in December. She was so grateful that her dad had lived long enough to see her married and Jessica born.

Alistair was cooing gently, gazing at his baby daughter, love and affection pouring from him and she was gazing back at him with her big blue eyes. She watched as he stroked her tiny tuft of russet and gold curls. Alistair looked up and grinned mouthing, 'I love you'. George, her father-in-law, caught her attention as he was doing his best to balance a cup of tea and eat a sandwich at the same time. She jumped in to rescue the rattling cup just as Alice began fussing over George and everyone else. Her mother-in-law, Alice, had a natural mothering instinct, although some would say interfering and overbearing. Molly couldn't help a grin spreading across her face and bit her lip to hold it back as Alistair shrugged, hand on one hip, but he said nothing to his mother throwing a smirk in Molly's direction instead.

"No, sorry girls, but I will not change my mind. I've thought of nothing else and I'm going back to Spain." Molly and Stella looked at each other in exasperation. Molly raised her eyebrows. Sandra only ever did what suited Sandra and this idea was no exception. "The villa hasn't sold and I miss our friends. We had a good life, your dad and I, in Spain and, let's be honest, there's nothing to keep me here. I might just as well go back." She made to get up putting an end to the subject saying, "You have your lives and we are both proud of you. but you have to understand that I need, no want, to live mine too. So that's the end of it." Sandra moved away and began talking to the other mourners who had come back to the farm. Molly and Stella were gobsmacked. Of all the things she could have said, this would take some beating and not what they were expecting at all.

"I don't like to think of Mum going back to Spain on her own, but…" Molly picked up a mug of tea and took a sip. "Yuk, sugar, must be yours, Stella?" She laughed and pulled the kettle onto the hot plate to make a fresh pot of tea.

"You're right, I worry too, but you know Mum; once she's made up her mind, we might as well give in." Stella tried the tea, "Mmm, must be mine. We should talk later. I don't think that it would do any good right now, not when she's like this." Heaving a sigh, Molly agreed.

"I'm sure that it will be a few weeks before she goes anyway and she may yet change her mind." Although Molly struggled to believe her own sentiment, knowing her mother very rarely changed her mind.

They headed towards the food. Molly watched her sister as she picked up some sandwiches and inspected the cakes. Stella had her own successful business making mainly wedding cakes but she also made birthday cakes or anything that people wanted really. She had quite a reputation for her designs using edible flowers and had started growing them herself. Her creations were stunning and she had appeared in magazines and been interviewed on local radio. Molly made her tea and waved her mug at Alistair who shook his head, rubbing his stomach making her giggle. She wandered over towards him but was caught by Alice.

"Molly dear, how are you coping? So much has happened in these last few months, getting married, having a baby and now your poor father…" Alice smiled encouragingly at her and Molly knew that she meant well, but she had missed out in her long list, coping with a new mother-in-law too. Molly was always careful with her reply as Alice often asked 'trick' questions.

"I couldn't have managed without Alistair; he has been wonderful," she spotted him, hoping for rescue, but he was clearly trying to free himself from his own mother-in-law, Sandra. "Sorry, Alice, I think Alistair needs me and Jessica will be ready for her feed. I'll catch up with you later." She slipped away from Alice and made her way towards them needing a hug from her two favourite people.

"Molly, thank goodness I don't think Jess would be able to wait any longer, she's starving!" He curled his arm around her waist squeezing her, gently nuzzling her neck and whispered, "I can't wait to get you alone, Mrs Warren; what do you say we get out of here?"

"Another day, another time." She leaned over and kissed him, whisking Jessica out of his arms, avoiding the electricity that shot through her at the thought of Alistair's warm kisses.

"I'll take her upstairs; can you help Bertie and Lucy please? They look like they could do with some," Molly grinned at him and turned to find Sandra blocking her way.

"Why don't you let me do that for you? I would love to take care of my granddaughter before I go back to Spain," her smile, sugary sweet, merely straightening her lips. Molly knew that look only too well, her mother was very good at getting her own way, but Molly was in no mood for giving in, not today.

"… And whose fault is that, Mum?" she snapped. "You don't have to go to Spain, you could stay here and see ALL your grandchildren more and no, you can't take Jess; I am breast-feeding, remember?" aiming a barb she knew wouldn't penetrate her mother's crusty exterior. Grabbing her bag, she made for the stairs, leaving Sandra open-mouthed. Molly was sick of her mother thinking that she was always right and doing as she wished, expecting everyone else to meekly fall in step without arguing. No, this was one battle she was not going to win. She crept into her old bedroom with a wriggling, crying Jessica. She cooed quietly as she organised herself to change Jessica's nappy. The door opened and in walked Lucy, "… Am I glad to see you." Molly beamed up at her best friend. Lucy had been fantastic, taking the pressure away from Molly, organising the food, getting flowers, a thousand and one little things that had helped with the trauma of the last few weeks. They knew each other so well that Molly could always rely on Lucy.

"Thought that I might escape too, just for five minutes, Alistair and Bertie seem to have the food and drinks under control, how about you? How are you doing?" she asked, sitting on the side of the bed. Jessica was now suckling contentedly and Molly sat by the window on an old nursing chair inherited from her grandmother, rocking gently.

"Mother has decided that she is going back to Spain. In some ways I'm pleased, she can be a bit pushy, you know she knows best and I'm useless. She can be infuriating at times," she laughed. "But I can't help worrying, she will be on her own, it's not the same as when dad was there." Molly had never ventured over to Spain to see them feeling abandoned and she consoled herself with the fact that she was too busy to 'pop over' to Spain.

"I know what you mean, but you will have to let her find out for herself. She'll be back, you'll see." Lucy turned to tidy away the detritus of baby changing. Molly wasn't so sure.

She leaned back in her chair looking out over the farmyard. The hens were scratching around, clucking and pecking at the dry earth. Her gaze led her to her beloved allotment, it was getting overgrown. She had neglected it since Jessica's birth and her father being so ill. She turned back at Lucy.

"… And what about the farm? I moved out to suit Mum and now she's going back to Spain," she said, her voice rising. "I suppose, being selfish, I would like her to stay but also thinking about it what would she do? I can't blame her in a way, but still…" Molly turned her attention to Jessica hiding the tears that threatened to let her down. Lucy sat quietly watching. "I know Alistair's flat isn't ideal, but it is above his business, oh, I don't know, I'm beginning to lose the plot myself. I can't bear to think of the farm empty and neglected and then there's Rex!" she let out a gasp in frustration, lifting Jessica onto her shoulder and patting her back.

"Anyway, enough about me and my woes. Come on, I'm dying to hear about you and Bertie," she said, changing the subject.

Lucy and Bertie had finally got together last year after Molly and Alistair's wedding, disappearing off to Oz for a month. Lucy had a couple of part-time jobs, but really needed something full time and poor Bertie had reluctantly started working for Alistair again. It was obvious that his heart wasn't in it anymore.

"Everything is just great; I'm thinking of asking him to move in with me. Well, it is silly of him still living in the cottage and now that the season is starting, he will have to leave very soon anyway. So, I thought, why not?" Lucy shrugged her shoulders, throwing Molly a sly smirk.

"… And what about his other plans, I know he didn't want to work for Alistair again, but do you think he is happy or pining for something new?" Molly changed Jessica into a very pretty pink dress that George and Alice had bought her when she was born. It had embroidered pink rose buds along the edge of the hem, Alice's favourite flowers. She picked her up and gave her a cuddle before settling her into her crib.

"He doesn't know yet, he really enjoyed doing up my place and he loves gardening but you can't make a living out of that, can you, as hard as he might try?" She looked gloomily down at her feet before brightening up again. "I have an interview next week in Poole hospital. I am keeping my fingers crossed. I need full-time work too. It's not that I didn't enjoy my caring job but the pay is awful, the other girls are lovely, I don't know how they do it and as for the garden centre…" she rolled her eyes, "my allergy has left my eyes streaming all the time, I'm not green-fingered like you," she sniffed as if to further make the point. "I will not miss it one bit." They both laughed as they crept out of the room leaving Jessica fast asleep. Alistair met them at the bottom of the stairs, his eyes flashing wildly as he gasped.

"Thank goodness, I was just coming to find you. Your mother is attempting to make a speech." Molly quickly squeezed passed him and into the kitchen to find Sandra gesticulating melodramatically, panic gripped her, as her mother could be announcing anything.

"So, thank you all again for coming. I have already informed Stella and Molly that I have made up my mind and I'm going back to Spain to live." There was murmuring all around the kitchen. Molly looked at Stella for help, but she was beaten to it by Sandra. "I love living in Spain, it's my home now and I have decided to sign the farm over to Molly and the holiday cottage to Stella," she turned and looked at the girls one to the other, both stunned, staring back at her. "You two can decide what you want to do with them, I'm going to pack and leave tomorrow." In a final flourish, she left the room and loud chatter ensued.

"I'm sorry, Molly," said Stella. "I had no idea she was going to do that." Stella squeezed her arm by way of apology and resignation, as it was impossible to argue with their mother so used to getting her own way.

"Me either. Now what are we going to do?" Molly had no idea what this new situation might entail and how they were going to deal with it. It had always been assumed that Molly would inherit the farm as she had always loved it and worked it and Stella had no interest in it at all, preferring to bake cakes.

"I suggest we get together next week after Mum has gone and try to sort this mess out. Can you come up to me one day as I have a major order on and I've already taken too much time out?" *Ever the sensible one,* thought Molly as she agreed. People began to leave and Molly and Lucy cleared the tables, Alistair picked up Rex's lead and Rex leapt from his basket needing no further encouragement and followed Alistair and Bertie out into the farmyard.

"Let's get out of here," he said to Bertie, shooting a grin at Molly. She watched them as they trudged through the farmyard and down the lane towards the woods wishing she could be with them. The woods are wonderful at this time of year with birds busy building nests and the trees bursting into bud and blossom.

15

"Look, Molly, we need to get back home," Stella broke into her daydream. "If you're sure you can manage, we'll go." She picked up her coat, helping Abigail and Tabitha with theirs. "The girls are getting fractious. Call me next week, okay?"

"Yes, of course, you go and I'll call you later." They disappeared and Molly raised her eyebrows at Lucy. "Looks like you and me again," she gave a stilted laugh and began to shake as the tears of exhaustion rolled down her cheeks. Lucy dashed over to comfort her and guided her to the settee.

"Sit here, I'll get you a drink." She poured a slug of brandy and handed it to Molly. "Come on, drink this."

"I can't, Jessica, remember." Molly blew her nose, looking up at Lucy pleadingly.

"Yes, you can, just this once. For medicinal purposes, of course." Molly took the glass and sipped. She half smiled at Lucy and took a bigger gulp. Lucy sat down beside her, handing her the box of tissues. "Do you want to talk or I can clear up while you put your feet up for a while?"

"You're a good friend, Lucy, do you mind if I just take five minutes?" Molly lifted her feet up onto the couch and Lucy pulled the red fleece, scattered with holly and snowflakes, a gift at Christmas, over her. Molly's eyes fell shut instantly.

* * *

Lucy began to clear away the dishes, putting cakes into tins and chairs back into the dining room. She stood surveying the room, it was one that she had admired since the first time she came through that stable door. The Aga was always warm and inviting, the welsh dresser a mishmash of plates and china from every era, mainly blue and white but the odd pink mug, the 'world's greatest mum' written on it and some old letters and photographs stuffed in between where they were tumbling out, forgotten. She let out a sigh and turned on the taps in the big old butler sink; she pulled on the marigolds and tried to be quiet as Molly had nodded off to sleep. An hour later, Molly stirred and looked at Lucy, rubbing her eyes.

"Better?" asked Lucy with a grin, waving a mug in her direction.

16

"How long have I been asleep? I am so sorry, I only meant to have five minutes."

"I know but I'm not surprised you were exhausted. I'll make a pot of coffee and before you ask… Jessica is fine; she is still asleep so you stay right where you are." Lucy busied herself with the coffee and two slices of cake. "I noticed that you didn't eat much earlier, so come on, eat up and tell me what is going through your mind."

Chapter 2

Lucy had a precious morning off from the care home, deciding to visit her mum and dad who lived in Trentmouth, a few miles from Wareham. She pulled up outside the cottage, the wisteria was in bud clinging and climbing its way over the front porch. Lucy beamed to herself; she had always loved this place with its tiny windows and pokey rooms. The cottage had been extended many years ago before the war and a shop created. It had been a bakery, post office and now her mother ran it as a general store. The door was open making Lucy smile; her mum loved that shop, it had become her life. It had metal buckets stuffed with flowers on the doorstep and a sign proclaiming the latest news. Not that much ever happened in Trentmouth and that's how they liked it. The windows looked grubby and she could see cobwebs on the inside floating in the breeze that wafted in through the open door. Lucy decided to go and see her dad first, he would be tinkering in the workshop with some lump of metal or other. He volunteered part time on the Swanage steam railway. He loved it, doing any task that came his way from sweeping the platform, working in the ticket office or getting covered in oil trying to fix something on an engine. To her surprise, he was sitting by the inglenook in the sitting room, his head in his hands.

"Dad... what's wrong?" she dropped her bag onto the settee by the door, dashing over to him, squeezing onto the edge of the couch and putting an arm around his shoulders.

"It's your mum, Lucy, love, she is getting so forgetful and I am worried about her." He turned to look at Lucy, his eyes red giving away his sense of concern. He looked tired, his shoulders sagged as he shook his head in despair. Lucy instantly felt concern; her father was never like this normally, but he had clearly not shaved and his clothes were crumpled and grubby. Thoughts of him being ill flashed through her mind.

"Being forgetful is hardly surprising, Dad, she works hard in that shop, she looks after you and it can't be easy. Why don't you offer to help her a bit? Look, let me put the kettle on, I'll take Mum a coffee and we can see what we can do." Lucy took some mugs out of the cupboard, switched the kettle on and was rather surprised to find that there was a pile of dirty dishes in the sink; not like her mum at all. She rolled up her sleeves and set to work, washing, clearing and tidying the kitchen. Her dad had not moved when she returned with his coffee and a chocolate digestive. "Here you are, Dad, I will take one through to Mum and will see you in a bit, okay?" She laid out a tray and carried it next door.

***

"Hello, Mum, I've brought you a coffee, how are you?" She wandered into the shop, kicking a bag of potatoes and nearly spilling the drinks. "Where should these potatoes be, Mum? I nearly fell over them; they shouldn't be here by the door." She gave her mum a hug and kissed her cheek.

"Hello, love, how nice to see you, they are alright there. I've nowhere else to put them anyway. I'm ready for that coffee though; what with your dad being down Swanage, I haven't had time to make one." Lucy opened her mouth to tell her that Dad was next door, but changed her mind, wondering how forgetful her mum had really become, concern growing.

"I have the morning off today, so I thought that I would come and help you. I could clean the windows if you like." She looked around the shop, everywhere was untidy, tins were piled on the floor, newspapers still tied up with string, the calendar hanging up behind the till was last years. Lucy let out a long sigh, saying, "Oh, dear. Mum, look, do you want to go next door for half an hour with your coffee and put your feet up? I can look after the shop; it's quiet and I can take care of things for you."

"Alright, love. I am tired. It's getting harder to look after the shop and your dad's no help at all. See you later." Lucy watched her mum slowly trudge back to the cottage noticing that she still had her slippers on, raising alarm bells shrilly in her ears. She turned back to survey the enormous task of sorting out the shop shaking her head, wondering if her mum was just truly exhausted or something else more sinister.

"Where do I start?" Lucy asked herself, scanning the shop. She picked up her coffee and munched a chocolate digestive, she realised that she had rather neglected her mum recently and had no idea that the shop was becoming such a clutter. Behind the desk was an old battered stool and Lucy plopped herself down with an enormous sigh. There were cobwebs everywhere and bits of rubbish littered the floor. The magazines were curling at the edges, well-thumbed and out of date. Birthday cards shoved into a twirling stand all higgledy-piggledy, a tray of fresh bread and cakes had been left on top of the newspapers and a fly was buzzing around, she gave a swipe at it and missed. Her iPhone gave out a tune, playing 'This is the life' merrily. She knew it was Bertie and thought how ironic to hear that tune, she grinned to herself flicking her hair as she placed it to her ear.

"Hi. What are you up to on your morning off?" he asked cheerfully. She began to relay the story to him, watching the fly as it flew straight into a spider's web. It began to get entangled and fought to free itself, getting more caught up.

"I don't know where to start, to be honest, everything needs doing and I'm just sitting here, staring at it."

"Well, why not start right where your feet are and move forward from there?" he said helpfully.

"Good idea, I have to work myself later, but I can at least make a start. Do you fancy coming over tonight and I will make dinner?"

"No, why don't you come over to me and I will cook. Oops, sorry, the other phone is ringing, talk later." Bertie had gone, but the thought of him cooking and a cosy evening in cheered her. She found a black sack and started filling it with old papers and magazines, clearing the counter. It was a lovely old mahogany display cabinet with glass doors, inside were children's beach toys, buckets and spades, bundles of paper flags, net bags filled with shells, plastic bats, tennis balls and Frisbee's. A loud tinkling noise brought Lucy off her knees as someone entered the shop and tripped over the bag of potatoes. Lucy jumped up, thinking that moving that sack had to be her next job.

"Alice! Are you alright?" She nipped around the counter to steady poor Alice who looked dazed for a minute.

"Yes, dear, I'm fine, no bones broken. What are you doing here?" She smiled warmly, placing her own bags on the floor, now making it almost impossible to walk around the shop at all.

"Just giving Mum a break, as I'm not due to start my shift till 2. What can I get you today?"

"Well, I just came in to catch up with the latest gossip, and get some bread. Have you heard any more about poor Sandra, is she alright in Spain? Molly keeps you up-to-date, I'm sure." Alice turned to sit down on the chair by the counter. She pulled out her handkerchief and gave a flick at the dust before settling herself with a smile on her lips. Lucy raised her eyes, shrugging as she watched this little performance.

"I don't know, to be honest, I haven't seen Molly since the funeral. I must go and see her, but I'm sure she's fine. Which loaf do you usually have, Alice?"

"Oh, I'll have a small malted brown loaf today and I was wondering if your mum would take a few copies of the *Parish* magazine for me. It is the AGM soon and we are having a meeting about finding a new vicar, now old Reverend Sykes is retiring." Lucy saw her precious time disappearing fast, normally she would love to chat to Alice, but today she cut her short.

"Yes, that will be fine, Alice, just leave them on the top of the counter. I'll find somewhere to put them. That's 75 pence for the loaf, please." Alice paid for her bread and departed the shop with a clear harrumph of disappointment. Lucy felt guilty at getting rid of her so quickly and really did not have an update about Sandra, something else she felt guilty about. The bell clanged again and a man stood there, carrying a briefcase and holding a folder.

He wore a dark suit with a white shirt and a rather jazzy, multi-patterned tie that was slightly skewed. His straw-coloured hair had been blown about in the wind, making him look dishevelled, but rather attractive. Lucy smiled at him.

"Oh," he said, "I was looking for Mrs Hamilton, is she here?"

"Sorry, she's having a few hours off, can I help you?" Lucy was intrigued.

"Err, yes, I represent the makers of 'Lovely Legs' stockings and tights…" he pointed to yet another twirling stand that was overflowing with all manner of things as well as the 'Lovely Legs', "…and I was wondering if Mrs Hamilton needed more stock. It's a courtesy visit actually, and you are?" He walked across the shop, holding out a hand towards Lucy. She shook his hand, pushing a wisp of hair behind her ear.

"I'm Lucy, but as you can see, there is plenty of stock. I don't think that tights and stockings are as popular as they used to be, perhaps you can leave your card and I'll make sure that Mum gets it." He pulled out a card and handed it to her. Lucy glanced at his name and looking up, she said, "Okay, Jasper... thanks." She couldn't help herself grinning as Jasper headed for the door. He stopped with his hand on the latch and turned, he threw her a wide smile.

"Thanks, Lucy. Nice to meet you, maybe I'll see you next time. I'm in the area." He closed the door.

"What a smoothie," she laughed to herself, placing his card in her jeans' pocket. The next few hours Lucy busied herself sorting out the shop, clearing out out-of-date stock, cleaning windows and shelves. She filled black sacks with all manner of rubbish, placing them in the boot of her car, ready for the refuse centre. There were, however, no more customers and Lucy began to worry about the shop takings, making a mental note to have a look at the books. Time passed quickly, with no sign of her mother's return. Feeling quite pleased with her morning's work, she glanced at her watch and slipped next door to find her mother.

"Hello, Lucy dear, what are you doing here?" said her mother. Lucy raised her eyebrows in disbelief as her mouth dropped open.

"Hmm... come to see you, Mum, I've been looking after the shop for you."

"The shop... but it's Sunday, the shop is closed, you don't need to do that, come and have a cup of tea and we can have a nice chat." Lucy glanced at her dad who just shrugged his shoulders, shaking his head.

"Well, actually I have to get to work now myself and it's Monday, Mum. I'll pop back later." She turned to leave, "... And Dad, the shop door is open." Lucy walked down the garden path, tears stinging her eyes. Her mobile buzzed and she pulled it out, not recognising the number. "Hello," she almost whispered and a voice said,

"Miss Hamilton, this is Poole Maternity Hospital. I'm ringing to offer you the full-time post of a midwife here in Poole."

***

Alice flounced into the kitchen dropping her bags onto the floor with a clatter. She grabbed the kettle to fill it up, she needed a coffee, urgently. She stared out of the window fuming; not even the sight of her colour-filled garden eased the anger she felt inside. She pulled out two mugs from the cupboard and crashed about finding the coffee and putting cake and plates onto a tray. Nothing seemed to quell her fury.

"Alice! I heard all the noise and thought that we had burglars. What on earth is the matter?" George stood in the doorway, glasses and a newspaper dangling from his hand, he smiled at his wife. His hair a little dishevelled, indicating to Alice that he had had the snooze he said he didn't need, making her feel a little guilty at the noise she had created.

"I'm furious, that's all. I don't know where to start. You wouldn't believe the morning I've had." She pulled hard on the kitchen drawer to find a spoon and cake slice. Everything rattled including her nerves. George came over and slipped an arm around her waist to comfort her. She felt the warmth of him flow through her veins and she relaxed despite her fight not to and to remain cross. Damn it, she deserved to be cross. Instead, she dropped her arms and defences as she snuggled in for a welcome cuddle.

"Go and sit in the snug, I'll finish here and bring in the tray and you can tell me all about it." Alice loved him so much, what would she do without him? She gave him a wan smile and a peck on the cheek before gratefully heading for the snug. She collapsed into her chair immediately wondering why she was being so cross. George deserved an explanation for her silly mood and she was ready to give it.

"I just don't understand, I always thought that Lucy was such a lovely girl," she wailed.

"And she is, dear; you must have caught her in a bad moment, that's all."

"You can be annoyingly right sometimes, George, and I love you for it," her face changing into a warm smile that crinkled her eyes. "It's just, well, you know…" she turned to look out of the window gulping down her embarrassment. The garden was coming to life with the azaleas in full bloom looking stunning in hot pinks and delicate whites, birds were flying madly about picking up bits of moss and twigs. She smiled to herself, saying, "I was just thinking, George… George, what's the matter?" She put her cup down and jumped up just as George screwed up his face and rubbed his chest.

"It's nothing, just a bit of indigestion, that's all."

"I'm going to send for the doctor and no arguing," she galvanised herself into action despite his protests, panic coursing through her veins. George tried to grab her arm.

"Please, I'm fine, honestly." Alice dashed into the hall.

"Take this as a bit of a wake-up call, George. I want to see you in my surgery next week and I'll run a few tests. That waistline of yours is getting bigger, too much of the good life, eh?" He shook hands with George and left. Alice returned to the snug ready to confront George but he was snoozing. She added a log to the wood burner and covered him with a multi-coloured crocheted blanket that she had made years before from left-over scraps of wool. She smiled at him, kissing his forehead. Her heart jumped on hearing a loud knock at the door. Alice, puzzled for a moment, looked at her watch.

"Oh dear, the PCC meeting, I'd forgotten all about it." She kissed George's forehead again, pushing his hair back and crept out of the room, quietly closing the door behind her.

***

The members of the Parochial Church Council sat around Alice's kitchen table. Doris leaned back in her chair arms folded. She was a tiny woman somewhere in her 80s, no one was quite sure, with short, cropped hair and a few white whiskers above her top lip which she kept smoothing and touching, much to Alice's disgust. She was no pushover though and had a powerful voice and temper. Lady Isobel tried to calm things down following some heated words from all concerned. Ted, David and Maureen all nodded and in turn agreed with everyone else instead of voicing their own opinion. Alice was still feeling anxious about George.

"Look," said Alice, "all I'm saying is that we should give all the candidates a chance and not just the men."

"There's always been a man vicar at St. Michaels'; it's tradition and that's how it should stay." Doris heaved up her, out of proportion to her tiny frame, ample bosom and looked Alice straight in the eye. "None of this new-fangled women ministers nonsense here, there will be happy clapping next!" Alice hid a smirk with her hand. For a moment, there was silence as everyone looked down and stole glances at each other. Finally, Alice rose from her chair.

"Any more tea anyone?" she busied herself switching on the kettle and pulling out another packet of biscuits, trying her hardest not to laugh out loud. Doris was being very silly and old-fashioned, but Alice had to admit that she was entitled to her opinion.

"The way I see it," said Lady Isobel in an attempt to get some order and decision from the committee, "…is that we hear who the Diocese come up with and recommend, of course, and after the interviews, we have another think about it. Don't you agree, Alice?" She turned to look at Alice who knew the cue she was thrown.

"Good idea and don't forget, every member of the congregation who is on our Church electoral role is entitled to vote too," her lips smiled sweetly, but her eyes remained doubtful.

There were mumbles of agreement around the room except for Doris.

"No woman is going to get my vote. I would rather leave and go to St. Bartholemew," amused but changing the subject.

"We need to start thinking about our summer fete, any thoughts on a theme for this year anyone? George and I are happy to host it again in our garden and we have in mind the last weekend in June." The meeting continued in a more civilised manner, ending with no further decisions except to agree to the fete being at the Warrens. David was to make the posters and put them up around the village. Ted and Maureen agreeing to organise the cake-making competition and the usual vegetables, flowers and crafts stalls as well as coming up with new ideas.

They needed something different to bring people in and promised to think of a theme for the next meeting. The WI always did the cream teas and Doris felt it her duty to oversee the WI as she wanted to ensure that the standards didn't slip.

***

Later that afternoon, Alice and Isobel sat on the veranda with a glass of chilled chardonnay, recounting the events of the meeting, chuckling about Doris and her out-dated ideas.

"I don't know why we put up with her," she laughed, "and you handled her very well, Alice.' She leaned over and squeezed Alice's arm. Lady Isobel and Alice had been best friends for a long time; they knew each other very well. Alice thought back to that dreadful day when Rufus had suffered a massive heart attack never to recover, leaving Isobel a widow with no children, in her early fifties and the responsibility of running the Trentmouth Manor estate. She smiled at her friend warmly. Although Alice was some fifteen years older than Isobel, they had enjoyed a close friendship with George and Rufus, making up a successful bridge team.

"I suppose the only thing we can do is to wait for the AGM and see who volunteers for Church Warden. If enough people show an interest, we can hold an election that might do the trick. I think it's time to remind people that the posts are open to all members of the church, you never know." She turned and gave a wan smile at Isobel.

"Yes, you're right, but who?" Just at that moment, George walked out through the French doors, Isobel shot a look at Alice and beamed up at George. "George! How lovely to see you."

Chapter 3

Molly drove over to the farm as she did most days but today was different as she had a decision to make. She had thought that moving into the flat would be easy, romantic even. Instead, the confined space had only proved how hard it was to bring up a new-born baby and adjusting to married life at the same time. Sandra had moved back to Spain giving Molly the farm. She had been in quite a dilemma as to what to do. She wanted to move back to the farm, as it was difficult with Jessica, a pram and shopping to climb up to the first floor flat above Alistair's business at Poundbury. He, however, wanted to stay at the flat, as the commute was great… she smiled to herself, but that did not solve the problem. Alistair just did not seem to understand, nor did he try to, the difficulties that living in Poundbury caused her. She had her business in Trentmouth, the farm and the constant driving backwards and forwards with a new-born baby was making her tired, very tired. Bertie had been a brick; he was still living in the holiday cottage and was looking after Rex, which seemed to suit them both. The season was starting soon and Bertie would have to leave the cottage, there was another decision, she mused. She glanced at Jessica who had nodded off to sleep, blissfully unaware of the chaos around her.

Molly was on her way to discuss the future with Bertie and how it affected not only him, but her other plans too – decisions, decisions.

"Hey," Bertie called out as she climbed down from the battered old Land Rover she loved so much. Her dad had bought it new before Molly was even born and she just couldn't bear to part with it and she had insisted on keeping it, much to the chagrin of Alistair, who didn't think that it quite matched the successful impression he was trying to portray at Poundbury.

This had caused Molly to laugh, as it suited perfectly her image of a country vet!

Rex bounded over skidding to a halt, yelping and jumping for joy up at her. She ruffled his fur and patted him affectionately.

"Hey, how are you?" They hugged and Bertie lifted Jessica out of her seat.

"She's gorgeous." He kissed her head and she stretched and yawned before dropping off to sleep again. "You are so lucky; she is the sweetest little thing I have ever seen." He cooed over her as they walked up to the house, Rex ran around trying to get attention and failing, so he padded along behind them, his tail down.

"I will put the kettle on, Bertie, can you put Jess in her crib, please.' A few minutes later, they were sitting at the kitchen table with mugs of coffee and slices of fruit cake.

"So," asked Bertie, "what are the options and more to the point, how do they involve me?"

"It's hard to know where to start, we can talk about the farm, my practice, your tenancy, Alistair and the business or we could talk about you and Lucy.' She looked at him for inspiration. Bertie leaned back in his chair, hands behind his head, stretching his long lean muscles like a cat, a Cheshire cat. He grinned.

"Hmm, I can't deny that all of the above have chased around in my head too, but, purely thinking of myself," he chuckled, "I know that I have to leave the cottage next week and I could move here into the farm..." he paused, "however, I can't afford the rent, as I am sure it would be much more than the cottage, so..." but before he could continue, Molly leaned forward, saying.

"We could come to some arrangement about the rent, but I want to move back here too," she paused, looking at him for some indication of agreement or otherwise, but seeing no startled looks, she pushed on, "it is so tight at the flat for the three of us, plus everything is up and down the stairs. Alistair wants to stay at Poundbury. I just don't know what to do." She scraped her chair back and lifted the coffee pot up as she gave a long, long sigh.

"Is everything alright between you and Alistair? It did come rather a shock to him and changed his life completely, marriage and a baby… and giving up his lifestyle in London," proffered Bertie by way of defence.

"Sorry, yes, we are fine, he adores Jessica and his new business is going well. Of course, you know that and that reminds me, I want to know about you, you kind of slipped back into the old routine, didn't you? What about your plans and dreams, come on, tell me, money no object, what would you love to do?"

"Phew, now that's a question. I would give up my work with Alistair for a start, I'm finding it a bit tedious, been doing it too long, I suppose. I really did enjoy working on your allotment last year and gardening for George and Alice. I haven't the time now and I miss it," he pinched the fat creeping onto his waistline by way of explanation, grinning up at her.

"Also, if I'm honest, I still have a hankering to own and run my own organic café."

"Oh, dear, I can hear Jessica crying. It's time for her feed. Anyway, hold that thought and we can talk again later." She got up and collected her bag to go upstairs. "If you like, I can rustle up some lunch for us and it's such a lovely day; do you fancy taking Jess for a walk later?"

"Good idea," said Bertie, "…but leave the lunch to me as you are a bit busy." He grinned as Molly disappeared up the stairs.

***

After lunch, Molly and Bertie set out to take Jessica for a walk stopping first to look at the sorry state of the allotment. There was a fine crop of nettles, dandelions and all manner of wild flowers and weeds. They sat on the bench staring at it; the only good thing was the rhubarb.

"It's not too late to get it back and even have some crops this year. I'm so sorry that all your hard work seems to have been for nothing." Molly felt guilty that she had neglected so much of her life in the last 6 months. She looked up at the sky for inspiration but none came.

"I have an idea," said Bertie with a grin, "it's cheeky I know but I could give my notice to Alistair, move into the farm, rent free, and get to work on the allotment. I can also give George a ring and see how he's coping with the garden. I might be able to pick up some work there. Then when you have persuaded Alistair to move into the farm, I'll move out. How does that sound?" He grinned at Molly, who for a moment stared back at him open-mouthed. Not that she objected, in fact it was a good idea, it was just such a surprise and took a moment to sink in.

"Well, I know I said no limitations, but, wow, you have thought about it and I have to say that, in the short term, it sounds good to me, however…I think that I will have to charge you £1 a week rent and you pay all the bills," she put out her hand, "deal?"

"Deal," said Bertie shaking her hand, "and, of course I'll look after Rex and the rest of the farm animals for you." He jumped up and whizzed the pram around ready for their walk.

They trundled down the bumpy lane with Rex running ahead and Bertie trying to avoid the many potholes so as not to wake up Jessica.

"One thing bothers me though."

"Oh, what's that?" asked Bertie, looking sideways at Molly.

"Where will you live when we move back in? Assuming that I can persuade Alistair that is, which I'm sure I can, as I also have to start working again soon."

"Oh, I don't know, I would live in a shepherd's hut or a yurt in the middle of a field if I had to, to make my dreams come true."

"You really are determined, aren't you?" she smiled. "Now, I want to know all about you and Lucy."

***

Back at the farm, Molly set to work clearing out cupboards, dusting and cleaning, determined to get the place ready not only for Bertie but also for herself. She was convinced that Alistair would fall into her way of thinking and move into the farm; after all it was the best solution. She had mounds of old clothes, for the recycling centre, books and ornaments for the charity shop and black sacks of rubbish already piled into the back of the Land Rover.

Her iPhone began to ring out and she grabbed it quickly not wanting to disturb Jessica. It was Alistair.

"Hello, darling, how's things?" she said, bouncing out into the farmyard.

"I've had Bertie on the phone, I don't know what you are playing at but he's handed in his notice and tells me he is moving into the farm!" he paused for a breath, "and on top of that, he is going to live there for £1 a week until we move in... have you gone mad?" his temper rising with frustration he let rip, "I don't want to move to the farm, I've told you that. I'm quite happy here, so what the hell's going on?" He stopped to catch his breath and Molly stood shaking, she had never heard him like this before; it was a revelation and one she didn't like at all. She thrashed around her brain to assimilate what she had just heard, jumping in with,

"It's a good plan for Bertie, me and the farm and you know, we can't continue as we are at the flat with Jessica; it's just not practical. I have to get back to work and it makes more sense to live here." She pleaded, hoping that he would see her point of view.

"Look, we will have to talk about it later, my office phone is ringing." He hung up and Molly was left staring at her iPhone, wondering what had just happened. Bertie appeared at the stable door leading to the kitchen and stood resting his arms on top of the closed bottom half.

"Hey, I'm so sorry, Molly, I didn't think. I just got on the phone to tell Alistair, then I rang George and Lucy. Half the village will know by now. I don't know what to say," he hung his head kicking the door, "I really am sorry to cause you any bother."

"It's okay, Bertie, it's not your fault," she heaved a sigh, put her iPhone down and looked at him. "I should have consulted him; you know how he likes to make the decisions."

"Only too well, but with Jess and everything, I thought he would be pleased," he raised both arms and dropped them by his side before shoving his hands into his pockets, "what can I do to make it up to you?" Molly gave a half laugh.

"Why don't you make us a cup of tea and I will go check on Jessica. I need to think."

Molly trudged up the stairs, her head racing, thoughts churning around totally puzzled by Alistair's outburst. It would solve lots of problems moving to the farm and okay Alistair would have to drive to Poundbury everyday but it would be an easy commute in comparison to what she had to do just now. She returned to the kitchen carrying Jessica and found Bertie looking very dishevelled a cheeky grin on his face.

"Look what I found down at the allotment!" He placed a box on the table with new potatoes, a half-nibbled cabbage, a few peas and a bunch of rhubarb. "Not bad for a garden full of weeds? And I'm sure that I can get it back into shape in no time." Molly was thrilled. She flopped down onto a chair, tears stinging her eyes.

"Bertie, that's wonderful. I only wish I could be working on it too."

"Aww, come on," he patted her arm. "You can come and help me whenever you like."

He threw her a lopsided grin and Molly had to laugh.

"Well, thanks, I will check my diary."

***

Molly drove back towards Dorchester after stopping at a charity shop with her haul of goods and calling in at the recycling centre. She had tried to contact Lucy, but she was busy working at the garden centre, so no time for a girlie chat. Lucy had been seconded to the café for the day as they were extremely busy serving cream teas. Molly didn't feel like driving back home just yet, Alistair's words still gnawing at her, so she turned off the road and up the country lanes towards the home of Stella at Beaminster.

"What a lovely surprise," declared Stella when she opened the door, "you should have let me know you were coming. I may have been out delivering. Never mind though, it's wonderful to see you, but I can tell by the look on your face that something is wrong." They hugged for a moment and Stella took Jessica, saying, "Come on, let's get the kettle on and you can tell me all about it." Molly dutifully followed her into her newly fitted kitchen diner the bi-folding doors were open onto the patio with its beautiful garden and vista of the hills beyond.

"How's business?" asked Molly as they sank into the comfy sofa. Jessica cradled in an armchair surrounded by cushions watching her mum and blowing contented bubbles. Stella cut into a lemon drizzle cake and handed a slice to Molly as she rolled her eyes in exasperation.

"Fine, now tell me what's really bothering you." Molly launched into the whole sorry tale, adding a bit of her own concern into the mix and watched as Stella merely went from looking shocked to amusement and back again. She was beginning to think that she was overacting a bit, as the story didn't sound that important when she said it out loud.

"Anyway, I don't know what to do now," she finished, looking at her little sister, Stella, for words of wisdom and inspiration. "I just needed someone to talk to I'm sorry to dump all my problems on you. Gorgeous cake though, I'm putting on weight." Molly pinched the roll of fat that was now bulging over the top of her jeans. Stella just laughed.

"Well, for one thing, you are not fat and that's the result of having this wonderful little bundle here, so stop worrying." She gave Jessica a tickle extracting happy noises from her and more bubbles. "I think that you are just tired, it's been a lot of adjusting all round, what with Dad and Mum going off to Spain like that, marriage, babies, so much has happened and you haven't adjusted to it, that's all and I'm sure that Alistair is the same."

"You could be right, I am confused and maybe not thinking about it from Alistair's point of view, just my own." She looked out onto the garden, watching a blackbird tugging at a worm in the lawn and smiled. "I miss having a garden, the flat is lovely, but I can't breathe sometimes living in such a built-up environment. Alistair is used to it, of course, and can't understand why I don't love it."

"I think that you need to sit down with Alistair and tell him what's bothering you just like you have told me and sort it out together. I also think that you need some time to yourself, give yourself a break Molly you can't do everything. Go and have a facial, or go to the cinema with Lucy, let Alistair look after Jess for a day and go shopping, anything to give you some down time. I bet you haven't started your yoga class again yet and I know you had designs on entering the summer fete this year with your art, so come on let me see my big sister Molly back," she grinned.

Molly put Jessica into the Land Rover and hugged Stella thanking her for listening and set off back home feeling more able to tackle Alistair thinking that it wasn't such a major problem after all. They loved each other and that was what really mattered. She checked her watch as she lit the candles on the table, dinner was ready and Alistair would be in soon. She looked in the mirror and smeared on a touch of lippy, feeling satisfied, she turned just as Alistair opened the door.

"Hey, darling, you look done in." She put her arms around him and stood on tiptoes, wading in, her lips puckered up. He gave her a cursory peck on the cheek, pushing her away, pulling at his tie, he flopped down, looking at her.

"We need to talk," he said.

Chapter 4

Bertie carried the last of his possessions into the farm and stood at the barn door, arms folded, with a stupid grin on his face. His dream was starting to become reality. Lucy crept up behind him and slid her arms around his waist. Bertie smiled, pulling her in close as they embraced.

His life could not be better.

"I love this place," he exhaled and took in another deep breath, "even if it's only for a short time, I just know I'm so happy here." He pulled Lucy toward him, snuggling her into his arms. "Just look at that view. Ah, this is the life," he breathed contentedly.

"I like this view," she teased, reaching up to nibble his bottom lip, "and which is your room?" Bertie swooped down on her kissing her face, her neck, her lips. She pulled off her top and fumbled with her jeans.

"Never mind that," said Bertie, scooping her into his arms and heading for the stairs. He put her down, pulling off his own clothes, kicking his boots into the corner of the room. With a clatter, he slid his fingers through her hair, devouring her mouth.

"Hello… is anyone in?" they heard a shout from downstairs. "Bertie, are you here?"

Bertie stared in disbelief at Lucy; his feelings getting the better of him, he wanted to ignore his visitor. Lucy giggled. Bertie pulled on his shirt and boots and thundered down the stairs, bursting into the kitchen to find Alice holding a dish covered in a tea towel.

"Alice! How… lovely to see you. How can I help you?" he spluttered as he dragged his fingers through his hair in an attempt to make it look less dishevelled… hoping to calm his voice and cool his burning skin.

"I brought you an apple pie," she said, whisking the cover from the pie, "…thought you could use it today. Are you moving in alright, do you need any help?" She looked so sweet and innocent, but Bertie had learned from past mistakes that she always had a hidden agenda.

"Fine, that pie does look good though, thanks," his mouth began to water as he put the pie into the larder. "Can I get you a coffee, Alice?" he asked as he filled the kettle.

"Oh, let me do that for you, Bertie, you must be tired due to all this moving and I brought you some chocolate hobnobs too," she grinned. He dutifully moved aside just as Rex jumped out of his basket and nuzzled his hand.

"Good guard dog you turned out to be," he ruffled his ears and Rex gave an appreciative grunt.

"So," said Alice, "how is everything with you and Lucy?" Bertie had a flashback to a few moments ago, letting a smile slide onto his face and quickly trying to bring his expression back to now and his visitor.

"Great, she's here actually, unpacking for me upstairs," he glanced at the door just as Lucy clicked it open, strolling in, looking slightly less dishevelled than he had.

"Hi, Alice, looks like I'm just in time for coffee. How are you?" Lucy and Bertie exchanged a grin and Alice tutted as she unhooked another mug from the dresser.

"I came to ask Bertie if he would like to enter the competition for home produce at the church fete. I've brought an entry form and there are lots of categories if you want to enter a craft, Lucy. The theme this year is 'Vintage' so you can read into that whatever you wish."

She said turning back to the coffee making clattering the spoon. Bertie clutched Lucy's hand.

She threw him a cheeky grin.

"I don't have any time for hobbies, Alice, now I'm working full time and I help Mum at the shop whenever I can too," she said, aiming a sideways glance at Bertie.

"I'll give it some thought, thanks, Alice. What are you going to enter?" said Bertie as he picked up the entry form scanning all the categories in an effort to look interested.

"Actually, I can't I'm afraid being on the organising committee, but we do need some new members," she hesitated turning to look in their direction, "we are all getting older and could do with some young blood if you are interested in helping Bertie or you Lucy?"

"Whoa! I don't think so. I don't know anything about that sort of thing, you will have to find another victim," they all laughed, leaving Bertie wondering if that was really behind her visit or something else.

"Lady Isobel is on the committee, you know, from Trentmouth Manor, but I understand, I'm sure that there will be plenty of other willing volunteers," Alice said huffily.

"I'll give it some thought anyway. Thanks for the entry form. I don't know what I'm doing at the moment apart from your garden, of course," he turned the form over between his fingers wondering if he had missed something, she was a wily old bird and the last thing he wanted right now was to be caught in one of Alice's traps.

"How's your mum, dear?" asked Alice, patting Lucy's hand.

"She's fine; we are keeping a close eye on her and Dad is giving up working on the Swanage railway so that he can be in the shop more."

"Good idea. I must pop in and see her," she sipped her coffee. "We are planning a big party this year as it is our 40th wedding anniversary and of course George will be 70. We thought that we would take advantage of the marquee on our lawn for the Church fete so I will need you to do some extra work for me in the garden Bertie," she eyed him over her coffee cup, "if that's convenient, of course."

"Sure thing, Alice, just let me know what you want done and what about the food? And a cake, I assume," he eyed her carefully as she was coming around to something.

"How wonderful, Alice," interrupted Lucy. "Congratulations and anything we can do to help, just let us know. Molly's sister Stella would make you a cake; she creates some spectacular cakes, you know." Lucy's iPhone pinged. She took a quick look, throwing Bertie a sideways glance, but said nothing.

"Yes, thanks; that's a good idea. I haven't got that far in planning yet, I will give it some thought," she swirled the last of her coffee and smiled, "do I hear wedding bells for you two?"

Both Bertie and Lucy spluttered at the same time and looked at each other. It was Lucy who spoke first.

"Alice, my goodness! We've only known each other a short while; give us chance and no you can't hear wedding bells; that is not on our agenda at all." Bertie shifted uneasily in his chair for a moment, wondering if that was a challenge or did Lucy really mean it? He would have to give it some more thought as the truth was it had been turning around in his mind to ask her to marry him.

The door crashed open, taking them all by surprise. Molly came stumbling in through the door carrying Jessica and dropped a huge bag onto the floor. Rex leapt out of his basket and began barking with excitement, running around the kitchen and jumping up at Molly. Bertie clambered from his seat to try and calm the mayhem, grabbing at Rex; Jessica began to cry and Molly, whose face was puce and stony, burst into tears.

"Whatever is the matter?" asked Alice, trying to wrestle Jessica out of her arms and making shushing noises.

"I've left him…" she sobbed.

"Don't be silly, Molly, dear, you've only just got married," declared Alice. "I'm sure whatever it is, is just a misunderstanding." She began jigging Jessica up and down which did nothing to calm her. Lucy put out her arms to rescue Jessica and took her outside to a more peaceful atmosphere. Bertie grabbed the kettle and gave Lucy a gratifying look as she shrugged her shoulders and disappeared.

"Now, come on, Molly, tell me what's wrong. I know my son better than anyone and I'm sure that this can be sorted out quickly. Now do stop crying, dear; this is not helping."

"Alice," snapped Molly, "you have no idea about Alistair or you wouldn't say that. I think you should go." Alice grabbed her bag.

"Well, I've never been spoken to like that in my life, I will go and console my son," she headed for the door without looking back.

"Alice… I'm sorry," sobbed Molly at her disappearing back, but it was too late; Alice had gone. She turned to Bertie and he held out his arms, Molly fell into them sobbing. He rubbed her back and held her head tight against his chest. They stood still for a moment as Bertie waited for her tears to subside and as she stopped shaking, he let her go and she flopped into the nearest chair.

"Does this mean I'm homeless before I've moved in?" he said grinning.

"I'm so sorry, Bertie, but no, you don't have to move out, I'll just be a house guest for a few days if that's alright with you?" she blew her nose. "I just had to get away. I've made a big mistake. I thought he loved me, well us, but not enough to consider me and my needs. He's only thinking of himself," she began to sob again.

"I don't think that that is completely true, he does love you both, but the farm is a bit… rustic and not his style at all. You just need to find a compromise that you will both be happy with that's all," he tried a wan smile and Molly wiped her eyes, smudging her mascara across her face.

"I've tried, I really have, but what other choices do we have? I can't keep lugging the pram upstairs and Jessica is growing, okay, she's not crawling yet, but what then?" she looked pleadingly at him.

"I don't know. Sorry, Molly, but not my area of expertise. I can console but after that you're on your own. I can make a mean cup of coffee though, want one?" She nodded and looked around to find Lucy back with a fast-asleep Jessica cradled in her arms.

"Thanks, Lucy, you're a star. I wish everything could be fixed as easily." She took Jessica and laid her on the couch. Bertie made three strong cups of coffee, opening the chocolate hobnobs that Alice had left for him.

"So…" began Lucy, "what now? I presume Alistair knows you've left him and where you are."

"No, I was just so furious that I packed a bag and left, but I'm sure by now that he does know as Alice would have gone over there to 'console my son'." She rolled her eyes and a smile cracked her face. They all laughed. "Poundbury is a great place; it's young, modern and vibrant with some really good pubs, live music, shops not unlike London in many ways, but I want to get back to work. The locum I've got wants to know when I will be returning as he has other commitments and I just can't function from Dorchester." Her phone began to ring and Molly looked at them both, "It's Alistair."

"Okay, come on, Bertie, we will take Jessica out and leave Molly to talk." She picked up Jessica who stirred slightly, yawned and went back to sleep. Bertie grabbed Rex's lead, he leapt from his bed, needing no further encouragement and they disappeared.

***

"Alistair," said Molly.

"What are you playing at? I've had Mother on the phone telling me she is so sorry that we have split up! What is going on and where are you, no, let me guess, the farm…" he gasped, "that bloody farm is all you care about, what about me and what I want? I'm trying to run a business here and you're not helping," he fell silent, "…well?"

"Well, nothing and thanks a lot for asking how I am and asking about Jessica," she fumed, "we are fine by the way, I just need some space to breathe and figure out what I want. You already know what you want and it doesn't seem to include Jessica and me, so you can have your space too and we will all be happy." She snapped; her heart was beating so fast, she thought that her chest would burst.

"Molly, I'm sorry, I didn't realise you felt this strongly, please, come home and I promise that we will talk this over, together. I want you to be happy and…I do love you," he paused. "I want you and Jessica more than anything else in the world."

"… And I love you too, but you have a funny way of showing it. I need to get back to work and then there's Jessica," she sobbed, hating herself for being so needy. "It's all about your business, as if mine doesn't matter."

"I admit that I've been absorbed in establishing myself here and maybe not thought about you as much as I should, but you don't need to go back to work, you know, I make enough to take care of us and you can concentrate on our daughter."

"You see… that's what I'm talking about," she snapped, beginning to lose her temper again. "I can concentrate on our daughter, she's your daughter too and she needs a father as well. Bertie plays with her more than you do," Molly heard his intake of breath and knew that that stung but she had to make her point, "…and I need my life too…" she broke off, gulping for breath.

"Okay, okay I get it. Will you please come home, so that we can talk? And Molly…I mean it, I do love you…both."

"I'll see you later," she looked around her beloved farmhouse and sniffed, "What next?" she asked herself as she packed her bag, once more, ready to leave.

Chapter 5

George stepped out of the French doors carrying two glasses of sherry. Alice was asleep on her Adirondack chair; he picked up her book from the floor and laid it on the table. A smile slid across his face as he settled back into his own chair and shook out the paper ready to do the crossword. Alice had a good heart, but she frequently ended up getting things wrong. She loved to help other people; it was just her way however misguided at times. George tried his best to console her and delicately point out that other people didn't always need her help, but here they were again with her 'other people always misunderstood her intentions' act; he loved her so much.

Alice stirred.

"Oh, George, I must have fallen asleep for a minute," she smiled at him, "What time is it?"

"Time for sherry, my love. You have had a nice long nap; it will do you good. You have been worrying far too much about Alistair and Molly; let's just leave them alone and let them sort it out eh? Now what about this crossword," he peered at her over the rim of his glasses, reaching out to lovingly squeeze her hand.

"I know you're right, darling, but I can't help worrying some times and I'm not interfering just trying to help like any concerned parent." George said nothing scrutinising the paper, he tapped the pen puffing his cheeks in and out. They sipped their sherry companionably, George reading out the clues as Alice surveyed the garden.

"I've been thinking," she exclaimed.

"Oh… oh, what about, my dear?" he lowered the paper to give her his full attention; he never knew what scheme Alice could have dreamt of this time.

"Well, as we have the marquee up for the church fete, why don't we keep it for an extra day and hold our 40th there?" she lifted an eyebrow in expectation, waiting.

"Excellent idea and I've been thinking too. You know this old house is far too big for us; why don't we downsize, maybe move into town?" he smiled, reaching for her hand again.

He was thinking of her health, although there was no lasting damage from her stroke but still, they should consider their health more, he had had his own scare recently too. He watched her as her face crinkled, he knew that twitch in her cheek only too well. "You see, my dear, the Doctor said that I am fine, but I won't be if I don't lose some weight and get some exercise," he patted his belly now overhanging his trousers.

"Why didn't you tell me, George? Oh, darling, here I am worrying about other people and I didn't know you had a problem, you should have told me. We can cut out all these cakes for a start and I will make some salads, I have a few extra pounds myself to get rid of. We'll start today."

George grinned.

"That's why I love you, Alice, but slow down; we can work it out together. I have decided to sign up for walking football, there's a club in Wareham and see how that works out," he sipped his sherry and tried again, "…and think about downsizing too, my love. You could walk to the shops and to church…" sensing he wasn't going to succeed this time he chuckled and changed the subject. "How is Tricia by the way? I know that Lucy is quite worried about her."

"How do you know that, George, I haven't been in the shop recently and we don't have as many visitors as we used to for some reason? I think that we will have to give up the sherry too," she announced, changing the subject.

"Never, my dear, sherry is our favourite time of day and Bertie told me, about Tricia, I mean. He has been working very hard in the garden; he has a knack for it and he tells me that he is considering entering the fete." He felt smug, turning her attention away from his one indulgence. He knew he could not give up the sherry.

"George, you're a natural salesman. Have you decided about being a church warden yet?" she quizzed.

"Not yet. Let me think about it some more." He knew that it was futile to resist, but he liked the idea of keeping his decision to himself for a bit longer. "Perhaps you should visit Tricia tomorrow, my dear, she would like that and forget about the young ones; they will visit when they are ready, you'll see." He shook out his paper and returned to his crossword.

***

The next morning, Alice took a gentle stroll down the lane towards the village. She stopped to admire the buds on the wild dog roses and the daisies pushing up through the grass on the road side. The birds were in full nest-building mode, picking up bits of twig and straw. She watched with amusement as she saw a blackbird tugging at a bit of moss. "I love the spring," she mused and swung her bag as she headed down the hill. As she turned the last corner, she could see a blue light flashing in the middle of the village and wondered what poor soul was in trouble but as she got closer, she could see that there was an ambulance and a fire engine outside the shop. She tried to hurry up to find out what had happened and seeing Donald with his head in his hands, she hurried towards him.

"Donald, are you alright? What on earth has happened and where's Tricia? Have you phoned Lucy? I must get hold of George," she panicked, fumbling in her bag to retrieve her mobile phone.

"Alice, stop worrying, Lucy is on her way and the paramedics are with Tricia now. I don't know exactly what happened, but I think that Tricia caught her foot in the electric cable and pulled the fire over. She fell and was knocked out, probably hit her head on the counter, some paper caught fire and well, you can see for yourself," he pointed towards the smoke still curling up out of the windows as the firemen were hosing the walls. A paramedic made his way over to Donald.

"We are ready to take her to hospital now, Mr Hamilton. Would you like to come in the ambulance with us? Your wife is suffering from smoke inhalation. She has some minor burns and a rather nasty cut on her head which should be x-rayed and you need to be checked too." The paramedic lifted his arm to guide

Donald into the waiting ambulance. He stood up, turning to Alice,

"Will you wait for Lucy and put her in the picture please, Alice? She will know what to do and I will go with Tricia." He turned and slowly climbed into the ambulance, looking very dishevelled. Alice let out a gasp as fear trickled down her spine, staring at the sad scene.

"Of course, I will, Donald. I'm so sorry and give Tricia my love. We will come and see her in hospital as soon as she can have visitors," Donald gave her a tiny smile and as he turned, she saw that his hands were also bleeding and his clothes were singed. Her hand flew to her mouth as she pressed the number for George, but nothing happened. "Damn," she said as she realised that the battery was dead. She couldn't go back home and the phone box in the village had been removed some years ago, so she sat on the bench and waited for Lucy. She didn't have long to wait as Lucy's car came skidding around the corner and screeched to a halt, spitting stones in its wake. Alice got up and put her arms up to Lucy.

"I'm so sorry, my dear, your dad has gone to hospital in the ambulance with your mum and he said to fill you in on what has happened," Alice said breathlessly, her hands trembling.

"Oh, dear, I need to sit down."

"Thanks, Alice, let me talk to the fire officer and then we'll go next door for a cup of tea, you look as though you need one." She put her arm around Alice's shoulders as she was clearly shaking. She guided her towards the cottage and went in search of the chief officer. A few minutes later, Lucy emerged into the cottage and put the kettle on.

"I've taken the liberty of calling George and he's on his way, you do look white, Alice, and Bertie is coming over too to fix the window and secure the door. Now, you can fill me in with what the paramedic said." George arrived first and immediately fell back into his doctor mode, fussing Alice and checking her pulse.

"I'm alright, dear, just a bit shocked that's all, I got quite a fright seeing poor Tricia on a stretcher like that. Oh, I'm sorry, Lucy," seeing Lucy's face ringed in concern, "I'm sure she'll be fine, I only came down to have a chat with her and well... you know the rest."

"Come on, Alice," said George helping her to her feet. "Let's get you home. I'm sure that Lucy wants to get to the hospital and see Tricia for herself and Bertie will be here soon." He guided her to the door. George turned to glance at Lucy, raising his hand.

***

A rap on the door made Lucy jump and she quickly pulled it open.

"Bertie, since when did you knock on the… oh, Jasper, I wasn't expecting to see you," she stared at him for a moment, puzzled.

"I'm sorry, Lucy, I was in the area and thought that I would stop by to see your mum and saw, well, obviously, you've had a problem. Is your mum alright?" he made a move as if to put his arms around her, but she stepped back with a jerk.

"Yes, well, no, she's in the hospital and she won't be ordering any more tights I'm afraid. Would you like a coffee? I need one myself."

"Thanks," he stepped into the cottage. "Wow, what a lovely old place. I love the beams," he enthused. Lucy cautiously watched him as he wandered around, taking in the room with a sweep of his eyes.

"Yes, thanks. Mum and Dad live here. I have my own place in Wareham. Sugar, milk?" she asked, waving a mug in the air.

"Both. Thanks. Two… sugars." He continued to look around the sitting room, picking up a picture, he waved it towards Lucy, "Who's this? Bertie, was it, I heard you say?"

"Yes, he's… hem… a friend," she bit her tongue, what was she doing flirting with Jasper when Bertie would be here any second. "He's coming over actually to fix the door and window for me." Just then, Bertie crashed in through the door, banging it as he went dashing, straight to Lucy.

"Are you okay, my darling, what happened? Come here," he put his arms around her and she dropped her head onto his shoulder, swallowing hard and glancing at Jasper.

"Hi," said Jasper. Bertie spun around.

"Who are you?" he stared at him for a second and looked back at Lucy.

"Oh, sorry, Bertie, this is Jasper, a rep, came to see Mum."

"Oh, right, sorry, mate," Bertie put out a hand, "didn't mean to snap like that." Jasper put down his mug and turned to Lucy.

"I hope your mum is okay. I'll see you next time maybe?" he lifted an eyebrow and left. Lucy curled into Bertie's arms, resting her head on his shoulder once more; how stupid of her to even look at anyone else. He clutched her hair and rocked her gently for a moment. She pulled back.

"I don't know what I'm going to do, the shop is a mess and Mum clearly can't carry on like this anymore and I've just had to run out of the maternity unit leaving a mother giving birth to twins. What am I going to do, Bertie?"

"Hey, let's not worry about that just now, you go and see your mum. I will take care of things here and we can talk later. Come over to the farm and I will cook dinner," he lifted her chin, tilting her face up to him, kissing away her tears, softly placing his lips to hers.

***

Bertie looked around at the mess, hardly knowing where to start. Water dripped down from the ceiling landing on his face. He wiped it away. There was more water damage than fire. He stood hands on hips, staring at the awful sight.

"Hello," a voice from the doorway startled him for a moment, "Ben Fox, fire investigation." He walked over towards Bertie to shake his hand.

"Hi, well, I was just about to start clearing up. I thought it was Tricia falling over the cable that caused the fire?"

"I still have to write a report and I can't let you clear up until I've finished. Okay if I get started?" he quizzed.

"Yes, sure. I presume I can fix the window and the door?"

"Yes, sir, go ahead; it won't take me long and then you can," he waved his arm around the shambles, "…do what you wish." Bertie picked up his tool kit and began to measure up the window, he watched the Investigator out of the corner of his eye wondering what the consequences might be regarding the insurance. He kept his thoughts to himself thinking of Lucy, her mum and what might happen next. He let out a huff bending down to retrieve a hammer and set to work. His iPhone began to ring and he grabbed it when he saw Lucy's name.

"Hi, how's everything?" he glanced over at Mr Fox and slipped outside to give Lucy an update.

"Mum will be fine but they are keeping her in overnight for observation and some further tests," she told him. "I'm thinking of staying with Dad tonight, he's very shocked, sorry, can I take a rain check on that dinner?"

"Of course, I'll miss you, maybe tomorrow?" He couldn't help letting his voice show his disappointment.

"Probably, I'll let you know. Thanks for making everything safe. Bye." His shoulders dropped as he stared at the phone wondering what was really happening now and did it include him. He knew how fiercely loyal Lucy was and protective of her parents. He felt empty inside feeling more acutely the loss of his own mum and disappearance of his dad. He would have to wait.

"All finished, sir. You can start on the clearing up now." Mr Fox wandered back to his car, whistling and Bertie found it unreasonably irritating.

"I need a drink," he told himself and walked into the cottage next door. He opened the fridge looking for a beer, he slammed the door rattling the jars and bottles, "...coffee it is then."

"Make it two, would you?" a voice broke into his rapidly downward spiralling mood, making him spin around; *twice in one day*, he mused.

"Molly... hi... I am so glad to see you," he kissed her cheek and gave her a squeeze. A gurgling noise took his attention and he crouched down to tickle Jessica, "...and this little sweetheart too." He straightened up, a smile returning, "Come to give me a hand? Next door is a terrible mess."

"Not really, I haven't got long but when I heard from Lucy, I thought I would come over and give moral support at least. I'll have that coffee though."

"Sure, coming up. How's everything with you and Alistair, if you don't mind me asking? The farm's fine by the way, in case you were wondering and Rex too, but I think he misses you." He switched the kettle on, clattered in the cupboard, finding mugs and coffee.

"You don't seem too happy, what's the matter?"

"I don't know, I thought that I was getting through to Alistair, but he has clammed up again, doesn't want to discuss it," she flopped onto the sofa with a heavy sigh.

"Well, do you want to talk about it with me or should I butt out?" he blew on his coffee before dunking a rich tea biscuit. He offered her the packet. "That's all I could find. You wouldn't think there was a shop next door," he laughed.

"You always understand, Bertie, you're a good friend… for a bloke," she smirked at him over the lip of her mug.

"Yes, well, for a bloke, I'm happy to listen and try to give a bloke's point of view. If I can," he grinned, dunking the last of his biscuit. "Alistair is very single minded and I bet he hasn't even considered that you have a point of view that isn't his." He smirked looking at her over the top of his mug.

"Well, I've had enough of it, he tells me he loves me, us," she smiled looking at the now sleeping Jessica, "and I know he does, but how am I going to get him to see that I had a life before him and I want to get on with it, not just be his little wife at home," she moaned in exasperation.

"Hmm, tricky one that, I don't think I can help you there, above my pay grade I'm afraid," he chuckled.

"You're no help at all, I should have known," she threw a cushion at him.

"Hey, watch my coffee. I'm sorry, Molly, but I have no idea what to say. If it was me married to you then, obviously, I would want you to go back to work as soon as, but I don't have Alistair's income, not much at all, actually," he put his hand into his pocket, pulling out a pound coin, handing it to Molly, "I can pay my rent this week though," they both giggled.

"Well, I must go, Bertie. Thanks for the coffee and chat," she grinned. "Jessica will be waking up and be hungry. See you soon." She got up handing Bertie her mug, collected Jessica and kissing Bertie on the cheek, headed for the door. Molly turned and with a wistful look, said, "If only I were married to you, Bertie…" she didn't finish her sentence and left.

Chapter 6

Molly struggled up the stairs into the flat with Jessica perched on her hip, leaving the pram and her shopping downstairs. She moaned and groaned to herself feeling more and more agitated at not only having to carry everything up the stairs but having to travel so much when Alistair didn't seem to notice her exasperation at all. Jessica began to grumble and whinge, not surprising as she was constantly jostled and Molly felt at times like she was slipping from her grasp.

"It's alright, my darling, Mummy will feed you soon." She went back downstairs picking up the post and shopping, leaving the pram just inside the door. She rifled through the junk mail dropping it straight into the bin and tore open a large white envelope addressed to her in her maiden name. She was excited to find out what, if anything, would transpire from her enquiries. Jessica began to wail. Molly quickly scanned the contents smiling to herself and picked up Jess ready to give her a feed. With Jess suckling away happily, Molly opened the letter once more and began to read it thoroughly. She put it to one side and began to scrutinise the attached plans and estimates from her architect. Molly beamed and tickled Jessica under her chin to encourage her to suckle as she had nodded off. "Mummy is going to become a property developer," she began to grin widely, "it's exciting, well, I'm converting the old barn next to the practice anyway, which could be described as a property development. I can't wait." Molly beamed at Jessica, tickling her chin to stimulate her awake to feed once more.

"Can't wait for what, Molly?" asked Alistair as he opened the door pushing into the flat, sounding very tired, "… And please, don't leave the pram in the hall. I nearly fell over it just now." Molly harrumphed.

"I've got planning permission on the barn and I can't carry that pram upstairs; it's just too heavy." She turned back to Jessica stroking her cheek and change from one breast to the other.

"I don't know why you're bothering with that old barn; we have a perfectly good home here. What's for dinner?" he walked over to the cupboard and poured himself a glass of red wine.

"I have no idea, I'm feeding Jessica, why don't you have a look in the fridge and make something," she glowered, "...and for me too." She was furious and felt her temper rising, her cheeks flushed hot.

"Hey, what's got into you? I was just wondering. You're not still talking about moving back to the farm, are you? I've told you how I feel about that. I don't understand why we can't just settle down here."

"And I've told you how I feel. Now let me change Jessica and we can have a proper talk. Okay?" Molly walked into the bedroom, slamming the door rather more loudly than she had planned. She muttered to herself and Jessica began to grizzle again, Molly picked her up and cuddled her to her face rocking backwards and forwards. "I'm sorry, precious," she cooed.

Molly relaxed and concentrated on Jess; she would tackle Alistair later. Couldn't he see that living here wasn't good for anyone but him?

Back in the sitting room, Alistair sat sipping his wine, watching the news as Molly walked over to him and held out Jessica, "Why don't you cuddle your daughter and I will look in the fridge?" she asked encouragingly.

"What? Sorry, later. Can't you put her in her seat for now; this is important."

"The news is more important than our daughter... since when?" Molly could feel her anger erupting. "I don't think you care about us anymore. This whole thing is past talking about, Alistair; why did you bother marrying me if you didn't want this?" she spluttered, indicating the room with a sweep of her hand.

"Now you come to mention it, I don't know either. Since Jessica was born, you haven't shown much interest in me, you know, where do I fit in with your plans?" he threw the letter on the floor, "... Or was I just a way for you getting pregnant? Very convenient, and I fell for it. I should never have left London."

Jessica started to cry. Molly stared in disbelief; how could he be so heartless?

"Now look what you've done. Come to Mummy, darling, Daddy didn't mean it," she shushed Jess and turning to Alistair, calmly said, "If you don't want us, then we will leave."

"Don't bother," he snarled, "I'm going." He got up banging the door and disappeared.

Molly burst into tears and Jessica cried even more. Mayhem ensued. Molly walked up and down comforting Jess and trying to understand what was wrong with Alistair. One minute he said he loved them and the next, he... Molly sobbed and sobbed. Once Jessica was down in her cot for the night, Molly searched the fridge for something to eat, settling on a bowl of casserole left over from the night before with some fresh bread. She picked up the phone pressing Lucy's number.

"Hey. How is your mum and everything?" said Molly as she curled up in the corner of the couch, tucking her feet under and trying to sound relaxed.

"Hi, Molly, well, Mum should be home tomorrow but after that I don't know where to start. Dad is distraught, Mum has been diagnosed with dementia as I suspected, the shop is a complete mess, I should be having dinner with Bertie and I'm here with Dad tonight instead. I've just started my new job, which is great by the way, and now I'm wondering what to do," she paused, "any ideas?"

"Wow, and here I was ringing you for a chat because Alistair has gone and I don't know where he is or even if he's coming back," she let out a sob. Lucy jumped in.

"Wait a minute, rewind and run that by me again. Alistair has left you? I don't believe it, what has happened?" she gasped.

"It's a long story but I think he might have gone for good; we had an almighty row; we both said things we didn't mean and well you have enough to worry about without me adding to it. I'm going to move back to the farm and see what happens after that."

"Are you sure that's the right thing to do? You can't sort it out if you're not there and I'm sure that Alistair will be back soon. I mean he has to, doesn't he? To run his business, I mean."

"That's true, I just don't know what to do," she took a deep breath, "...anyway I do have some good news, I have my planning permission for the barn and am really excited about that. Alistair isn't, by the way, pleased, I mean, about the planning permission, he thinks it's a waste of time and money."

"That's brilliant news, about the planning. I am really pleased for you. Look shall I come over? Dad's had his dinner and I could do with some girly time, you know, take my mind off all this mess here."

"That would be good, I'll put the kettle on, see you in a bit." She clicked off her phone and checked on Jess before going to the kitchen to put the kettle on and see if she could find the remains of any cake.

***

Alistair drove down the road out of Dorchester in a fury. He swung his sports car around the lanes sending stones flying into the air not knowing where he was going and not caring. He was fed up of having his day interrupted, his work was suffering and he was trying to support a wife and child without any help or even thanks. A car came up behind him, its blue light flashing. Alistair slowed and pulled onto the grass verge; he thumped the steering wheel.

"That's all I need," his anger not abating in the slightest. He watched the police officer walk slowly around the car; his colleague was on the radio. He lowered the window.

"Evening, sir, you were driving a bit erratic back there; is everything alright?" he asked politely.

"Yes, I'm sorry. I have had a row with my wife and well, I know it sounds pathetic, but I just, well, stormed out of there. I wasn't thinking, I just drove away," spluttered Alistair.

"Step out of the car, please, sir, have you been drinking?'

'No. Actually, yes, but I only had a few sips before…" he looked at his feet.

"… You stormed out. Yes, we know that, sir. As you have admitted having a drink, I would like you to take a breathalyser test for me if you don't mind?" His colleague now joined them, hands on hips, surveying the car.

"Nice car you have, sir, yours I presume, not borrowed it at all, have you?"

"No, I mean, yes, it is my car and is this really necessary? I have my documents with me and I haven't been drinking, so can we please get on with it." He handed his papers to the second officer and took the breathalyser from the first.

"I want you to take a deep breath and then blow continuously till I tell you to stop."

Alistair did as he was told, trying to calm down. The police officer looked at the result.

"Well, sir, you are not over the limit, but I suggest you sit quietly in your car for now and calm down before you cause an accident."

"Yes, officer, I will. Sorry I was being an idiot." The two police officers looked at each other and strolled back to their vehicle. Alistair watched them drive off before he sat back in his car; he gripped the steering wheel and dropped his head onto his hands. With little idea of where to go, he started the engine, driving distractedly down the road, his head whirling with a million thoughts and talking to himself. "What have I done?" No answer came. It was growing dark as Alistair found himself heading towards the farm. The lights were on, but only Bertie's old Jag was parked in the farmyard. He felt stupidly relieved that Lucy was not there; he wouldn't want to interrupt something and was strangely jealous of Bertie's independence.

He climbed out of his car and as he walked towards the door, it flew open and Rex came bounding over barking like a lunatic.

"Hey, boy, come on, it's only me." He ruffled his fur and Rex jumped up and down like a puppy. Bertie stood in the doorway, arms folded, leaning on the doorjamb.

"To what do I owe this pleasure, Alistair? And at this time of night," he glanced at his watch. Alistair could see the stupid grin on Bertie's face and wondered if he had made a mistake coming over, but he was here now.

"Thought I would come and keep you company for a bit, you know, indulge in some man's talk," he attempted to swagger over, raising his hand for a high five.

"Bloody hell, you must be ill. Come on in, mate, want a beer?" Alistair followed him into the kitchen, the old familiar smells assaulted his brain. Nothing had changed. He half expected to see Molly come through the door as Rex settled at his feet. There was something familiar and comforting about the farm, but he would never admit it, to anyone.

"Come on then, out with it," said Bertie handing him a beer, Alistair put out his hand and couldn't stop himself shaking. "Hey, what's happened? You look white, mate, and all done in."

"Sorry, I'm hungry, that's all. You wouldn't have a biscuit or something, would you?"

"I can do better than that, how about a bacon sandwich? And I always keep in a packet of chocolate hobnobs, in case an old mate comes around." He grinned at Alistair and he had to laugh.

"Yes, well, I'm sorry about that, I have rather ignored you recently but I'm here now," and began to tell Bertie the whole sorry tale as he watched him cook the bacon, put the brown sauce on the table and cut the two thickest slices of white bread he had seen in a long time.

He gulped in anticipation as his mouth watered and his nostrils sniffed in greedy expectation.

"You are a mate and I would have come before if I'd known about this," he said waving the sandwich in the air and licking brown sauce from his chin. Rex was sitting up staring at him licking his lips and swallowing at the sight of the bacon.

"It's not for you, mate," he said to Rex ruffling his ears, "…have you any treats for him, Bertie? I don't think I can stand him staring at me; I feel guilty." Bertie whistled to Rex and shook his box of treats. Rex retreated to his basket munching on a biscuit.

"Ironic, don't you think?" said Bertie at length.

"What do you mean?" Alistair looked up in surprise.

"Well, I thought that you couldn't stand this place and yet, here you are, in need of a bed for the night. I presume you want a bed for the night, right?"

"Please if it's not too much trouble? I didn't know where else to go. I couldn't go to Mother's… obviously."

"Obviously," said Bertie taking another pull on his beer, "and technically the farm's yours too now you're married to Molly."

"I suppose, I hadn't thought of it like that. Anyway, I'll have to sort something more permanent tomorrow."

"Don't you think that you should let Molly know where you are? She will be worried."

"No, I don't think so. I need time to think about all this and anyway I will have to go back in the morning to open up the office. If you don't mind, I'm exhausted, I'd like to get to bed."

"Okay, this way."

***

Molly's phone gave a ping. She grabbed it quickly. It was from Bertie, telling her that Alistair was at the farm and not to worry. She looked at Lucy, swiping a tear away.

"That was Bertie. Alistair is with him."

"I need to go," she stood up and pulled on her jacket, "he'll be back tomorrow, all smiles and apologies, carrying a big bunch of flowers, you'll see."

Molly wasn't quite so sure.

Chapter 7

Lucy stared at the shop with its blackened windows, bits of charred wood strewn across the lawn detritus of her mum's dream. She pinned a notice on the door saying CLOSED TILL FURTHER NOTICE. Dropping her shoulders and with a heavy heart pulled away from the kerb giving a final glance at the cottage next door. Her mum was now home and quite oblivious to what had happened in the shop. She had a few scrapes and bruises but the whole episode seemed to have catapulted her into her current state of mind. Her dad seemed unable to accept the situation and insisted that she should be able to remember and accusing the doctors of not doing their job properly. She felt as if her head was full of smog as she pulled into the farmyard. She had not intended to come here at all, she had been driving home realising that she had driven on autopilot and couldn't remember the journey. She switched off the engine bursting into tears. She put her hands over her face and just let it go, the pain, the worry and her feeling of desperation. Bertie yanked open her car door, she looked up at him mascara streaking her cheeks, red puffy eyes and sniffing.

"I'm so sorry, Bertie, I must look a mess," she sobbed.

"Hey, come on, let's get you indoors. I have a bottle of red open with your name on it," he smiled as he wrapped his arms around her tightly. "You can tell me all about it."

Lucy attempted to chuckle and let Bertie help her indoors, his arm comforting around her shoulders, the one person she could rely on. In the kitchen, Rex sat up in his basket whining but he didn't move. Bertie poured a large glass for her and she took an appreciative sip, then another and another.

"Slow down, there's no hurry. Come on tell me, is it your mum?" Bertie turned to the stove and began to stir something; Lucy took a deep breath watching him and feeling such warmth for him. She admired his calm approach to everything. Nothing seemed to bother him. Am I falling in love with him? She wondered. No, I can't be, he's just a wonderful man. She continued to gaze at him, trying to deny what her heart was telling her. He turned giving her a smile. Lucy jumped up and in two strides, was by his side.

"Will that spoil if we leave it for a while?" she asked, wiping the tears from her eyes, replacing them with lust.

"No," he pulled the pan off the heat. "Never, come here," he devoured her mouth with kisses, gentle at first and then becoming deeper and more urgent. She pulled away.

"Is Alistair due back?" she said, looking anxiously at the door.

"No, he's finally gone to see George and Alice so he won't be back for hours.' He took her hand and they dashed up the stairs pulling at clothes as they went falling onto his bed. Satiated and relaxed Lucy turned over reaching for Bertie. The bed was empty and she sat bolt upright disorientated for a moment. There was a clatter somewhere downstairs. Lucy looked at her watch. She must have nodded off to sleep. Quickly pulling on her clothes she headed downstairs to find Bertie back at the stove and cooking.

"There you are, I thought that I would let you sleep, you looked all done in," he grinned. Lucy crossed the stone-flagged floor, her heels clicking. Rex lifted his ears and watched them, gave a grunt and closed his eyes again. She slid her arm around his waist

"Hmmm that's why I love you," she squeezed him nestling her head on his back.

"What? Run that by me again. You… you love me?" he let the spoon drop, turning to enfold her in his arms. She couldn't help herself; she hugged him tightly and planted a quick kiss on his lips. "You said you love me, have you any idea how long I've waited to hear you say that?" he was grinning at her now, little lines crinkling the corners of his eyes. She touched them with her finger to smooth them away.

"You could have said it to me first," she giggled, "…but yes, I do love you, so much." She reached up on tiptoes, her lips seeking his.

"And I love you too," said Bertie between more kisses, "so much, so very much." He pulled away looking into her eyes. "Dinner or back upstairs?"

"Dinner," she gave a laugh. "I'm starving and back upstairs later, if Alistair doesn't come back," she threw him a cheeky grin.

"Who cares about Alistair, this is the best day of my life," he kissed her again, smoothing her hair, tucking a wayward curl behind her ear. "You are so beautiful, did I ever tell you that?" he said, letting a smile crease his lips.

"No, I don't think so, that smells really good, what have you made?" she peeped over his shoulder to look into the bubbling pan changing the subject.

"It's just vegetable stew and dumplings with homemade bread."

"Homemade bread, I didn't know you could bake as well!" her eyebrows shot up in awe.

"Alice, actually, she keeps turning up with food, I'm not sure if she's checking up on Alistair, or thinks that I need fattening up. She's always saying that I look thin and anyway it is welcome. I've even got some ginger cake that we can have with ice cream if you like."

"Yes, please, I really am starving. I do feel better already just being with you but I can't help worry about Mum and Dad," said Lucy reaching for bowls, picking up cutlery and pulling out the breadboard. She cut the bread into chunks and lathered some butter onto one corner, biting it off with relish. Bertie spooned out the stew.

"I should buy you an apron, then my vision would be complete," she laughed, tapping his bum, "…obviously with nothing underneath."

"Naughty," he pretended to be affronted, "you buy the apron and I'll see what I can do." He placed the bowls of steaming food onto the table and squeezed her hand. "The best day ever," he said again. Bertie patted his stomach and downed his glass of wine. "Top you up?" he asked picking up the red wine. "Oops, nearly all gone I'll get another, I suppose it should be champagne," he tipped up the wine into her glass.

"No more for me, I am driving remember," she glanced up at him, "and I ought to be getting back I am working tomorrow, the early shift."

"Stay. Stay with me tonight, I'll make sure you're up early. You won't be late. Promise," he laced his fingers through hers, his eyes pleading.

"I suppose I could but…"

"No buts, I'll open another bottle and I want to hear all about your mum and dad." She watched him jump up and smiled to herself, wanting to stay, to be as happy as this, forever.

"I feel like I've suddenly become the adult, which I know sounds weird but Dad is just looking to me to take over, sort everything out, be in charge and he just sits there, holding his head, not knowing what to do." She flopped back on the couch, glancing around the warm familiar room. "You know, I finally understand what Molly sees in this place. It envelopes you with a life of its own, makes you feel safe as if the world outside doesn't exist." She trailed her fingers along the worn arm of the sofa tracing the edges of the now faded pattern of hydrangeas and peacocks.

"I know what you mean. It feels comfortable, protecting," sighed Bertie. She watched him surveying his new home, he turned to look at her, "You could move in, live here with me." She jolted forward for a second and looked him straight in the eyes. She could feel that he meant it she swallowed hard.

"Maybe, one day, but right now I have to take care of things for my dad. The insurance has agreed a settlement and that has to be my priority right now," she caressed his arm gently fearing his rejection.

"Yes, sorry you're right I wasn't thinking. So what's next? At the shop, I mean." Lucy launched into her ideas telling Bertie about the different options for the cottage and shop.

"But the first thing is to book some time off and start clearing out and cleaning. I can't get Dad to consider moving, he won't hear of it but they will have to sooner or later. Mum clearly can't run the shop again, the two come together. It makes sense to sell up and move into Wareham then at least they are near to everything they need."

"Big decision that, I can understand your dad he must be in total shock at the moment. It's hardly surprising that he can't think straight. Look I can help too we can salvage what we can have a closing down sale maybe once the place is empty it might make things easier for him to see what he needs to do next. What do you think?" said Bertie. Lucy could feel the love in his eyes as they carefully searched her face for her response.

"Good idea," she said fondly, "come and have dinner with me tomorrow and we can make some plans. You could stay over and I won't be worried about Alistair turning up." She leaned over to kiss him.

"Love your thinking, it's a date," he returned her kiss, taking hold of her face in his hands, his kisses becoming more urgent. The crunching of wheels on gravel made them pull away.

"Alistair," they said in unison as he crashed in through the door, looking annoyed, grumbling to himself and dropping his bag on the floor, oblivious to them. Lucy and Bertie looked at each other.

"Nice evening?" asked Bertie as sarcastically as possible, grinning at Lucy.

"My mother, my mother…" he paused as his voice was rising in tempo, "my mother should keep her nose out and leave people alone." He stood hands on hips, before pacing back and forth.

"Hi, Alistair," said Lucy.

"Oh. Hi, Lucy, sorry. Sorry, am I interrupting something?" he rubbed his forehead, staring at them.

"I was just going actually. See you tomorrow Bertie." She got up and kissed him perfunctorily, picked up her bag and made to leave.

"I'll come outside with you…" he looked into her eyes regret written all over his face.

Bertie turned to Alistair, "Back in a minute, pal, okay?" He followed Lucy out to her car. "I could kill Alistair at times," he growled. "I wish you didn't have to go," he caressed her cheek.

"I know. See you tomorrow," he kissed her very gently and closing the car door he raised his arm in a wave watching her disappear down the lane. Rex was by his feet yawning and stretching.

"Sorry, mate, you need a walk, don't you, boy? Come on, let's get your lead and leave Alistair to calm down." He pushed open the door to retrieve Rex's lead hanging on a peg just inside the kitchen only to see Alistair downing a glass of his red wine and pouring another. "Save one for me, won't you? I'll just take Rex for a quick run, won't be long." He closed the door again not waiting for a reply and set off down the lane Rex padding along beside him. He decided to take the long route down to the sea and up along the cliff path.

There was a full moon and he could see one or two boats on the horizon wondering if they were fishing or just enjoying the warm spring evening. His head was doing somersaults thinking of Lucy and her declaration tonight then on to Alistair. "How could he be so stupid?" he asked Rex who merely lifted his ears and gave a little woof. "He has it all, a wonderful wife, a gorgeous little girl, a thriving business…" he stopped to watch some people skimming stones down on the beach, "…and he's risking it all, for what?" he stared down at Rex who was now panting from the climb. "Because he wants to stay living above the shop and yet, he's not, he's living with me. It doesn't make any sense at all!" he shook his head. "Come on, boy, let's go home before Alistair drinks me dry."

Bertie clicked the latch on the kitchen door and not hearing a sound crept inside. He saw Alistair fast asleep on the couch, mouth open, snoring gently. The empty wine bottle on the table told its own story.

"Hmm, I should have known," he picked up the bottle, "at least he didn't find my best whisky." He grinned at Rex who was now turning round and round in his bed trying to make it comfortable before crashing down letting his head drop onto his paws. Alistair made a snorting sound and woke himself up.

"Bertie…? Oh, Bertie, sorry mate I didn't know where I was for a moment. Did I hear you say whisky?" he rubbed his eyes and squeezed the bridge of his nose, shaking himself awake.

"No," he grunted in reply, "I said do you want a coffee? I was just putting the kettle on but I might be able to find a nightcap. Have you sorted anything out yet? With Molly I mean, you can't carry on like this." He turned to retrieve the mugs and pulled the kettle onto the Aga.

"Oh, not you as well, I've heard nothing else from my mother all evening. Molly won't even talk to me, I've done nothing wrong; all I want is to keep things as they are," he sounded exasperated and continued, "I just don't understand,

Molly is a good mum; she can do what she wants. I'm really busy, there is so much business in this area and all she keeps saying is she wants to get back to work and move over here to this old place," he looked around, derisorily nodding and waving his arm in an encompassing manner.

"It's her family home, she was brought up here," he poured a tot of the cheap whisky into the two mugs of coffee and handed one to Alistair, "you must be able to understand her need to get back to work. That practice is her life and you don't have to carry a baby, shopping and a pram up to a cramped flat." He took a swig of coffee wincing at the cheap taste of whisky as it hit the back of his throat.

"She's got to you, hasn't she? I suppose it was inevitable, no one seems to be able to see my point of view," he took a gulp of coffee, "I don't want to split up, but I can't live here, Bertie. Look at this place, everything needs doing to it, it would cost a fortune and anyway, I don't want to live here." He drank some more, "Got any biscuits, mate, take the taste of this rubbish whisky away?" Bertie opened the cupboard and took out a tin, handing it to Alistair.

"Listen to yourself, who's living here?" he paused pointing a finger at him, "… You. You are, mate, not Molly, if you're asking me and, I guess you are, then I would say, get back to Poundbury and talk to your wife. You know you should, if you mean it, about wanting to stay together, then it's down to you." He wagged his finger at Alistair in utter exasperation

"… And another thing, little Jessica is gorgeous; you are a bloody fool, mate, she won't know who her dad is if you don't do something about it." He stood up as he finished his rant partly out of frustration with Lucy going home and Alistair whinging like he has nothing, when if he took a good look at himself, he would see that he has everything. "I'm going to bed," he snapped, taking a last look at Alistair who appeared to be nonplussed and staring back at him.

He pulled out his phone as he climbed the stairs; he needed to talk to Lucy, bring his sanity back.

***

The next morning, all was quiet and Bertie assumed that Alistair had gone to work and maybe back to his wife, he shrugged picking up Rex's lead for their morning ritual. Rex obliged and they set off down the lane towards the village. Rex bounding by his side with excitement watched as Bertie picked up a stick throwing it into the field and climbing over the stile. Rex dodged underneath and took off lolloping his way through the mud after his prize. Bertie noticed a wisp of smoke coming from over the other side of the hill and headed towards it wondering who could be lighting a fire this early. Climbing over the next stile, Bertie put Rex onto the lead as there were sheep in the field. They began bleating and looked flustered as they moved away from them. He rounded the bend, only to see the back end of a car sticking out of the ditch he hurried towards it there was a distinct smell of petrol in the air. He could see that it was a sports car, his mind began to race… it was Alistair's car.

"Alistair," he called, "Alistair… are you alright?" He grabbed the nearside handle; the door was jammed and he could see Alistair slumped over the wheel. Bertie pulled out his mobile and pressed the number for Molly, then disconnected, pressing the number for George.

"Idiot," he said out loud and disconnected again and pressed 999. A paramedic was first on the scene quickly followed by George. Rex ran round and round, barking and trying to give everyone his stick. Bertie grabbed him and reluctantly put him on his lead and into George's car out of the way. Alice began to wail.

"Alistair, Alistair, what happened?" without waiting for a reply, she turned to the paramedic, "Is he going to be alright? Please tell me he will be alright."

"Alice, dear," said George, "let the girl do her job. Of course, he will be alright, just a bump on the head and a damaged ego," he smiled at the paramedic as he pulled Alice gently away. He patted her hand, "You are more in shock than Alistair. Now sit down and let them do their job."

"No bones broken," declared the paramedic, "but I would suggest we take you to A&E to check you over, that is a nasty bump you have there."

"No, honestly, I'll be alright. I just skidded on some mud, forgot I was in the country," he huffed, "need to get to work, the office won't open itself," he threw a glance in Bertie's direction.

"That's up to you, sir," grunted the paramedic as she packed away her bag just as Molly pulled up screeching to a halt. She jumped out of her Land Rover leaving a crying Jessica in her wake. Bertie rescued Jessica who was soon cooing happily.

"Oh, Alistair, what on earth happened to you? I was so worried when Bertie phoned."

"I'm fine, will everyone please stop fussing. I need to get to work."

"Not in that, you won't," said Bertie pointing at the dented car with its buckled wheel and half-missing bumper.

"I think you should come home with us," Alice sobbed.

"Mother, I'm fine. If everyone would just stop overreacting, my head's pounding, I can't think straight," he let out a sigh as he rubbed the back of his neck, twisting his head from side to side.

"That settles it," declared George taking charge, "Molly, dear, if you would bring Alistair down to our house, Alice will make some tea and can I ask you Bertie to arrange for the car to be towed into the garage in Wareham, please? Then we can all get some rest."

Bertie placed Jessica back into her seat and collected Rex. He sorted out Alistair's prized possession and set off back to the farm, pressing the number for Lucy and filling her in on the morning's drama.

"Are you still coming over this evening? I promised to cook remember?"

"Yes, definitely yes, I'll bring some veg from the allotment. I must get over to George and Alice's. I'm gardening today and find out about Alistair."

"See you later; I'll be home just after five, so come over when you're ready," she disconnected and Bertie turned to Rex,

"This is turning into a funny old day, mate," he patted Rex, "come on let's get you back to the farm, I have work to do." They trotted off back up the lane; Bertie felt a spot of rain, he looked up at the sky to see the gathering clouds.

"That's all I need," he told Rex.

Chapter 8

George and Alice sat on their veranda watching the glorious sunset. The sky was streaked with orange, red and gold. Starlings were gathering over the trees performing a wonderful murmuration across the sky before diving to the trees for the night. Alice sipped her sherry, a ritual they had perfected since George had retired. She looked across at him and opened her mouth to speak. George was snoozing quietly and she didn't have the heart to wake him. She reminisced about their life, so far, and wondered how Alistair was going to reconcile his differences with Molly. God only knows she thought that Molly was right but she would never admit it to Alistair. You can't cope with a baby in a flat not one upstairs with only one bedroom, she knew only too well. When she and George were newlywed and couldn't afford anything else, how she had struggled in those early days. George grunted, turning position, waking himself up, he pulled off his glasses and rubbed his eyes, sitting up.

"Sorry, dear, I seem to have nodded off. All that exercise at the football. Hmm sherry…" he took a sip, "…what were you saying, dear?" Alice laughed. How typical of George.

They had been married for forty years; her love had never diminished but grown over the years. She didn't know what she would do without him.

"I was just thinking that's all. You know you mentioned downsizing? Well, I've been considering our options." George sat up straight, giving her his full attention.

"Was that wise, my dear, and on your own?" George teased. Alice let out a chuckle and gently placed a fist on his arm as if to box him. She loved his little ways. There was a time when they hardly saw each other, especially when George was on call at all hours of the day and night; thankfully, that was behind them now.

"It occurred to me that maybe we could consider it although I shall miss this place. Are you sure that we are not too young? I mean we are not even seventy; well, almost I know but we could stay here easily for another ten years or so, there's no hurry, is there?" She turned and looked at him, her eyes pleading. Alice really couldn't bear the thought of moving out of her beloved home. True it was a bit large for just the two of them, but a better home she couldn't imagine.

"No, we don't have to do anything; it's just that we have both had scares recently and—"

"—But," interrupted Alice. George raised his hand.

"Let me finish, my darling, please, I just want to say that there is a whole wide world out there and no we are not old but I want us to have that retirement we always said we would and visit some of those places you have always wanted to go to. I know you have a little notebook with them all in and I just think that it is time we did it. Let the young ones sort themselves out. I know you're worried about Alistair but no worrying in the world will make him change his mind. He's as stubborn as you, so no we don't have to do anything you don't want to do. But you could think about it." He sipped his sherry sitting back again and resting his head. Alice did the same. After a few moments, she took another deep breath, considering what her response should be.

"That was quite a speech there, George, I can tell you have been waiting to deliver it and I know you're right; it's just that we have been so happy here… however, I'm not going to argue; can I think about it some more… please?"

"Darling, I love you so much, of course, whatever you wish." Alice smiled.

"Actually, I do need to talk to you about something, the Church fete, our wedding anniversary, a new vicar and you becoming a church warden."

"Oh, dear," said George, "let me get the sherry bottle, I'm going to need a top up." The cane chair creaked as he heaved himself up, he disappeared into the dining room, reappearing waving the bottle at Alice.

"Okay, my dear, I'm all yours, what first?" he smiled and kissed her cheek lovingly.

***

Alistair's mood was no better. He prowled around the office, rubbing the bump on his head.

He could hear Molly upstairs, vacuuming and occasionally, he heard Jessica cry. He leaned on the window ledge watching people walking by, he wondered if he had made a mistake in leaving London, but then, he did love Molly and Jess, but he did not want to move from Poundbury; it felt like home although not at the moment he was still at the farm. He let out a laugh. Bertie, his mother everyone seemed to think that he was in the wrong but hey his business is here what do they know? He balled his hands into fists and shoved them into his pockets in frustration. He glanced around thinking that he ought to do some work. He swung off his jacket and threw it onto the back of his chair pulled at his tie and opened the top button of his shirt. There was a knock on his door and Molly walked in.

"… Coffee?" she asked walking in with a steaming mug and a packet of biscuits.

"Thanks. Where's Jess?" Molly pulled out the baby monitor and waved it at him before placing it on his desk.

"… Fast asleep. I wondered if you could listen out for her. I need to go to the supermarket and I didn't want to wake her up. She's teething." Alistair dropped his papers and pushed his chair back.

"I'm trying to work; can't you go later?" He quickly realised his mistake, thinking better of it. Seeing the pained look on Molly's face, he relented, 'Okay, but please don't be long. I'm expecting a call." Molly slipped out and disappeared. It wasn't long before he heard Jessica start to cry and thinking that he could ignore her, tried to carry on working. Her cries grew louder and louder, then suddenly stopped. Alistair jumped up and raced upstairs only to find Jessica playing with a teddy bear. He picked her up with such relief and cuddled her to him.

"I'm so sorry, Jess, you frightened me for a minute there." He kissed the top of her head, she wriggled blowing bubbles at him. "My dear sweet little darling Jess, I love you so much. This thing with Mummy and me is so stupid. I will sort it, I promise." He kissed her again, rocking her and smoothing her hair. "… Sometimes Daddy makes a mistake, but you are not one of

68

them," he told her as Jess just gurgled and rubbed her eyes. Alistair heard his phone ring and put Jessica back into her cot, racing downstairs. The minute he grabbed the phone, he heard Jessica crying again, but he had to speak to his important client and turned the monitor off.

***

Molly pulled onto the drive and could hear Jessica from outside, she was horrified. She shot up the stairs two at a time and dashed into Jessica's room. By now, she was bright red in the face, tears rolling down her cheeks and howling as if she had been abandoned forever. Molly picked her up and shushed her, rocking her gently and cooing.

"I think you need a clean nappy; that is a lovely smell you have there. Come on, let's get you sorted out and then we can have a drink." Once finished, she took Jessica with her, remembering that she had left the shopping in the Land Rover. Cradling Jessica on her hip, she carried the shopping, one bag at a time, into the house and up the stairs. She could hear Alistair talking on the phone. She waited. Eventually, all was quiet and Molly went to confront him.

"Baby alarm broke?" she asked, picking it up.

"No, just turned off."

She glared at him, "Well, that tells me everything…"

"… I did hear Jess, but I couldn't put the phone down on a client now, could I?" he raised both hands, palms uppermost and looked from Molly to Jessica.

"Well, I've made up my mind, Alistair. You can move back in and before you get too excited, I'm moving to the farm… for good." She turned on her heels and marched out.

Alistair jumped up to follow her.

"Come on, Molly, I'm sorry." Molly turned and stared at him then continued upstairs; she had heard it all before and this time it wouldn't work.

"Tonight…" she called back down the stairs without turning to look. "Come on, my precious, we are going to move to the farm, go and see Bertie; that will be fun, won't it?"

Alistair raced after her, gasping for breath.

"Please, don't do this, Molly, I… don't want you to leave," he hissed, trying not to raise his voice. "Look, I'm sorry, I don't want you to go, I need you and I've missed you," he cajoled, his voice melting like ice cream covered in hot chocolate sauce, "…and I love you. You know I do, don't you? Come on, we can work this out, for Jess." Molly swung around to face him, anger and anguish boiling up together.

"Alistair, can't you see that it's not working out here, I can't even trust you to look after her for half an hour; anything could have happened. I'm going and that's it, you can have the flat, I'm sure you will be much happier here and we can get on with our lives." She turned away pulling cases out of the cupboard and grabbing clothes. She heard the door bang downstairs; Alistair had gone. Tears started to trickle down her cheeks, she sniffed and swiped them away. "Well, that answers that question," she told Jessica who was sitting playing on the rug. "Let's go see Bertie and Rex." Molly pulled away from the drive but couldn't see Alistair. She took out her phone to speak to Bertie.

"I already know," he said before she could say anything. "Alistair phoned and asked me to pack up his things; he'll be over later to pick them up. What is wrong with you two?" He sounded exasperated and Molly knew that this ping-pong had to stop.

"Oh. Well, he didn't try very hard to make me stay, did he? I'm sure that answers your other question. I'm going to see Stella and will be with you later and, Bertie… sorry about this; you don't have to leave, in fact, please don't leave. Okay?"

"Okay, see you later." He sounded resigned to the situation and Molly realised that this could only be a temporary arrangement. She drove to Beaminster, feeling guilty that she only seemed to visit her sister in a crisis, but knowing that she would understand. She began to talk to Jessica, pouring out all her thoughts and feelings. In reply, Jessica made lots of happy noises playing with her toes and gurgling at her mummy. Stella was just as understanding as Molly expected her to be. They hugged each other and Molly sobbed.

"I know I should never have married him but I really thought that he loved me and wanted our baby," she moaned. "I have no idea what happens next; it's down to him I suppose."

"I rather think that it's down to you, but a break might bring you both to your senses. I've seen the way he looks at you and I'm sure that he does love you but he's nearly forty and fatherhood has rather taken him by surprise. I don't think he knows how to handle it."

"You always see the good in people, I hope you're right, Stella, but right now I have to put Jessica first, get her settled and then I have a barn to convert. The builders are starting next week and I really want to get back to work."

"Have you found a nursery yet?" Stella asked handing Molly a slice of date and walnut cake and a cup of Earl Grey tea.

"I haven't looked, but that's another thing on my list and I need to speak to Lucy; she is going to wonder what I am up to moving in with her boyfriend," she laughed.

"He's staying on at the farm?" Stella raised her eyebrows in surprise.

"I can't throw him out now, can I? It's not his fault that all this has happened. I'm sure it will be fine." Molly hoped that he would, as she could do with some support. Bertie had always supported her and she loved him as a dear friend.

"Good luck with that one is all I'm saying, Molly," she sipped her tea.

"That was delicious," said Molly, scooping up the remaining crumbs. "I forgot to ask you how things are with the cake business."

"Excellent. I have two weddings this week, a christening cake for Sunday and a birthday cake for tomorrow," she glanced at her watch.

"I must be going," declared Molly as she picked up Jessica. "Thanks, Stella, for everything." She put Jessica back in the battered old Land Rover and drove down the road back to the Isle of Purbeck. She thought about her sister's advice as she meandered down the lanes and finally into the farmyard. There was no one around so Molly let herself in and pulled the kettle onto the hob all the familiar feelings flooded her senses she felt happy and comfortable here. She walked around the kitchen picking things up and looking at them as if with new eyes. Rex yawned and settled back into his bed giving a little welcome snort. Molly smiled to herself, wondering why she had ever agreed to leave at all. She quickly slipped into her old routine turning the boys' pad back into a home fit for a baby. Her phone buzzed; it was Lucy.

"Hi, Lucy, I was going to call you later, I'm at the farm, for good this time and I wanted to talk to you about it. You're alright with it, aren't you? I mean, me staying here with Bertie. Alistair will be going back to the flat, obviously and well, what do you think?" she finally paused for breath.

"What can I say? Of course, it's your farm and Bertie always knew that it was only temporary, but well, it is a bit odd, don't you think? Anyway, I only grabbed a few minutes' break. I'll come over later, see you then." She sounded a little short and suspicious, thought Molly and who could blame her.

"Okay. Bye.' Molly shuddered, closing her phone. Lucy was a bit frosty, hardly surprising, but she felt sure that it would all work out. Over the next few hours, Molly busied herself restoring her room to the way she wanted it and making up Jessica's room. Alistair's bags were packed and piled up by the farmyard door. She ran a finger over them, thinking how it could have been, why was he so stubborn? He had been living here, couldn't he see how it would make life so much easier, she moaned. Jessica squealed and Molly raced into the kitchen to find Rex sniffing and licking Jessica on her ear. Molly picked her up. "Come on, you two, let's go for a walk." Rex padded along beside her and Molly turned first to inspect the allotment. She sat on the bench, thinking back to when she had first asked Bertie to help her with the digging. He had done a good job, there were neat rows of carrots, onions, beetroot and potatoes even lettuce, green beans and more. She twisted her wedding ring as tears pushed their way onto her cheek, she brushed them away, taking a deep breath, turned the pushchair away and began to walk down the hill. Rex was racing on in front, sniffing every few steps and making his mark. Arriving back at the farm, Molly was surprised to see three more vehicles parked up by her rusting old Land Rover. She had not expected a delegation, but, "Here goes," she told Jessica as she opened the door into the kitchen. "How lovely to see you all," she breezed, taking Jessica's coat off, endeavouring to sound calm; she could feel her heart pounding and her hands were shaking. She glanced around the room, but it was Lucy who broke the silence.

"I know you don't like living in the flat, Molly, but this is not the answer." Molly felt anger creeping over her at her best friend's first comment.

"How do you know?" Molly snapped angrily. "I'm not after Bertie if that's what you think; this is my house and I'm not living in that flat a minute longer." She turned and glared at Alistair. "What have you been saying?" she asked him, her nostrils flaring. Alistair jumped to his feet.

"Look, I get it and I'm happy, well not happy, but willing to move in here with you if that's what you really want," he attempted to put his arms around her, but Molly shrugged him off.

"Don't try to placate me and act as if nothing has happened. It's clear to me that your precious business is far more important to you than I am or Jessica," she took a breath, trying to gulp down the rising lump in her throat.

"Molly, please, of course, my business is important, but not more than you and Jess; but I have to earn a living, can't you see that and I know you want to get back to work, your business is important too, but we need to sit down and work it out together." He dropped his hands in resignation, "Not like this." Everyone looked at each other, waiting. Jessica began to wail and Molly picked her up.

"She needs feeding and changing." Molly turned to leave, but Alistair caught her arm.

"Please," he said, before letting go again.

"Need any help?" Lucy asked tentatively, sounding much more like the friend she knew and loved. Molly shook her head. Looking up, she caught Bertie's eye. He had remained quiet so far, but he grinned at her and jumping up, he asked,

"Shall I make dinner… for all of us? Or would you rather Lucy and me scarpered for a bit, let you two talk?" Ever the diplomat, Molly smiled at him.

"That would be lovely and please stay, I won't be long and… and you, Alistair," she climbed the stairs, cuddling and kissing Jessica. "Mummy loves you very much," she whispered. Later, Molly returned to the warmth of the kitchen, she could hear happy chatter as she opened the door. 'Something smells good,' she announced as cheerfully as possible, doing her best not to let her anxiety show.

"Here," Alistair held out a glass of wine, proffering a tentative half smile.

"Thanks." She took the wine, letting her mouth twitch slightly. It was as if he were trying to woo her all over again. Molly liked the feeling, but wasn't about to let him off so easily. Meal over, Bertie pushed back his chair, rubbing his stomach.

"Well, I hate to break the good mood, but where do we go from here? I mean I'm not sure if I still live here or what is happening." He looked from Molly to Alistair.

"Why don't you come and stay with me tonight?" suggested Lucy. "Let them talk and see what tomorrow brings," she squeezed his hand, a twitch playing with her lips.

"Yeah, that's a good idea, okay better wash up first and get a few things," he stood up and Molly saw the look of love on his face, her heart twisted, she swallowed hard.

"Thanks, Bertie, you're a mate," she answered. "I'll wash up you two go and I'll see you in the morning." Bertie made to move to the stairs when there was a screeching of brakes outside, they all looked at one another.

"Who on earth is that at this time of night?" said Molly, getting up to investigate. The door crashed open and Rex leapt from his bed, barking frantically and racing towards the door. Sandra stood there; her arm draped around a suntanned man half her age. She held up a bottle of vino and swayed manically.

"Surprise!" she announced unnecessarily. Molly stood frozen to the spot; her mouth open.

"Well, aren't you going to say hello to your Mum or something?" drawled Sandra

"… This is Enrico by the way, my, err… friend," she hiccoughed.

"Darling, I'm much more than that," he nibbled at her ear and Sandra giggled. Molly turned and looked at Alistair, her eyes staring blankly as if he had the answer. He put an arm around her shoulders and hugged her close.

"Mum…" said Molly, unable to say anything else; her throat felt dry and staring at the dark-skinned Enrico with his black greasy hair, heavy gold chains clattering around his neck and rings on every finger.

"I've come to get the farm back; I'm going to sell it. Enrico says that I should never have given it away and the cottage, of course. I need the money for Spain." There was a deathly silence as everyone stared at the swaying couple before them.

"But, Mum, you gave me the farm when Dad died and Stella the cottage, you can't do this."

"I can do whatever I like. Luckily, I haven't signed the papers yet and now I don't need to. That's right, isn't it, Enrico?" she giggled.

'Of course, my darling." He picked up her hand and began to kiss each fingertip in turn, lifting his eyes up at Molly. She cringed inwardly, pulling back further into Alistair's arms.

"I think it's time we left," said Bertie, taking Lucy by the hand and heading for the door.

Chapter 9

"What do you think of that little scene?" asked Lucy when they were back at her house in Wareham. She felt for Molly, that was embarrassing and that Enrico made her shudder.

"Beats me," he said, slipping his arms around her waist pulling her gently to him. "I can think of other things I'd rather talk about right now."

"… But." He picked her up devouring her mouth stopping her from further elaborating. She swung her legs around his waist, forgetting her next question as they feasted on each other. "Hmm… no interruptions, what bliss." Lucy stretched out on the bed tracing a finger across Bertie's chest. "We have been thwarted too many times up at the farm. Bertie…?" said Lucy, endeavouring to get his attention.

"Hmm…" he bent over her, licking her nipples.

"Why don't you move in with me?" she grinned at him as he abruptly lifted his head, his eyes darting around her face.

"That's a bit sudden, isn't it? I don't know what to say, I need to think about it." She stared at him for a moment, that was not the reply she was expecting. She battled on.

"There's nothing to think about. God only knows what's going on at the farm. You might not even have a home there anymore. It makes more sense for you to move in here with me," she paused as she saw the hesitation in Bertie's eyes and pressed a finger to his lips. He took hold of her hand taking a deep breath.

"Okay, I'm not saying 'no' but I need to get back to the farm today to find out what's happening." He swung his legs out of bed. Lucy quickly aimed a smack on his bum.

"Already…?" she said, throwing him a cheeky grin, pulling back the covers.

"Well, maybe not just yet." He slid back between the sheets and into her.

***

Lucy pulled on her dressing gown as Bertie headed for the shower. She yawned long and deep. Picking up the coffee pot and switching on the grill to make eggs on toast. She tugged open the fridge and took out tomatoes and mushrooms when her phone buzzed. It was Molly.

"Hi, how is everything over there today? Your mum and Enrico…" she said, drawling out his name in an exaggerated Spanish accent, "…still with you?" She pulled out the butter and marmalade pushing the door close with her elbow.

"No, thankfully Enrico said he couldn't possibly stay in this old place and they have gone to The Priory in Wareham," Molly released a yawn.

"Wow, he must be rich."

"I rather think that Mum is paying. Anyway, can you come over today? I really need to talk to you; Alistair has gone to work and I wasn't sure what time you started at the hospital today."

"Stop, back up a minute, Alistair stayed last night, does this mean what I think it means?"

"Maybe, he was really sweet and very supportive but he slept in the spare room."

"Well, that's a start, give him a chance, Molly," she hesitated before continuing. "I'm not due in till this afternoon so give me an hour and I'll be there. I know that Bertie wants to come over too and see what his position is now with everything that's going on. Is that alright?"

"Of course, see you later." She closed her phone just as Bertie enveloped her into his arms and began nibbling her ear.

"Hey, I might change my mind about you moving in, I will never get any work done!" she grinned, giving him a gentle push. "… And the toast is burning." She leapt to rescue the toast just as the deafening shrill of the smoke alarm started threatening to wake the whole neighbourhood. Bertie wafted the alarm with a tea towel and Lucy quickly opened the door ejecting the burnt offerings out onto the patio. They both fell about laughing before Lucy cut two more slices of bread wagging her finger at him saying, "… No, behave. I need to talk to you about Molly." Sitting at the table coffee in hand Bertie pushed his plate away.

77

"If that's how I am treated, I might never leave." He rubbed his stomach as he lifted his eyebrows at Lucy.

"No promises," she teased, "… Molly sounded a bit distraught earlier and I'm going over there in a minute. Do you want a lift?"

"I'll run if you don't mind and then you two can have a girly chat before I get there," he drained his coffee. "I've been thinking…"

"Hmm… What about, disappearing off to Lanzarote and becoming a beach bum and looking for wealthy widows, like Enrico?" she collected the plates and stacked the dishwasher.

"As attractive as that maybe," Lucy turned sharply and flicked the tea towel at him.

Bertie feigned a damaged arm and moaned in pain, "Ow, I… I was actually thinking about the shop. I'm a one-woman man and I already have everything I need right here." Lucy leaned in for a kiss and got rather more than she bargained for.

***

Later, Lucy drove into the farmyard, she looked at her watch. She was over an hour late. Rex came bounding across the farmyard expending more energy in that frenzied minute than he had all day. Lucy gave him a pat and he trotted along beside her back into the kitchen.

"I'm so sorry, Molly, I got held up," she felt her skin getting hot at the thought and she tugged at her coat, throwing it onto the sofa.

"No worries, I've had phone calls this morning anyway, both from Alistair and my solicitor and, of course, I had to speak to Stella. All hell let loose here last night, but thankfully, I've heard nothing from them today so far. I don't know what's got into mother." Molly poured out two coffees, cut some chocolate cake and put it in front of Lucy. "Well, I do of course it's that bloody Enrico. I don't know what's going to happen now and then there's Bertie," she burst into tears. Lucy jumped up and put her arms around her.

"Hey, come on let it all out. It will be fine, I'm sure," she rubbed Molly's back but wondered what could or would happen next. Sandra seemed sure of what she wanted to do and she did have the right; it was still her farm and if she wanted to sell it and spend all the money on Enrico there was nothing Molly or anyone else could do about it. It did throw up other questions though, who is this Enrico person? He was clearly years younger than Sandra; he could be genuine though. Molly blew her nose.

"I'm sorry, Lucy. I think I needed that; I feel like I don't know my own mother anymore. It's just that my problems with Alistair and then mother turning up like that," she let out an enormous breath, "what is going on with the world all of a sudden?"

"Good question. What did your solicitor say? Is there anything you can do?" Lucy picked up her chocolate cake and sat at the scrubbed pine table, Molly joined her, collecting two napkins for them.

"He needs time to look into everything. Stella and I are seeing him tomorrow. It would appear that the best thing to do right now is to stay put. I'm just thankful that I moved back yesterday and that I haven't started back at work yet. It couldn't have happened at a worse time as the builders start on Monday and I need to be there for that, but at least, Hugh, you know, the locum, can give me a few more months," she sipped her coffee. "What is wrong with Mum? Dad has only just passed away; he wouldn't want this... Do you think she was seeing this Enrico before Dad died?" Molly put her coffee down and started to sob once more.

"No, I'm sure not. I think that Enrico is just taking advantage of Sandra's vulnerability and maybe she's been bragging about the property she owns here and he came to see it for himself." Lucy tried to reassure Molly. "Tell me about Alistair."

"He was great last night, even fed Jessica in the early hours so that I could get some sleep. He's just as worried as I am and said that he will try and do some digging, see what he can find out about Enrico. Would you like another coffee?" Molly stood to get the coffee pot from the Aga.

"Please. Look if there's anything I can do, just let me know, I don't know what but...oh nearly forgot Bertie is on his way, he wanted to get a run in and he's worried if he is going to lose his home. I told him he can move in with me, but he wanted to talk to you first."

"What would I do without you two?" Molly tried a wan smile just as the door opened and Sandra walked in, in a cloud of Dune, followed by Enrico. Both girls turned, shooting a quick glance at each other. Lucy could see the look of shock mingled with love and despair on Molly's face.

***

"Walk right in, won't you, don't mind us," Molly immediately regretted what she said and bit her lip.

"Don't you start on me, Molly, my head is pounding this morning and I can walk straight into my house any time I like. Have you any paracetamol?" Sandra glowered at Molly and Lucy. Enrico put his arms around Sandra, squeezing her rather intimately. Molly was dumbfounded, how could her mother be so cruel?

"Don't upset yourself, my darling, sit down and let me massage your shoulders." He pulled out a chair and helped her to sit down. Molly just stared in utter amazement before reaching for the paracetamol and a glass of water on autopilot, pushing it in front of her mum.

"Is that better, darling? You know how these little things can give you a nasty headache."

Enrico said kissing the top of her head and lifting his eyes menacingly in Molly's direction.

"Oh, yes, Enrico," she reached up and patted his hand before picking up the tablets and swallowing them. She turned to Molly.

"When are you moving out, Molly? I want to get an estate agent here as soon as possible and return to Spain."

"Mum, I can't believe you're doing this to me and Stella and no, I'm not moving out. Stella and I have an appointment with our solicitor tomorrow and you haven't even asked about your new grandchild yet." Molly gulped, feeling herself get more agitated by the second.

It didn't help that Enrico was staring at her all the time. She wished that Alistair was here.

"You can see whoever you wish, but it doesn't alter a thing. I still own this house and the sooner things are sorted the better. Now, what about a coffee for me and Enrico? That cake looks good too.' Sandra settled herself by the table and Enrico slid onto a chair next to her, being very attentive. Molly felt at a loss, she had never seen her mother like this before… before this whole alien scenario and it made her feel sick. She was out of her depth and fighting the love for her mum, but was horrified at what she had become.

"Shall I take Jessica out in her pram, Molly?" Lucy asked. 'I think she has woken up and you can talk to your mum."

"Yes, thanks, Lucy, I'll just get a bottle in case she gets hungry and a change of nappy." Molly turned to pack the things into a bag, her hands shaking, dreading being left alone, but what choice did she have?

"Molly, dear," Sandra now sounded more like her old self and Molly turned to look at her, "why don't you let me and Enrico take her out? I would like to spend some time with her." Molly's heart began to pound as adrenalin surged through her body, she gripped the bag, she couldn't think of anything worse. Maybe it was Enrico's plan to kidnap baby Jessica and hold her to ransom in exchange for the farm, she panicked. *Don't be silly,* a little voice said in her head. She relaxed. Of course, that was nonsense, but how she hated this frightening man.

"No," said Molly, rather sharply. "No, it's okay, Lucy can take her, she knows Lucy and I think that we need to talk… err in private." Molly threw an apologetic look at Lucy who smiled back before settling Jess in her pram.

"Yes, you're right as usual, Molly. There are things that we need to discuss." Molly heaved a sigh of relief and tucked Jess up giving her a kiss and squeezing Lucy's arm.

"I'll be back in an hour, Molly, don't forget I have to work this afternoon," she whispered. Lucy manoeuvred the pram outside just as Bertie came running up the lane, he waved at Lucy and Molly.

"Hi. Going somewhere?" he puffed and panted as he stopped beside them his hands on his knees as he caught his breath. Molly quickly filled him in and Bertie said, "Look, I'll stay, I need a shower and change. Someone should stay with you. We know nothing about this Enrico fellow."

"Yes, you're right,' said Molly, 'come on in and see you later, Lucy." She watched Lucy walk out of the farmyard before taking a deep breath to gain some courage. She straightened her back and walked into the kitchen to tackle her mother and the lecherous Enrico.

"Hi," greeted Bertie with a wave as he followed her in and immediately disappeared upstairs without waiting for a reply.

"Good grief, Molly, how many men have you got living here? I presume he lives here too by the way he seems to be making himself at home." Sandra looked at Molly displaying her favourite disgusted look.

"He does live here as a matter of fact and he's a really good friend," Molly wondered why she was justifying herself, feeling defensive when she had done nothing wrong. Her mother always knew how to manipulate her, not like Stella; she wouldn't treat Stella like this.

She caught Enrico staring at her again and she gave an involuntary shudder, quickly looking back at her mother who didn't appear to notice Enrico's behaviour at all. "So, what is it you want to say, Mum?"

"Molly, you have to understand that life goes on. I loved your father, but now I can't manage on my pension, I should never have given you the farm, I wasn't thinking, it was the grief speaking. You have Alistair bringing in a good income, the practice and I hear that you are converting that old barn into a home... so where's your problem letting your old mum have the money from the sale of the farm, eh?" She looked at Molly with a downtrodden forlorn look on her face. Put like that, Molly felt a heel, her shoulders dropped and she began to wonder if she was the one at fault here after all. "You can't deny me some fun and a decent life, surely, see me not having enough to eat and struggling; what kind of daughter would that make you?" Molly saw red, this wasn't her mother talking, this was some radicalised person and she knew exactly who had done this to her. Staring straight at Enrico, she pulled herself up, reaching for the coffee pot, tempted though, she was to pour it over his head, she smiled sweetly.

"… More coffee, Enrico?" she said and then turning to her mum, "You could sell up in Spain and move back here, you have Dad's money from the sale of the land not to mention his pension, I think that you are rather comfortable actually and as you said yourself, Dad wanted me to have the farm and Stella the cottage." She shot a look at Enrico who was now staring at

82

Sandra, clearly, this was all news to him. "…I would say that I am a loving and protective daughter, actually one who loved her dad and is trying to look out for you too."

"I can see that we are getting nowhere." She abruptly stood up and turning to Enrico, announced, "I think we should leave, I'll come back when you are not so aggressive and more amenable to your old mum." She picked up her bag, "Your dad would turn in his grave if he knew how you were treating me." Molly's mouth dropped open. Then quickly she shot back,

"Have you been to the churchyard to talk to him yet, Mum?" Molly knew that was a bit mean, but she was trying to get her mum out of this deluded state of mind, "You remember where he is buried, don't you?" Sandra stormed out without saying another word, Enrico close behind. The door crashed shut and Rex gave a startled woof as he clambered out of his bed, shook himself and slunk around Molly's legs. Bertie clicked open the door, his hair still wet and clinging to his face, a towel draped around his shoulders.

"Is it safe to come in now? I could hear all the shouting and thought that I should stay out of the way." He shoved his hands into his pockets hunching his shoulders. He tentatively made his way across the kitchen picking up the coffee pot.

"Oh, Bertie, I'm so sorry. I forgot that you were upstairs." Molly sobbed of all the things her mother could have said. She was amazed at the awfulness of her language; this is not like her at all and Molly was left wondering more about who is this Enrico fellow. She knew she didn't like him and there was obviously more to it, but what?

"No worries. This is empty." He shook the pot, "Shall I make some more?" Molly nodded and dropped onto the couch. She looked around the kitchen, she had known and loved this room her whole life, it didn't matter to her that the Aga was chipped or that the flagstones needed re-setting or even that the sash windows rattled in the wind. She pictured her father coming in from milking the cows, being told off for not removing his boots and sitting at the scrubbed pine kitchen table eating meat and potato pie, carrots and gravy, onion gravy, to be precise. It was like only yesterday and now her mother walked around like she was gentry, making demands followed by her Spanish lapdog. Bertie held out a mug of coffee,

"Hey, where are you? Some distant place and time, I bet." She looked up at him and took the coffee a plan building in her mind. "That cake looks good." He grinned.

"Oh, sorry, Bertie, go ahead help yourself," she glanced at her watch, "Lucy should be back soon with Jessica and I have decided that I am not going to take this lying down, in fact, if it's a fight she wants, she is going to get it, so watch out when sparks fly." She gritted her teeth determined that somehow, she was not going to lose the farm. She got up from the couch with renewed determination picking up her iPhone. She needed to talk to Stella – urgently.

Chapter 10

Sandra sat in front of her solicitor. She pulled her coat up more tightly around her neck. It was the summer here in England, but she still found it chilly after the heat of Spain. Spain, she couldn't wait to get back there and sit under her veranda looking at the gorgeous turquoise blue of the Med, palm tree fronds gently moving in the cooling breeze. The sun glinting off the waves as they gently bubbled along the surface of the sea and Enrico, so attentive, massaging her shoulders. She let out a sigh and old Bradwood looked up at her over the rim of his glasses, sucking in his breath.

"Well," she said rather impatiently, "what do you think? I need to know as I want to get back home, to Spain, as soon as possible." She pulled herself up to her full height as a shiver passed through her; she crossed her legs smoothing her dress over her knees, clutching her bag. Sandra looked him in the eye, knowing what his answer would be, but she had to ask in case there was a glimmer of hope that she would get her own way. It wasn't easy being a single woman again, well a widow technically; however, she still needed money and in her mid-sixties felt she was still a catch. She smoothed her hair and pursed her lips, not that that would have any effect on old Bradwood she knew, in fact, what was he doing still practising, senile old goat, he must be seventy if he's a day. Sandra took in a deep breath and waited. Mr Bradwood took off his glasses and placed them neatly on top of the open file on his desk and got up, walking towards the door.

"Coffee… Mrs Craven? I should have asked when you arrived, very remiss of me," he opened the door without waiting for her answer. "Two coffees, please, Jayne. Thank you." He closed the door again and sat down. "When are you planning to go back to Spain, Mrs Craven? Only these things take time." He pulled on his chin, causing Sandra to feel agitated and annoyed with him. He was prevaricating.

"As soon as possible," snapped Sandra. "I don't want to stay here too long. I had forgotten how cold it is and this is the summer!" She glanced at him only to observe the amused look on his face. There was a knock on the door and Jayne came in carrying a tray neatly laid up with coffee and biscuits. She placed it on the corner of the desk and retreated, the door clicked shut. Mr Bradwood set about handing her a coffee and offering biscuits.

"Look, Mr Bradwood, please stop prevaricating. I need to know when I can sell the farm and where I stand, no sugar for me thank you," she took the coffee from him taking a sip.

Sandra pulled a face, wincing at the disgusting taste of instant, yet another reason for going home.

"Mrs Craven… Sandra…" Mr Bradwood put his glasses on again resting them on the end of his nose and peering at her over the top. She felt as if he were treating her like a naughty child or worse, a complete imbecile, but she smiled weakly, looking him in the eye. "It is complicated, but basically, your and your husband's estates were equalized and…"

"Yes, yes, I know that, all I want to do is sell up, so when can I do that?" She put the coffee down took out a tissue and dabbed her mouth, not wanting to smudge her lipstick.

"I think that I need to explain what exactly yours and your husband's wills mean. It's not as straightforward as that. Your husband's half of the estate, meaning the farm and the cottage and land within its curtilage have been left to Molly and Stella."

"You mean that I only own half of it? But I can still sell it, surely?" she asked, now feeling quite anxious about the whole thing.

"No, any sale has to be with the full agreement of Molly and Stella and also, you must allow them first refusal to purchase the whole."

"But what if they say 'no'? How am I going to get my money?" Sandra did not hide her annoyance at the situation, clearly escalating by the second, as she sighed over and over again.

"I suggest that you speak to Molly and Stella as soon as possible and find out what they want to do and if you need me to facilitate a meeting, then please make an appointment with Jayne."

"This is ridiculous," Sandra furiously scraped her chair back staring at Bradwood and stormed out of the office without another word. In reception, Enrico, who had been lazily flipping through a magazine, leapt to his feet, Sandra's face crumpled at the sight of him, she pulled out a tissue to dab her eyes.

"My darling, what on earth happened?" He put his arms around her and led her outside. "Let's go for a coffee back at the hotel and you can fill me in. Please don't upset yourself. It's your property, you can do whatever you wish with it, can you not?"

***

Stella and Molly walked up the main street towards the office of Humphrey Bradwood in Wareham, just as a car shot out of the car park, narrowly missing them. Molly threw her arm out to protect her sister as it careered passed them and down the road towards the river.

"I think that was Mum, with Enrico driving like a madman. I wonder what Bradwood told them?" They pushed open the office door for their appointment with dear old Mr Bradwood. Jayne met them with a smile. An hour later, Stella and Molly sat drinking Earl Grey tea in their favourite teashop by the quay.

"I can't believe it, good old Dad, he must have known something like this might happen," said Molly. Stella put her cup down, picking up the crumbs from her chocolate and beetroot cake.

"No, I don't think so, he just wanted to make sure there was something left for us. I don't think Mum was involved with Enrico or anyone else before Dad died, I'm sure of it." She poured another cup of tea looking forlornly out of the window. Molly lazily sipped the remains of her tea, considering the situation they now found themselves in.

"Maybe not, but she didn't tell us about the equalization of the estates and that we had inherited Dad's half, did she?" declared Molly. "Unless of course, she didn't understand what it meant. You know Mum, she left all the finances to Dad, she couldn't be bothered… until now, that is." They grinned at each other.

"No, you're right and I think that it must have been quite a shock to her to find out that she can't push us out and sell up. What are we going to do though, we now own half of all of it? So, that changes everything."

"Good question. Do you want to buy the other half and then we can separate it out properly? Mum can't buy us out, she wants rid of the place and she can't sell half to someone else without our say so. On the other hand, I don't want to hurt her, but I do not trust that Enrico at all," declared Molly. She watched Stella as she picked up her cake, writing a reminder on her phone.

"Neither do I, not one little bit..." said Stella, looking into her teacup, swirling round the last dregs. "That cake was really good. I think, I will try that one at home. Did I tell you I'm thinking of starting a mail order business online? For my cakes that is," Stella grinned, changing the subject.

"Brilliant idea, I'm surprised that you didn't do it before. When does it all happen?"

Molly straightened, giving her full attention to this innovative news.

"I have a website being designed, so am nearly ready for a launch date, then I'll see how it goes. The girls are very excited. They think that we will be millionaires tomorrow," they both laughed. "So, come on we had better get back to the farm and I need to get home I have a lot to do." They left the teashop and walked through the cobbled alleyway from the quay back to the car in silence. Molly desperately wanted to keep the farm, but with the expense of the barn conversion, she just didn't have the cash right now and Stella's new business venture could mean that she couldn't do it either. Once they were in the car, Molly broached the subject again.

"We should try and meet up with Mum, on her own, and try to discuss it without getting heated, don't you think?" asked Molly.

"Yes, I do, but I've been thinking, as much as I would like to buy her out, I don't think we can at the moment what with the online launch and everything and I can't think of a compromise unless we sell the whole lot. At least, then mum can have her half and I have to admit the extra cash would be useful," she paused, throwing a sideways glance at Molly.

"I can't let the farm go, I just can't," Molly gulped, not realising till now how much she really loved the place, "it would break my heart." She turned and looked out of the window and across the water meadows that led to the harbour. Stella turned left into the lane that led down to the farm.

"Oh, dear," she announced. Molly shot up her head and seeing her mother's hired car in the farmyard, her heart sank. "Looks like we have company, are you ready for the fireworks?"

Chapter 11

Alice threw herself into the arrangements for the church fete and the celebrations for their wedding anniversary, calling a meeting of the church wardens and organising committee.

She cleaned the house from top to bottom, even the rooms that no one would see, but she knew that not one speck of dust remained. Even the oven had seen a clean and George had been dispatched to clean the windows amid much complaining and suggestion of finding a window cleaner! Alice was only too aware that Doris, in particular, had a habit of trailing a finger along any surface and carefully inspecting her fingers for any sign of dust. Alice had always found this habit very rude, but nevertheless, she was determined that no one would find anything amiss with her house. Lady Isobel was the first to arrive, bringing with her a tin of chocolate brownies, it was the only thing she could make successfully and they were always appreciated.

"Isobel..." they air-kissed each other. "I'm so pleased that you are early as I need to talk to you before the others land on us," beamed Alice as she helped Isobel with her jacket.

She took out a plate and arranged the brownies onto it, piling them up into a pyramid before putting them onto the centre of the table. The door opened and George walked in, his glasses up on his forehead and holding the morning paper.

"Morning, Isobel," he glanced at the table, "ooh, one of these for me?" He leaned over, removing a brownie from the bottom, causing the pyramid to topple over. Alice tapped his hand.

"George, now look what you have done and they were not for you," she said crossly as George shoved the last crumbs into his mouth, giving Isobel a conspiratorial wink. Her face crinkled into a smile and she lifted her hand to her mouth to stifle a grin from Alice, just too late as Alice had seen the little exchange.

"Be off with you," she remonstrated, "… unless, of course, you want to volunteer for the committee?"

"I have to be somewhere," said George hurriedly, turning to Isobel, "sorry, Isobel, catch you next time." He disappeared, leaving mayhem in his wake. Alice tutted.

"Let's retire to the other room, Isobel; we need to talk about the new vicar; I want to know what your thoughts are." She led the way into the snug room, carrying a tray. "I quite like the sound of the latest two applicants and the Bishop complimented them both. I know that we shall have the opportunity to meet them soon, but I wonder if you have had chance to think about them yourself?" They settled down in the two wing chairs and Alice poured the tea.

"They are both quite different, Reverend Timothy Wagstaff is married with two children; it would be nice to have a family man. I don't know how involved his wife might be, but she could take some of the church duties off our shoulders," she sipped her tea before continuing, "the church fete, the Christmas bazaar, the Harvest supper and all the other fund raisers that we do are quite a responsibility, not to mention the workload, but, of course, these days, many have careers of their own and don't get involved at all. We need to know more about them, I feel."

"What about Reverend Suzanne Martin? Now she is young and apparently, full of enthusiasm. This would be her first parish, I think that she could be the one to bring the younger generation into the church, a real breath of fresh air, don't you think?" declared Alice with a smile.

"Hmmm, I rather think that you want to put old Doris's nose out!" They both laughed as a knock came to the front door.

"That must be the rest of the committee, perhaps you will stay to tea, Isobel and we can continue this chat later."

***

Lucy placed the tea tray in front of her mum and sat down. She gave a sigh and pondered how to bring up the subject of the shop. It had lain empty since that dreadful day of the fire and her mum either hadn't noticed the damage or maybe she couldn't be bothered anymore, but either way, something had to be done and her father, poor man, did not seem able to cope at all.

"Mum..." she ventured hesitatingly, "I was wondering what you wanted to do with the shop?"

"The shop...? What are you talking about, dear? There's nothing wrong with the shop and I will be back working as soon as I feel better." She picked up her tea and looked at Lucy with raised eyebrows.

"Don't you remember the fire, Mum? The shop is totally ruined. I was thinking of holding a sale of anything that could be rescued so that it can be rebuilt by the insurance company and..." her mum broke into her flow, gasping, a terrified look in her eyes.

"Fire! Who did this? Some vandals from Wareham, no doubt, have you told the police?" she put her cup down standing up. "Let me see the damage, why didn't you tell me before? I never get to know what's going on and where is your father? He's always disappearing." Lucy jumped up, grabbing her mum's arm.

"Sit down, Mum. It was weeks ago; you have been in the hospital. You knocked the heater over and caused the fire."

"Don't be ridiculous, Lucy, that's impossible, I would never do a thing like that," she snatched her arm away from Lucy. "I'm going to see this for myself, now let me go." Lucy dropped her arm and followed her out to the shop. The damp walls had dried out, but tins were strewn across the floor, charred papers had been swept into one corner, the glass counter was blackened from the smoke. Only a pile of beach buckets and spades seemed to have escaped the devastation. Her mum walked across the shop, she picked up a tin placing it on the counter, wandering around in silence. She spun the sails on a windmill once destined for a sandcastle down on Trentmouth beach. Staring at the mess, she burst into tears, grabbing a handkerchief, she sobbed and sobbed. Lucy put her arm around her shoulders and guided her back into the cottage, sitting her down by the inglenook. Tricia wiped her eyes and took a sip of tea. "Yuk, this tea is cold, dear, can you make a fresh pot and where's your father?"

Lucy retreated to the kitchen, stunned by her mother's reaction. She did not understand dementia; all she knew that there were many types of dementia and it seems that everyone is different. She had not expected her mother to act as if she hadn't even seen the shop. She glanced out of the window, relieved to see her dad walking up the path. She needed to talk to him and get things moving.

"Just making a pot of tea, Dad, would you like one?' she called out to him.

"Yes, please, love. How's your mum?" he appeared at the kitchen door, leaned against the doorjamb, looking weary. He had just finished his stint at the railway and his hands were covered in oil and grease. He loved it there, but he was looking weary and not just from hard work Lucy knew and was beginning to understand his worries over Tricia.

"I'm really worried about her. She knew nothing about the fire and insisted on seeing the shop then came back in here as if she hadn't seen it at all. What are we going to do, Dad?" she asked anxiously.

"I don't know, love, I don't know," he rubbed a hand across his forehead, smearing some oil down his cheek. "Let me try and talk to her. You get off and see Bertie."

"Thanks, Dad. I'll ring you tonight." Lucy put on her jacket and went to kiss her mum.

Tricia sat totally still, not reacting to Lucy at all, her eyes on her empty plate. "Bye, Mum. See you tomorrow." Lucy left without looking back, tears stinging her eyes.

It was Lucy's day off and she drove over to the farm, wondering what the latest was with Sandra and Enrico, not to mention the problems that Molly and Alistair were having. She thought about her mum and how her dad was going to cope. It was clear that they would not be moving as she wanted them to do, her mum would never handle it, not now. She knew that it was going to be down to her to make the decisions from now on; she let out a heavy sigh.

Lucy drove on towards the farm, passing the duck pond, narrowly missing a mother duck followed by her brood of ducklings as they crossed the road, making her smile. She resolved to put on a happy face and try to push her thoughts away, for now. Driving into the farmyard, Lucy slowed and stopped, staring at a car she didn't recognise. The farm door opened and a woman stepped out. She was smartly dressed in a dark navy suit and way too high killer heels. She was carrying a briefcase and shook hands with Bertie saying something to him before she walked, swinging her hips, Lucy noticed, to her car –

a smart red convertible, no less. Lucy hesitated and put her car in reverse, imagining the worst, ready to disappear. Bertie waved, was it to her or that woman, Lucy seethed. She swung her car up into the farmyard and watched the woman disappear. Bertie opened her door.

"Hey, this is a surprise, a nice one, I might add. I thought you would be ages yet," he grinned.

"Clearly," Lucy said, her face betraying her thoughts.

"Wow, you jealous?" Bertie smirked, almost triumphant as he held the door open for her, struggling to stifle an even bigger grin, she noticed.

"Well, who was she then?" Lucy was horrified at her own reactions, spluttering an apology, "Sorry… I mean, I didn't know you were expecting another visitor this afternoon. Sorry, that came out wrong, of course, you can see whoever you like. She looked very nice, she must have a good job, driving a car like that and…"

"Whoa, stop," Bertie held up a hand and leaned in for a kiss. "I'm very flattered that you are jealous and you think that she was here for me but, alas, she is an estate agent, sent by Sandra," he pulled her close, "…and she is not a patch on you," he kissed her deeply, "ever."

Lucy snuggled up to him, feeling very foolish.

'The ones I've met never looked like that or drove a sports car, so can you understand why I was err… suspicious!' she attempted a pleading look of innocence which only made Bertie laugh even more. He put an arm around her shoulders and guided her indoors. Rex lifted his head to look at her and then, as if from the effort, dropped his head once more and went back to sleep.

"I've missed you," Bertie said, lifting her chin up and looking into her eyes.

"I've missed you too. I want to hear all about this… this estate agent."

"Later," Bertie kissed her again, pushing her coat off onto the floor. Lucy let her bag fall, kicked off her shoes, tearing at her top. Bertie grabbed her hand and led her up the stairs.

The sun was falling behind the trees when they arrived back in the kitchen. All was quiet.

Only Rex stirred; he yawned and padded towards the door to be let out. "I'll cook," exclaimed Bertie, "can you open a bottle of wine please, then I will tell you all about this afternoon's visit."

"Okay," Lucy smiled, contentment flooding through her. She watched him deftly get out the various cooking pots, vegetables, eggs and cheese placing them onto the kitchen table.

She poured two glasses of wine and sat down. There was a rap on the door and in walked Sandra, followed by Enrico. Rex pushed his way between the two of them looking for attention. Lucy and Bertie stared at the sudden intrusion.

***

"Bertie, I want to know all about the estate agent, what did she say, when can it go up for sale and when are you leaving?" she made to sit down at the table picking up Bertie's glass of wine, taking a sip.

"Well, hello to you too," he declared, hands on hips, a wooden spoon waving in the air.

Lucy placed a hand over her mouth to disguise a grin. Bertie had no reason to be accommodating to Sandra and was not afraid to show his disgust at her actions.

"Looks like we are just in time for dinner, Bertie, what are you making?" Sandra took another sip of wine, peering at him expectantly as if she had not even noticed his curt tone.

Lucy stared at her with a flabbergasted look on her face.

"No, I am not making supper for you and Enrico and that's my wine you're drinking. You can't just walk in here as though…" he hesitated slightly.

"Like what, Bertie? Like I own the place," she said gulping the wine, throwing a triumphant look at Bertie.

He squirmed. "Well, politeness wouldn't go amiss, would it," he felt stupidly defensive racking his brain as to what to say next. Then an idea hit him, "Actually I think that Molly and Stella should hear what she had to say, as I believe they own half the property too," he let a smirk slide onto his face, regaining the upper hand as he smiled at Lucy.

"Oh, don't worry about that, Bertie. Molly will be back soon and I've already phoned Stella and she should be here in an hour, just in time for whatever you are cooking for supper." She raised the glass and downed the wine, turning to Enrico, "Pour me another, darling, would you? I'm really quite thirsty." Bertie stared in utter disbelief, throwing a quick glance at Lucy and raising his shoulders in surrender. Lucy went to the dresser and collected another glass and a bottle, pouring a drink for Bertie. Bertie just watched Sandra, anger boiling through his veins he wondered how long he would have to put up with this... this situation.

"...and a glass for Enrico too, Lucy. I'm sure it was just an oversight on your part," she patted Enrico on the arm, "I must say, the old place hasn't changed at all. It will have to be tidied up a bit before it goes on the market, can't have it looking such a mess." Bertie banged his knife on the table.

"Right, that's it. I want you out of here now. You can come back when Molly and Stella are here," he spluttered, sending a shower of spittle in Sandra's direction. Sandra dabbed herself, her lips curled, glaring at Bertie with triumph in her eyes.

"I think you are rather overreacting, don't you? Considering this place has nothing to do with you." Bertie clenched and unclenched his fists, his face now bright-red. He gulped hard. Lucy leapt to her feet.

"Why don't we just all calm down? Molly will be here soon and then we can talk about it in a civilised manner." She put her arm around Bertie's waist and he managed a wan smile at her as he turned his back on Sandra, pulling a tea towel from the front of the Aga.

"Can you do something with those apples, Bertie, for dessert? I hear you are quite a good cook... for a man," Sandra dripped sarcasm as Enrico chuckled.

Bertie felt himself bristle and he so wanted to throw this bitch of a woman out on her ear, Molly and Stella being the only reason not to. He collected his thoughts and after a few moments, he turned to look at both Sandra and Enrico, who were cuddling up to each other as if she had said nothing. "I give up," he mouthed to Lucy.

"I'm sure I heard a car," he looked across towards the door just as Molly arrived, struggling with Jessica and a bag of shopping. He dashed to help her, diverting the adrenaline that was coursing around his body. Lucy put her arms out to Jessica and took her, giving her a squeeze. Jessica gurgled in response.

"Mum, hi, Enrico. What's going on?" Molly looked at everyone in turn.

"I think it best if Sandra answers that one," said Bertie, "would you like a cup of tea or a glass of wine, Molly," he leaned over and kissed her cheek, wrestling the bag of shopping from her hand.

"Tea, please, Bertie, I have to feed Jessica in a minute. So come on, why the atmosphere, what have I missed?" Molly busied herself removing her jacket. She raked her fingers through her hair, pulling out a chair and sitting at the pine kitchen table.

"We were just waiting for you, darling and Stella, so that Bertie can tell us all about the visit from the estate agent today and he's making supper for all of us, isn't that kind of him?"

Molly looked over at Bertie, her eyebrows raised. Bertie placed the tea in front of her banging the mug onto the table, grinding his teeth, but staying silent, afraid of what he might say next.

He took a deep breath, his head swirling with what he would like to say.

Pulling himself up straight, he looked at Lucy then Molly, before finally saying, "No problem," although still seething, but not prepared to give Sandra any more excuses to have a go at him. He caught Lucy's eye again, attempting to send her a hug with his eyes.

"I'll just text Stella to see what time she will be here and then we can sort something out," said Molly, diplomatically. Bertie, unhappy with the way he was being treated by Sandra, set about making preparations for six people now, instead of the romantic dinner for two that he had planned. He could hear whispering between Sandra and Enrico, he chose to ignore them. Molly had retreated upstairs to feed Jessica, with Lucy in her wake on some pretext or other. He wondered how he had gotten into all this and more importantly, how he was going to extricate himself from it. He had felt so sorry for Sandra when Molly's dad died and then he thought her quite brave to go back to Spain on her own. Now he was seeing a different side to her altogether and one he despised. He began turning figures over in his mind and thought about the shop and the dilemma facing Lucy. They had planned to discuss the shop and how to get rid of all the damaged goods and salvage what they could. He thought of this odd couple behind him and turning, asked.

"Enrico, I have been rude to you, I'm sorry. Tell me about yourself, what are you doing in Spain and how did you meet Sandra?" Bertie moved to the table and picked up some beef tomatoes, cucumber, lettuce, red onions, peppers and radishes and began preparing them to go with the cheese soufflé he had decided to make, together with some tiny, baby Jersey Royals.

"I err…well, I have been working in a bar on the beach, you know, enjoying the sun, some swimming and some nightclub work too. I am very busy." Bertie watched him as Enrico became lost in the pictures in his own mind; he waved his arms about as a wide smile spread across his face, "…and well, I met Sandra there, you know, on the beach, it is near her villa. She was very sad and told me about her husband. In the beginning, I felt sorry for her, but then I get to know her better, she is a wonderful lady and now I love her." Enrico placed a protective hand on Sandra's shoulder. Bertie wanted to puke, but he took a sip of wine instead and continued his questioning; this was turning out to be very interesting.

"So, where do you live then, Enrico?" he chopped the cucumber into little pieces, not wishing to look at him and trying to give the impression that he was just making polite conversation.

"With Sandra, of course, we love each other very much and are so happy. So, tell me, Bertie, how long have you lived here in the farm with Molly and her husband. He is not here, no?" Bertie, though a little startled by this turn in the questioning, took it in his stride.

"Oh, I think you know the answer to that one, Enrico, and I, of course, love Lucy. Have you always lived in Spain, Enrico?"

"Of course, I was born in Spain."

"Your English is very good. Did you come to England to learn English?" Bertie found himself more and more curious about Enrico. He was sure that something was wrong and he was determined to find out what it was that was niggling at him.

"I speak to many people at the beach. It is very popular with the British tourists and I learn quickly, you know." He turned to Sandra, letting his fingers trail down her arm.

"Have you been married before? I would have thought that a handsome bloke like you would have his pick of all the girls. No children, Enrico?" Bertie picked up the bowl of salad and put it into the fridge.

"So many questions," Enrico exaggerated his arms, waving again.

"Yes, Bertie, that's enough. You're just trying to trick him and I won't have it," Sandra looked at her watch, "Stella should be here any minute and then we can get this matter dealt with."

Bertie allowed a grin to crease his lips. He had lots of information to share with Alistair. He pulled out his phone and sent him a text suggesting that he get his butt over to the farm as soon as possible and closed his phone.

***

Lucy sat watching Molly feed Jessica, wondering when she would be a mother too, not that anything on that subject had been discussed with Bertie. She sat twiddling her hair round and round her finger. Bertie, the man of her dreams – he truly was wonderful, but hey ho... she glanced over at Molly who was grinning at her.

"Come on, Lucy, I know that look, what are you thinking? If it's polite enough to share, of course," she gave a chuckle, swopping Jessica to her over breast. "You were on some other planet just then, anything to do with Bertie, perhaps?" Lucy stopped twiddling her hair and stood up, stretching, giving herself time to return to now and Molly, who was her priority after all.

"Okay, you got me. Guilty as charged," she stretched some more and sat down again, "I was thinking about Bertie and also at my own chances of motherhood, but that's in the future. I really wanted to talk about you." She neatly switched the subject away from her raging hormones.

"Me?" Molly raised her eyebrows to look straight at Lucy, "what on earth about? I'm fine." she looked down at Jess and rubbed her cheek as she had stopped suckling and nodded off.

"Yes, you. What's happened to you? Since you became a mother, you have no time for Alistair. You're grumpy half the time and you certainly don't spend time on yourself – just look at your hair, it needs cutting and you haven't been to see George and Alice for ages. So come on, talk to me."

"Well, don't hold back, will you. Just tell me the truth. I can handle it," she laughed.

"Alistair just does not seem interested in me or Jessica and I can't visit George and Alice, as Alice will try and tell me how to run my life and inform me about what I am doing wrong!"

Molly glared at Lucy and a second later, her face crinkled, as tears pushed from her eyes and dribbled down her cheeks.

"Molly, I'm sorry," Lucy grabbed the tissues. "I didn't mean to hurt you, but come on, what happened to your dreams? You had such plans and now they seem to have been forgotten. I know that there's all this with your mother and Alistair isn't helping, but I thought you loved him. What do you truly want from your life?" She looked Molly in the eyes, waiting for a reply.

"Wow, that's a big question. You'll have to give me time on that one. I don't know, it's just that everything has become a bit much. I don't want to lose the farm, but it looks as if I will and I haven't time to think about Alistair at the moment... and as for my dreams," she paused, "...are they still mine? I don't know anymore. Everything has changed and maybe my dreams have too." Molly lifted Jessica onto her shoulder and began patting her back. "I think I can hear Stella downstairs and I am expecting a huge row to erupt at any minute, I don't know if I can face it. Trust Alistair not to be here when I need him, it's always been business first with him, second and third when I think about it. Even though I love him to bits, I probably shouldn't have married him or even told him I was pregnant," she rocked back and forth as Jessica gave a burp and squirmed, pulling up her knees.

"Come on, Molly, I'm sure you don't really mean that, I know you're tired. Do you want me to change Jess for you and you can go downstairs and... well, you know?" She put her arms out to pick up Jessica, Molly handed her over and headed for the door, she stopped, turning to Lucy.

"Wish me luck," her shoulders drooping along with her voice, she turned and went downstairs.

***

Sandra stood up scraping her chair across the old flagstone floor, pulling her coat tightly around her.

"That's all I have to say on the matter. I hope that you girls will understand I need to sell this old place and move on with my life," she picked up her bag, throwing her hair back with a swaggering determination. "I would have thought that you two would want to do the same." She swept her eyes over them. "I will speak to old, what's his name, and tell him my decision. I trust that you won't interfere with the agents selling the farm," she looked at the assembled crew who said nothing, nothing at all, "…and I won't accept a penny less than £300,000 for my share, the sooner the better." She turned to Enrico, saying, "Come on, let's go," and they left without another word.

"I'm sorry, Molly, but I must go to get back to Tony, so sorry to leave you with this mess. Give me a call soon, let me know what's happening." They kissed and hugged. Stella picked up her keys and left.

Molly plopped down at the table, all manner of thoughts raging through her head, not least her mother's attitude and the smug look on Enrico's face. Alistair rose from the couch to stand behind her and massaged her shoulders. Molly looked from one to the other and back again.

"Well, I'm starving. I don't know about you all, but it's a shame to waste this food when Bertie has gone to so much trouble. I suggest we eat."

"Great idea," said Bertie, "this soufflé is just about ready, so let's tuck in."

"I brought some more wine, it's out in the car," said Alistair and he popped out to get it. A buzz started around the kitchen as they all relaxed and shared a lovely meal together, chatting about each other's day-to-day lives and not mentioning Sandra, her ultimatum or Enrico.

Chapter 12

Having come to terms with losing the farm, the next few weeks flew by. Molly threw herself into the barn conversion next door to her veterinary practise. She was thrilled with the progress, looking forward to moving in. She had only heard from Sandra when she wanted an update on the sale of the farm. No one was being obstructive, although Sandra didn't believe her, but the farm needed a lot of work and the position of the cottage made it difficult to separate the two properties. The architect had come up with a shared drive and not everyone who viewed the property liked that idea. She turned her attention back to her own project; the roof was about to go on and the building inspector was due. Luckily no bats were discovered roosting in the loft, so the builders were now moving ahead at a pace. Molly stood watching them for a few minutes, with Jessica asleep in her pram. She had popped down to see the locum and make arrangements to start work again.

"I really appreciate you giving me so much time, Hugh, I don't know what I would have done without you," she smiled.

"No worries, it's been fun, but I do need to get back home. I've been offered a partnership... unless, of course, you were thinking of a partnership here." he tapped his pen on the desktop absentmindedly, looking up at Molly.

"Sorry, Hugh, but there isn't enough business for that, not yet. If things pick up then maybe, but you probably won't be interested then. Anyway, thanks for the offer."

"Hey, you know what? This place could be a little goldmine. There are lots more we could do and offer by way of bringing in more business. I have some ideas that I would like to run by you. If you think that you might be interested... maybe." He half pleaded. Molly stared at him for a second.

"You know what? Yes, I am interested. Why don't you come over to the farm tonight? Say, about seven and we can talk about it some more."

"Sounds like a plan to me. See you at seven," he grinned.

Molly turned the pram around and headed for the beach. The season hadn't quite got underway and apart from a few people walking along the beach, it was quiet. The gulls were screeching overhead and Molly watched their antics as she sat on the sea wall. Trentmouth was a quaint little village, hardly a hotspot for tourism or much business and now that the only shop had closed, it was down to the hardened coast path walkers and locals who ventured down to the cove.

Promptly at seven, Hugh knocked on the farm door. As Molly let him in, Rex bounded up expecting a fuss. Hugh didn't disappoint.

"Would you like a beer or a glass of wine?" asked Molly.

"Err, yes, please, just a small one, as I'm driving and I haven't eaten yet," he exclaimed as he took out a pad and pen. Molly raised her eyebrows.

"You have come prepared, I see," Hugh smiled. "I have homemade bread and cheese if you would like some?"

"Love some, thanks." Molly put the food onto the table together with a Dorset apple cake and sat down.

"So, come on then, what are these ideas you have come up with. Not that I am promising anything… yet." She cut some cake, pouring herself a cup of tea and sat opposite Hugh at the kitchen table.

"Well, for a start, we could do a re-launch, for the partnership, I mean. You know, offer cheese and biscuits, a glass of bubbly, put some bunting up, that sort of thing. Invite all our, I mean, your existing customers and leaflet Trentmouth and surrounding villages, inviting people to come and say hello."

"Hmm, well, that sounds good for a start, but it's not enough to fill the surgery and cover two vets." She said sceptically.

"No, but we have to start somewhere and then we could take a stall at the church fete in June, have bowls of water ready for the hot weather. We could have dog treats to give away and lots of companies will supply us with free samples, you know, spread the word that we are local, people don't have to travel to

Wareham or Poole." Hugh was getting excited. He stuffed another slice of bread into his mouth, picking up a cherry tomato.

"You have given it a lot of thought and I can see that these things would be good, but I still don't know. It would be a big commitment and what about on-going business. I like the idea of the church fete. I've never done that before and I could set up a pen for the hens with their chicks, that always gets a crowd looking, even if they don't have a pet."

"Yes, that's a good idea and I'm sure that we could think of more. We could set up a pen outside the surgery at Christmas with reindeer in it and even have bunnies at Easter," he was getting carried away and Molly laughed.

"Next, you will be offering riding lessons, taking people through the surf down on the beach at sunset or romantic rides for Valentines."

"Wow, now I love that one. It's better than mine." He grinned. "So, what do you say? About a partnership, I mean."

"We need to look at incomes and what you expect to earn, and I thought that you had been offered a partnership elsewhere, what about that?" queried Molly.

"Ah, well, confession time, I think. Sorry, Molly, but I may have exaggerated a bit there. I haven't actually been offered a partnership, but I think that there is great potential here. I've got to like that place, quite a lot actually. I admit, I wasn't keen at the start, calling Trentmouth a backwater, but it's, well it's gotten under my skin," he paused, taking a sip of wine, "So, come on, Molly, what do you think? Partners?" He held out his hand, ready to shake on a deal. Molly hesitated, thinking that this could be good for her business, but what will Alistair say? Perhaps she should give it more thought. Hugh was well liked by her customers; he had a way with the women who came in and he certainly had kept the business running for her. She flew out her hand, grabbing Hugh's and shaking it.

"What the hell, yes. Yes, I will do it, why not?" She pushed her chair back, scraping it across the quarry tiled floor. "This calls for bubbly, but it will have to be elderflower pressé, I'm afraid." She collected the bottle from the fridge and two glasses. Jessica stirred, but fell fast asleep again. "I think that this will be good for both of us."

"Great, just great, I can't wait. However, I will need to go home for a week or so to sort out everything and find somewhere a bit more permanent down here. There's just one thing, as the fete is only a couple of months away can we get the partnership up and running before then, do you think?" He tapped his pen on his chin.

"I don't see why not, actually, that's a good idea, no need to wait. Okay, I will get onto it first thing Monday." Molly felt daunted, but to have a partner meant someone else to shoulder responsibilities and the work. She had forgotten to order supplies recently and she was behind with her accounts, a job she hated doing, yes this was a good idea. She smiled at Hugh.

"What do you think, to Craven and Gilmour or do you want to change it to Warren and Gilmour or even Gilmour and Warren," he looked quizzically. Molly shot her head up.

"I never thought of that. I haven't changed the name to my married name. Hmm, I think I prefer Craven and Gilmour. I like the sound of that. That's settled then, we have a lot to sort out and had better get started."

***

The next day, Molly was excited to tell Alistair about her plans. She had thought that Alistair might not approve. It was her business after all and Alistair had a good head for potential when he saw it. Still, she had gone ahead without consulting him. It was done now.

Her dreams were finally coming to fruition.

Alistair seemed keen on the idea, in fact, he thought it was a brilliant idea, saying, "Why don't we have dinner tonight to celebrate. I'd like to take you out, you know, spend some time together," he looked awkward for a moment.

Molly grinned to herself. It had been a long time since Alistair had suggested dinner for just the two of them. She missed him, but she knew she couldn't back down or that would be the end, causing her to have a completely different life. She acceded, saying, "Okay, I'd love that. I'll ask Lucy if she will look after Jessica and maybe we could try that new Italian on Wareham quay. What do you think?" She looked sideways to see his response. He had mellowed over recent events and rather less grumpy.

"Yes, fine by me. I'll pick you up at seven, if that's alright?" he still sounded hesitant, but Molly found that endearing. He was trying. Molly spent the rest of the day on a high. She called her Solicitor. Spoke to Lucy, who was delighted to look after Jess and updated Hugh.

Finally, she called Alice, arranging to visit later that afternoon.

"Molly, dear, how lovely to see you. Please, come in. We are outside on the veranda, go through and I will put the kettle on." Molly walked through the snug and found George lazing in the sun, newspaper in hand.

"George…" she exclaimed. He got up out of his chair and gave her a hug.

"My dear, I'm so happy to see you. We have felt neglected of late." He tickled Jessica on her cheek and she gave him a toothless grin, dribbling down her chin.

"Sorry, George, but things have been a bit strained recently and well, I felt awkward," she paused, "and I suppose, I wasn't sure how you and Alice would feel about me."

"Oh, Molly, with Alistair or without, we are always happy to see you, and little Jessica, of course. We are her grandparents after all." Molly felt a little told off in the nicest possible way and had to admit he was right and maybe she had been selfish not visiting them more.

"Sit down, please," he indicated a chair and sat down himself. "Arrh, here is Alice. We are dying to hear all your news. Aren't we dear?" he looked up at Alice, reaching for the tray.

"Oh, yes, we are. I want to know everything about everything." They all laughed, ice broken and settled into stories of Jessica, updates on the barn and the difficulty in selling the farm, carefully not mentioning Alistair.

"Actually, Alice, I wanted to ask you about a stall at the fete. Am I too late to book one? And I want to have a pen for some hens with their chicks, if possible, near the entrance. What do you think?" Molly had handed Jessica over to Alice who was happily gurgling away at all the attention. Alice looked up.

"What a lovely idea, Molly. Yes, of course, you can and I will sort it out for you and get back to you."

"Great. There's something else I want to tell you," she hesitated, glancing from one to the other, "but, please, don't get too excited, it's just that Alistair and I are going out to dinner tonight and…"

"Molly, dear, that's wonderful," exclaimed Alice.

"Now, dear," said George, "you know what Molly just said, so don't go getting yourself too excited. It's just dinner." he leaned over and squeezed Alice's arm, throwing a look at Molly. She gave a wan smile in reply.

"Thanks," mouthed Molly. "I do need to be going actually. I have so much to do before tonight. I want to get my hair cut." Molly saw the look that passed between George and Alice, but said nothing.

"Alright, my dear," said George, "and do come again soon."

"Yes," said Alice, "and I will get back to you about the fete." They said their 'goodbyes' and Molly headed towards Wareham and the hairdresser.

***

Alistair drove into the farmyard, spot on seven and Molly was ready, she looked in the mirror and put on an extra smear of lippy.

"You look great," said Lucy, "so, stop worrying and have a good time."

"Thanks," said Molly, "are you sure I look okay?" Molly tweaked her hair yet again.

"Yes. Now go. And Molly, if you decide to stay over tonight, I can look after Jessica for you," she grinned.

"Oh, I don't think we are there yet, but I will bear it in mind," she beamed, just as Alistair opened the door.

"Wow, Molly… you look… amazing, and I love the hair," he gawped at Molly.

"Thanks. Now let's go, I'm starving," she turned, throwing raised eyebrows at Lucy, together with a cheeky grin.

They drove down the road relatively in silence. Molly wondering what to say to Alistair as this was a most unusual situation, he was her husband but acting like it was a first date. Molly liked it. She began to wonder if they could get back together. Things had been very strained, but Molly had to admit to herself that maybe she had had a short fuse recently and it wasn't all Alistair's fault. They parked on the quay, facing the river and sat for a few moments, watching a couple throwing bread into the water to feed the ducks. The ducks looked at it, but quickly swam away, showing disgust. Molly chuckled to herself. She turned to Alistair.

"You're quiet, everything alright?" she looked at him as he sat half-slumped forward.

"Yes… I'm fine. It's just that I suddenly don't know what to say to you. You look beautiful tonight and I'm scared," he looked her full in the eyes.

"What do you mean? Scared of what?" she asked, dumbfounded.

"I've missed you so much and I love you and our daughter," he squeezed her hand. "I've been such an idiot; will you forgive me?" he pleaded.

"I love you too and I… I don't want to rake over old ground," she hesitated, "why don't we go in and talk about it over dinner?"

"Good idea," he leaned over, brushing her cheek with a soft kiss. He jumped out of the car, dashing round to open the door for her. Molly felt the old feeling of electricity shoot through her body. She shuddered slightly, letting Alistair help her out of the car, exhilarated, trying to stop the grin from creasing her face. They sat by the window, watching the sun slowly sink over the Purbeck Hills. Molly sipped her Prosecco and toyed with her tiramisu.

They had talked about her new business venture and Alistair's new clients, but not about themselves. Molly was reluctant to mention them, as in a funny sort of way, she felt that it should be Alistair, although she couldn't think why. She twiddled with her wedding ring, throwing a quick glance at the gorgeous square-cut diamond on her engagement ring. She wanted to say so much, wrestling with lots of thoughts, but none of them seemed right.

"So," they both said together and then laughed.

"You go first," said Molly, taking a fork full of the delicious coffee and cream concoction.

"No, please, Molly, I'd rather you go first," he said, caressing her hand very tenderly, "I don't want to say the wrong thing." Molly finished her dessert, giving herself time to put her thoughts into some kind of order.

"I'm not sure where to start, but the fact remains that I can't live in the flat. Jessica and I need to be at the farm, although I don't know for how much longer," she paused, taking a deep breath, "I miss you too, but I'm not sure where we go from here." She sat back fidgeting with her napkin, waiting for Alistair to say something.

"Oh, Molly," he took her hand, intertwining their fingers, "I get it, I finally get it, and you're right, I have been selfish and only thinking of myself. Can we try again? Come back with me tonight…" he hesitated and Molly knew that it was now or never. She desperately wanted to feel his arms around her; he was such a tender lover.

She pulled her hand away, saying, "You get the bill and I will text Lucy to make sure that she can stay over and look after Jess," she grinned up at him and Alistair leapt to his feet. She couldn't help a giggle as Alistair signalled the waiter and she pulled out her iPhone.

***

They woke early the next morning and Alistair made two coffees bringing them back to bed. Molly was already sitting up her knees pulled up under her chin glowing and feeling totally wonderful.

"Hey you look happy," said Alistair rather unnecessarily, but grinning all the same.

"I am. I was wondering," she took the coffee, sipping it and letting out a breath of pure contentment.

"Ye…s," grinned Alistair, looking at her with his obvious love spilling out of every pore. Molly took courage.

"Well, why don't you move into the farm with us? I know that Lucy would love Bertie to move in with her or maybe he could have the flat in Poundbury," she sipped more coffee, but as Alistair stayed silently caressing her arm, she pushed on, "…and I was thinking that when the barn is finished, we could move in there, our first proper family home together. So, what do you think?"

Alistair took her mug away from her, placing it on the side table; he turned back to her, saying, "Okay," as he pushed the covers back and made love to her again.

Some long-time later Molly's iPhone buzzed and for a moment, she couldn't think where she was, then the joy crashed in on her and she sat bolt upright, realising that it was her iPhone. Her heart thudded in her chest. She grabbed it.

"Lucy, hey, is everything alright? Is something wrong with Jess," she fumbled with her heap of clothes, trying to find her underwear.

"Everything is fine, Alistair rang earlier. I've never heard him sound happier," she laughed, "anyway, it's nearly lunchtime and I was wondering when you would be back, as I have to be at work at two."

"Wow, is that the time? I must have fallen asleep again. I'll be back as soon as I can."

"Fine, no worries, you don't have to rush if you are… you know, busy." Molly could see her cheeky grin down the phone and bit her lip trying not to grin too much.

"Thanks. I've got lots to tell you, see you later." She closed her iPhone and headed for the shower.

***

The next day, Lucy was on an early shift. She leaned over in bed to kiss Bertie who grunted an acknowledgement with his eyes still closed. Lucy chuckled.

"See you later," she whispered as she picked up her bag and keys, heading for the door.

Bertie had moved in 'temporarily'. He had said to give Molly and Alistair some space up at the farm. Apparently, they were like lovesick teenagers and from her brief chat with Molly, it would appear that things were even better than before. Lucy left Wareham behind, driving towards Poole, the radio on loud to keep her awake. Chris Evans was way too cheerful for the crack of dawn, but she couldn't help herself laughing out loud at some of the things he said.

She was tired. It was wonderful having Bertie to stay, but her lack of sleep was catching up on her. She planned to see Molly after work and get the full story, but for now, she had other things on her mind.

Her mum had retreated even more into herself, quite happy as if she didn't have a care in the world and, of course, she didn't. Lucy sighed because all those cares were now hers.

Her father wasn't much help either; all he kept saying was, "Whatever you think best." *Whatever that means,* she pondered, not knowing what was best, just bumbling along, hoping it was the right thing.

"Well, I know really," she told herself, "you can't help me with this one, Chris," she told the radio. She pulled into the car park and headed for the ward, her head down, still turning the dilemma over in her mind. Her phone buzzed, it was Molly inviting her and Bertie to dinner that evening. She quickly accepted and sent another to Bertie to let him know. He was quite the chef and had taken over her kitchen. She didn't mind even when he admitted that she was a guinea pig for the day he would have his own café. She grinned, slipping her phone back into her bag. The ward was chaotic already and it was only 7 a.m. An emergency overnight had meant that they had to send some patients home, as they now had no beds and another expectant mother was on her way in. Lucy shrugged off her own problems, putting them to the back of her mind, pasting a smile onto her face, ready to tackle the day ahead.

***

On her way home much later, the last thing she wanted was to go to the farm. It had been a difficult day and all she could think of was relaxing in a tub full of bubbles with a glass of wine. The team hadn't been able to save the baby from the overnight emergency and that always upset her, even though there was nothing anyone could do. She had tried to reassure the mother that it wasn't her fault, but she was inconsolable. The next mother had had a much happier ending, a premature baby, all had gone well. She pulled up onto the drive to find Bertie standing in the doorway, beer in hand, grinning at her.

"What's with the stupid grin?" she asked, reaching up to kiss him.

"Nothing," he exclaimed, the grin not diminishing one iota.

"Huh, a likely story, come on, tell me. I need a bath," she threw her coat down and kicked off her shoes.

"Already waiting for you and I put some of those smelly things in that you like."

"Oh, Bertie," she snuggled up to his neck, "I do love you." He folded his arms around her and held her close for a few moments. He kissed the top of her head.

"I love you too. Now come on into that bath." He took her hand and led her upstairs, helping her undress at the same time. "You are so beautiful," he said, stroking her back.

"Thank you," she smiled, "now let me get into this divine bath and Bertie… any chance of a glass of white wine?"

He pushed the door open and there, on the side of the bath, her dream had come true. Lucy turned to him, "You are perfect, did you know that? And I am not letting you go."

Bertie pulled the door, still grinning, and disappeared. Lucy let a tear roll down her cheek, too tired to care. She took a delicious sip of wine and climbed into the tub.

What seemed all too short a time, they drove up to the farm and Lucy had to admit that she was starving. Molly was waiting by the door with Jessica in her arms and Alistair with his arm draped over her shoulder; they looked like the perfect couple standing there, totally happy. Rex was spinning around in circles, woofing and trying to lick everyone. Bertie did the honours with Rex before shaking hands with Alistair, following him into the kitchen, collecting a beer as he passed the fridge. Lucy took Jessica, who was beaming and reaching for her hair.

"I hardly need to ask, but come on, I want to know everything," said Lucy.

"Let's walk down to the allotment. I have so much to tell you. Dinner will be fine for twenty minutes. Won't be long…" she called into the kitchen as they walked over to the bench by the allotment.

Molly couldn't help but grin, "Things are better than ever, Lucy, and I can't thank you enough for being there for me, even when I have been such a grouch."

"Think nothing of it. Most new mums struggle one way or another, mainly due to lack of sleep." She tickled Jess under her chin, making her giggle. "…and this one is worth every single sleepless night."

"You're right, I never realised how much it would change my life. Anyway, I want to tell you about Hugh, you know, the locum." Molly launched into her news, so excited that Lucy almost felt envious. She loved her job, but she couldn't bring herself to tell her about Tricia, deciding that it would keep for another day.

Chapter 13

Alice had agreed to hold the interviews with the candidates for the post of vicar at her house.

The village hall was having a new heating system fitted and not suitable to hold confidential interviews. Well, not really interviews, as such it was more an informal 'come and meet us' chat so that the PCC could see for themselves who the Bishop was recommending and ask their own questions. Alice looked around her dining room and nodded with satisfaction, quietly pleased at this change in venue. She placed a vase of tulips onto the table next to her Victoria sponge and an empty plate ready for the chocolate brownies that she knew Lady Isobel would bring. Someone rapped on the front door and Alice turned to greet her guests.

With all the committee assembled, Alice tapped the table.

"Ladies and gentlemen, before we get underway, I would like to welcome George onto our committee, as this is his first meeting," she turned and smiled at him and a flutter of polite clapping passed around the room. "Our first candidate will be here in fifteen minutes, but we need to discuss the repairs to the village hall. The new heating system is being installed as you know and we have had quotes from a number of builders for the other renovation work."

Alice paused and that was all that was needed for Doris to jump in and start grumbling.

"There is nothing wrong with the toilets, they are perfectly adequate. In my day, it was an outside toilet and we didn't complain. We can save money by not replacing the kitchen too. I can't see anything wrong with the one in there now. I had that put in back in the fifties."

Doris harrumphed; arms folded under her ample bosom. Alice let out a heavy sigh. Isobel jumped in to rescue the situation.

"Now, Doris, let's not go over that again, it has all been agreed and approved and we need to update the hall if we are to attract people to come and hire it." Doris said nothing, reaching for another slice of cake and grunting. "I think that we may need to look at other fundraising ideas at our next meeting. We will also go over the final preparations for the fete and now I feel that we should turn our attention to our candidates, as I think that the first one has just arrived." There was a murmur of agreement around the room and George got up to open the door to Reverend Timothy Wagstaff. George ushered him in and introduced him to the waiting PCC.

"Come in, Reverend Wagstaff," said Alice as she stood to shake his hand.

"Thank you," he said rather quietly. Alice smiled to herself as all eyes were on this poor man, weighing him up and assessing him before he could even speak. She rather thought that most minds were already made up, especially Doris'. He was a timid, dour looking man with thin wispy hair. He had slightly hunched rounded shoulders and looked as though he was carrying the weight of the world, rather than just meeting the PCC.

"Please, sit here," said Alice, indicating a chair at the top of the table so that everyone could see him, clearly putting him under even more pressure. "Tea?" she asked, lifting the teapot. He mumbled his thanks and Alice placed a china cup and saucer in front of him, cutting a slice of cake and pushing it towards him with a napkin and fork. They all asked various questions about his history, his family and other parishes, including church attendance figures and most importantly, his success with fundraising. Alice cleared her throat, ready to ask the one question that they all wanted answered.

"Your wife, Reverend Wagstaff, what part in the church life would you envisage that she would be involved with?"

"My wife?" he looked quizzically at Alice.

"Yes. It is usual for the vicar's wife to take on lots of different roles within the parish. For example, heading up the fundraising committee, organising Sunday school outings, organising the Christmas party, meet and greet parishioners, flower rotas, that kind of things." She smiled at him encouragingly.

"My wife is a very busy solicitor. She has her own career, being a vicar is mine and although she comes to Sunday service, Veronica, my wife, will not be doing any of those things," he cleared his throat and tugged at his dog collar, "...and, of course, we have two children who take up a lot of her time too." After a few moments of silence, Lady Isobel spoke.

"Of course... of course, we understand, Reverend," she glanced around at the crestfallen faces. "Are there any other questions?" she paused, "... No. Well, thank you so much for coming to see us today and I'm sure that the Bishop will be in touch." Reverend Wagstaff gave his thanks with a weak smile as he left the room. George showed him out. They all looked one to the other.

"I like him," said Doris, "he's just the sort of man we need, good family man. He gets my vote," she smiled and nodded, pushing up her bosom contentedly as if she had won the day already.

"Let's not be hasty, Doris, we have another candidate shortly and we must give them both an equal opportunity, that's only fair," said Alice. There was nodding and agreement around the room. "I'll make another pot of tea, as I'm sure that Reverend Martin will be here shortly." As Alice made her way to the kitchen, she heard another rap on the front door and George followed her, saying that he would let her in. Alice put the kettle on and George bustled in behind her.

"Let me do this, you get back to the dining room before that poor girl gets eaten by the Lions," he chuckled.

"Thanks, George," she placed a kiss on his cheek and made her way back to the waiting committee.

"Aar, hello, Reverend Martin," she held out her hand, "please, come and sit down. George is just making the tea."

"Hello everyone," she beamed, there was a mutter of response, "...and please, call me Suzanne. I am pleased to meet you all. And thanks, I would love a cup of tea." She sat down.

Alice noticed that she was wearing a coral-coloured trouser suit with her dog collar that really set off her long flowing, strawberry blonde hair and startling blue eyes; she was indeed a very pretty woman and young. Alice beamed to herself, instantly warming to her.

"Well," said Lady Isobel, "Do tell us all about yourself, please... Suzanne."

Suzanne gave a huge smile and began a potted history to the group of her career so far. She had gained a degree in Media Studies and for her first job, she was lucky enough to work for the local BBC. It was fun, she explained, and involved meeting a lot of people, but hard work too, at times. She also had a motorbike, which brought a gasp from Doris. However, she continued, she was not happy and felt that God was calling her to work for him. She resisted for a long time, but when she gave herself up to her calling, God had had her on a roller coaster of a journey ever since. She grinned at them, love shining out from her face. The group around the table were stunned.

"We don't want any of that happy clapping nonsense around here," Doris boomed.

"Err, Doris, that's not what we are here to discuss," Alice jumped in.

"I'm just putting her straight," Doris glared at Alice.

"Well, Doris, is it?" smiled Suzanne, looking directly at Doris and without waiting for a reply, said, "I am so happy to be of service to Our Lord and it makes me feel very happy to be in Church on a Sunday morning. Do you not feel the same way?"

Very clever, thought Alice, throwing a quick glance at Isobel, totally unable to hold back a smirk.

Doris muttered to herself, taking another bite of her cake without replying to Suzanne.

"Err, well," said Alice, "What about involvement in the general running of the Parish?"

There was a murmur around the room as attention was given over to Suzanne and away from the grumbling Doris. Alice knew that Suzanne would not be able to do it all on her own, but it was a question that everyone wanted answered. Things had become harder; they were all getting older and with illness, amongst other pressures, no one seemed to want to get involved anymore. She had tried to get the younger generation to take an interest, but everyone was so busy working and too tired for voluntary work in the community.

"Well, I will do my best to take things on, even if it's only in the capacity of Chairman. I would love to know what events take place and how best I can get involved. However, I understand from the Bishop that you have all done a brilliant job in that area of church life and I would not want to interfere. Also, I would like to think that you would want to ensure that life continues as smoothly as possible and I would welcome your support too." Suzanne looked at them all, especially Doris, before turning her lovely smile back to Alice.

"Thank you, Suzanne. I think that's all the questions that we have, unless you have anything to ask us?" Alice glanced around the room, avoiding Doris' eyes.

"I was wondering what your next event was and maybe I will be able to come along and support you."

"Our Church fete is in June and you are very welcome to come along and support us. Thank you again. I'm sure that the Bishop will be in touch." Alice accompanied her to the door.

"Doris is old fashioned; she doesn't like change." Alice spoke in hushed tones.

Suzanne laughed. "I've met worse, so please don't worry." Closing the door, Alice quickly returned to the dining room where she could hear Isobel trying to speak to Doris who was already barking her thoughts to the room.

"Now, Doris, we need a proper discussion about the two candidates. Let me make another pot of tea and we can discuss it properly. Is that alright with everyone?" said Alice.

"I'm not changing my opinion; I don't want a woman vicar. It's a job for a man and I will leave, you mark my words."

There was a collective sigh around the room as Alice picked up the teapot and headed for the kitchen. She already knew that this was not going to end well. She leaned against the kitchen sink, pondering how best to tackle Doris before returning to the dining room where heated words were already underway. Lady Isobel was rapping on the table.

"Quiet, ladies and gentlemen, please. Now we need to talk about each candidate in turn with equal thought and consideration. So, let's talk about Reverend Wagstaff. I thought that he was a very nice man, quiet, but it must be nerve wracking, sitting in front of us all."

"I want him," jumped in Doris. Isobel calmly ignored her, clearing her throat, she continued.

"My only misgiving is that he will not be supported by his wife. I'm sure that she is a very nice person, but we would not be able to rely on her at all for any contribution in any of our events." Everyone shuffled and glanced at each other. "We know what you think, Doris, but can we hear from you, Ted? David? Maureen?" Ted cleared his throat.

"I did like Reverend Wagstaff, but I think we need someone with more 'go' in them."

Both David and Maureen agreed, with Maureen saying.

"I think that Suzanne could bring new, younger people into the church. She is very bouncy and fun, maybe that's just what we need."

A further discussion ensued exactly as Alice and Isobel had expected. Finally, it was George who spoke.

"I know that I am the new boy around here, but," they all laughed, "I have listened to all the arguments and if I am right, then are we not just giving feedback to the Bishop and he will make the decision as to who will be our next vicar." He paused, fiddling with his fork, pushing the crumbs around his plate.

"Yes," said Isobel, "and in a general summing up, it would appear that we all, with the exception of Doris, feel that Suzanne is the best candidate for Trentmouth. Agreed?"

"I shall, of course, be speaking to the Bishop myself. He needs to know that women have no place in a church," declared Doris, rising and making her way towards the door. She turned and glared at them before leaving.

"Well," said Alice, "everyone is entitled to their own opinion, including Doris." She glanced at all of the faces looking to her. Alice shook her head and flopped down, wondering where to go from here. It was Lady Isobel who summed it up for them all nicely.

"Doris is just one member of this committee. Admittedly, she is old and stuck in her ways, but we need to decide what we believe is best for the parish and proceed, however Doris may take it is her decision."

"Yes. You are right, Isabel. I think, however, that that is enough for one day. With your permission, I will let the Bishop know our majority decision and we shall have to wait and see the outcome." There was a general agreement and Alice continued by telling them the news about Molly wanting a stall and the arrangements for their Ruby Anniversary afternoon tea. The telephone rang and George left to answer it. He came back a moment later, his face betraying his thoughts.

"It's the Bishop, Alice dear. He's already had a call from Doris and wants to speak to you." Alice quickly shot into the hall and picked up the receiver.

"Hello, Bishop," she said, squeezing the phone.

Chapter 14

Molly was in full swing, organising their move into the now completed barn. She was happy.

She had worked hard, choosing new furniture and furnishings. The kitchen had to have an Aga, of course, and she found it a joy replicating, in part, the farm, even down to an old rocking chair taking pride of place in the corner of the kitchen. The next daunting task was to clear out the farm, move some possessions, but having to leave most for Bertie who was due to move back in. The flat, too, had to be cleared. Alistair had suggested letting it and that was still a consideration, either to a long-term tenant, or even another business, but that was the least of Molly's problems at the moment. Her mother was due to fly in again and was decidedly unhappy. Claiming she desperately now needed the money. Sandra wasn't clear if Enrico would be joining her or not and Molly hoped not. Then there were the preparations for the church fete, she was trying to leave that task to Hugh and he was more than happy to take it on. Molly, however, found it difficult to delegate and insisted on being kept in the loop at all times. Exhausting, but Molly was enjoying it all, finding a new purpose and thrill to life.

Her phone buzzed.

"Hi, Lucy, how are you?" and without waiting for a response, she continued, "I'm up to my eyes in it, nearly finished at the farm and then Mother, next week…" She paused, realising that Lucy hadn't spoken a word, "Luce! Are you alright," she went quiet, listening hard to the silence.

"Luce, where are you? I'm coming over."

"I… I'm at home. Oh Molly," she sobbed.

"Okay, put the kettle on, I will be with you in ten." She closed her iPhone, scooped up Jessica and headed for the door, wondering what on earth could have happened. Rex bounded after her, frantically wagging his tail, woofing and rubbing her legs. "Sorry, Rex, not this time. I'll take you out later, good boy." He dropped onto all fours, his tail down and sloped off back to his bed. Molly closed the door, thoughts racing round her head as to what was making Lucy so upset? Could it be her mother or her dad? As far as she knew, her job was great and then suddenly, the thought struck her, had she split up from Bertie? She raced down the road, crunching on the broken tarmac at the verge. "This bloody road," she shouted at the sky, "why don't they fix all these bloody potholes before there is an accident?" She turned right at the traffic lights and sped off down the road. Molly began to feel a bit guilty having neglected her friend recently. She had been so happy, back with Alistair, her new business partner Hugh, not to mention the barn and she realised that she had not given much thought to Lucy and Bertie. She didn't have time to pick up some muffins and raced on, screeching to a halt on Lucy's driveway. The door was ajar and Molly quickly retrieved Jess in her seat and dashed in. Mascara was streaked down both cheeks, her nose was red and her eyes all puffed up.

Lucy had clearly been crying for some considerable time. Molly put Jess down and enveloped her friend in a hug, saying, "Oh, Lucy, what on earth has happened?" Lucy shook her head. She sniffed, gulping back yet more tears. "Is it your mum or… or dad?" Lucy shook her head. "Bertie… have you and Bertie split up?"

"No." Lucy pulled away from Molly, "Nothing like that. Bertie is wonderful. It's just, well, it's just…" she pulled a long, narrow box from her pocket and a little white stick. Molly stared at it; her mouth dry. She turned and looked at Lucy.

"Are the tears because it is positive… or negative?" she dragged her eyes up to look into Lucy's face.

"It's negative, but I so hoped it was positive." Molly drew breath and tried to swallow a smile, staring at her friend's face all crinkled as if she would cry again.

"Does Bertie know anything about this?" she searched her face to see if she could find the answer and Lucy shook her head once more. "Right, okay. Let's have a cup of tea and you can start at the beginning." Molly quickly made the tea, not wanting to leave Lucy alone for too long, as she might start crying again. They sat in the cosy little sitting room, with its wood burner gently warming them. Molly looked around, realising that she hadn't noticed before the high ceilings and very decorative cornice. She admired the intricate carving and delicate plasterwork around the centre light. "So," she said at last, dragging her eyes back to Lucy, "I guess you really wanted a baby, but what about Bertie, would he want one right now?" Lucy pulled another tissue from the box, glancing around the room. A shudder went through her; she tucked her feet up onto the settee, picking up her tea.

"It's a long story, to be honest and I've let things get on top of me. What with Mum being in her own world and Dad just going through the motions. He's just lost without Mum running everything for him. Bertie moved in, now he's going back to the farm and work... well, work is just awful at the moment," she sipped her tea again and Molly kept quiet to give her friend time to think. "So, I suppose when I thought that I might be pregnant, I got all excited, I dashed up to the chemist this morning and could hardly wait to do the test, but well... you know the rest."

"Hmmm," said Molly, her mind racing about what to say, to not only placate Lucy, but help her get back on track. "On a scale of one to ten, where would each of these concerns sit with you at the moment? I mean, you clearly can't deal with them all at once, so what is most urgent do you think?"

Lucy let a little twitch play on her lips, then she half grinned, "I think that I have created a mountain where one didn't exist, haven't I?"

"Maybe, all these things are bothering you and need sorting, so, one at a time. What's the easiest to deal with and we can start there." It wasn't long before Lucy had put each problem into perspective and was smiling again.

"That just leaves work. Why is that such a problem? You love your job, don't you?" Molly quizzed.

"It's not that. It's just that we are so understaffed and we just don't have enough beds. Do you know, one poor woman almost gave birth in the corridor last night? It was awful. People staring as they passed by, she was screaming, her husband was being abusive to me and it wasn't my fault. I did my best and apologised, but I think that he is going to complain and where will that put me? I could lose my job!"

"Surely not, that would be so unfair. If there are no beds and not enough staff, you can hardly take the blame. Is she alright after that trauma?"

"Oh yes. We found her a bed and mother and baby are doing fine, thank goodness, but, you know, when I think about it, a baby really wouldn't be right for us just now. I just got myself into a corner and couldn't see a way out." She finished her tea. "I know it's early, but do you fancy a glass of wine?"

"That's more like it, but just a small one, as I will have to drive back soon." Molly felt relieved that her friend appeared to be back on track and she ticked herself off for neglecting her. She had heard that there were problems at the hospital, not to mention the threatened closure of the maternity unit in Poole and move to Bournemouth, but had no idea it was as bad as it was.

"I've been thinking, why don't we try and have a night out? Alistair will look after Jessica and I'm sure that Bertie would help too. What do you think? We could go to the cinema or just out for a meal."

"Yes. Okay, I would like that and actually, I could cook here, make it a bit special. We are always coming to you. Jess would be fine upstairs, or you could always ask George and Alice. I bet they would be thrilled." She threw Molly a cheeky grin, making Molly laugh.

"You're on," *and welcome back,* she added under her breath.

***

Lucy busied herself making dinner for the four friends. It had been a long time since she had done any entertaining and it felt good, especially as Bertie was staying over too.

Molly had asked Alice to babysit. Alice was over the moon. Molly had told her and had insisted on practising a nappy change and feeding Jessica 'just in case she woke up'. Lucy laughed out loud. She danced around the kitchen, listening to Steve Wright on radio two, something she rarely did, but today was different. Today nothing could spoil her mood, everything had sorted itself out at work and the husband had apologised. The sun had been shining this morning and Lucy had walked into town to pick up some fresh ginger and lemons, but now clouds were gathering and she stared at the darkening sky, hoping that it would not rain.

Her iPhone bleeped. For a split second, Lucy's heart jumped, *Please don't let it be an emergency at work,* she thought. She picked it up, fingers crossed, relieved to see that it was only Bertie, saying that he was on his way. She checked on the time, two hours before Molly and Alistair would arrive. She could easily finish her dessert, shower and be ready. A sudden clap of thunder made her jolt and she turned just in time to see another flash of lightening streak across the sky, quickly followed by another loud crash of thunder. She shivered as she watched the rain now beating on to the windowpanes. The door shot open and Bertie stood on the mat, soaking wet. His hair was stuck to his head and drops of water trickled down his face. Lucy grabbed a towel and tossed it across to him.

"Thanks. That storm blew up out of nowhere. Something smells good though. I'm hungry," he dried his face and began to pull off his wet t-shirt and then his trousers.

"You're always hungry, but you'll have to wait, dinner is at seven. Tea and cake, do you?" She grinned at him, lifting out the cake and mugs from the cupboard. Bertie crossed the kitchen, slipping his arms around her waist, placing kisses on her neck.

"I could think of something else to do, however. Especially as we have plenty of time till dinner," Bertie kissed her cheek and then her forehead, undoing the buttons on her shirt as he went. Lucy tapped his hand and gently pushed him away.

"Behave, Bertie. I need to finish this," she grinned. Bertie feigned pain in his hand, quickly returning to his quest to divest Lucy of her clothes.

"Ooh, that hurt," he slipped his hand under her bra, gently squeezing her nipple. Lucy put down her knife, turning into his arms. Bertie enveloped her, slipping his fingers through her hair, kissing her deeply. He lifted her into his arms, taking her upstairs.

A loud ticking noise wove its way into her brain and Lucy couldn't think what day it was or even what time. She snuggled up to Bertie without opening her eyes. Suddenly, a thought trickled into her consciousness. She shot bolt upright, looking at the clock.

"Bertie," she shook him, "Bertie, it's nearly six-thirty, come on, get up, Molly and Alistair will be here soon." She leapt out of bed and headed for the shower, panic setting in. She wondered how she could be ready for their guests in only thirty minutes. It was still raining when Lucy returned to the kitchen. She turned on the oven, slipping her Homity pie in to warm. Thankfully, it was to be accompanied by a salad and her chocolate pineapple roulade only needed dusting with icing sugar. Bertie appeared in the kitchen, looking cool and relaxed.

"What can I do to help?" he threw her a cheeky grin.

"Open the wine, will you, please? And I think that we should relight the wood burner, as it is not very warm. It hasn't stopped raining for hours; I wasn't expecting this cold weather and I've made salad and a cold dessert. I do hope that it will be alright." Her voice was rising as she felt more panicked by the second. Whenever they went to the farm and Molly cooked, it was always perfect. Lucy felt inadequate, wishing she hadn't volunteered to cook for them all or gone for the vegetable stew and dumplings she had originally planned.

"Hey, stop worrying," said Bertie, "you're a good cook, it will be wonderful… and I have some ideas I want to talk to you about later."

"What… what about?" There was a rap on the front door and Bertie dashed to open it before Molly and Alistair got a drenching, leaving Lucy open mouthed. Lucy felt flustered, wondering not only if the food would be alright, but what on earth did Bertie want to talk about. She planted a smile on her face as she turned to welcome their guests, her heart racing.

Molly smiled, but Lucy could see dark circles under her eyes and she seemed listless. She pulled her into the kitchen on a pretext of checking the oven.

"Are you alright, Molly? You don't look your usual self. Is Jessica okay, and Alistair?"

"Yes. Yes, fine. I'm sorry, Lucy, I'm just worried, as Mother is due tomorrow and she has Enrico with her. I'm just expecting a bit of a showdown, that's all. It's not as if I want to keep the farm now, I am really happy about moving to the barn. We are good, better than ever and Jessica is adorable, but Mum has changed. I hardly know her anymore. To be fair, she was never very 'motherly', but now she is obsessed with getting money and keeping Enrico and you know what?" she paused.

"No," said Lucy, "…do tell, although I'm not so sure that this isn't all Enrico's doing. He might just be trying to get money and then push off. Sandra wouldn't be the first to be taken in by a gigolo, not that I'm saying he is, but it makes you wonder." Lucy cut the Homity pie into slices and carried the plates to the table that Bertie had set up in front of the wood burner.

"I know and it does worry me, but as she said, 'it's her life, nothing to do with us', and I have to respect that, but we shall see what tomorrow brings. Here, let me help you." Molly picked up the bowl of salad and followed Lucy.

***

Bertie stood washing up in the kitchen, crashing and banging the pots and pans, creating quite a fuss.

"Remind me again why you didn't buy a dishwasher," he asked over his shoulder.

"I wouldn't have the pleasure of watching you wash up with a dishwasher now, would I?" she slipped her arms around his waist and squeezed him gently. "Now I want to know all about the idea that you teased me with just as they arrived."

"Ah, yes. Tell you what, you make some hot chocolate, I'll finish here and we can sit down, as I have a proposition for you." Lucy pulled away and filled the kettle.

"That sounds awfully serious. Am I going to like it?" Lucy now clattered the mugs and took out the cream for the hot chocolate. She found a box of chocolate mints and piled up a tray to deliver into the sitting room. She opened the wood burner door and put in two more logs. It popped and spit, bursting into flame. She rubbed her hands together, snuggling up on the couch, kicking off her shoes and tucking her feet under her. She let out a long sigh, wondering if Bertie was about to propose, then dismissing the idea as she chuckled to herself.

She looked up and grinned at Bertie as he came into the room carrying his laptop. *Not a marriage proposal then,* she thought.

"I've been doing some calculations," he said, opening his laptop and logging in. Lucy said nothing. "If you don't like it, just say, it's only an idea." Lucy watched him, sipping her hot chocolate and dunking a mint. It began to melt and Lucy licked the delicious dark chocolate from her fingers before popping the soft mint into her mouth. She stayed calm; after the day she had had, nothing could surprise or upset her. Bertie took a swig of his chocolate, "Right here it is," he turned to Lucy, "the thing is I have quite a bit of money saved up, added to what dad left me and well, it's not enough and I know that I couldn't get a mortgage at the moment, so I was wondering…" he took a deep breath and looked deep into Lucy's eyes.

'Ye…es, and…?'

"Well, I was wondering if, that is, what do you think of me and you buying the farm?" he kept his eyes firmly on Lucy's. Lucy froze, her mug poised in mid-air, of all the things he could have said, it was the last thing she would ever have imagined. She stared at him for a moment, thoughts whizzing round her head. Then the words sort of tumbled out.

"I'm not saying 'no', but I have this place and we can't possibly afford the farm and as you said, you are not earning much at the moment and you know Sandra arrives tomorrow, don't you? This just might be the maddest idea you have ever had." She saw the hurt look in his eyes, relenting her tirade a little. She said, "…come on, Bertie, and come to think of it, why? Why buy the farm? I just need more information. Tell me your ideas, I know you well enough to know that you will have worked on this for weeks," she let a smile slide onto her face and Bertie visibly relaxed, a smile playing on his lips too.

"Yes, well, it's still a work in progress, but what I thought was if you sell this place, we could have enough together to buy it all," he was getting very excited, throwing his arms around in an all-encompassing movement, "you could carry on working and I will build up my gardening business. Did I tell you that Lady Isobel wants me to go over and take a look at her place? Anyway, I would still have the allotment and I was thinking of getting one of those Citroen vans and converting it into a mobile sandwich and cake shop. I would sell my old jag, of course," he took a deep breath.

"Slow down, Bertie. I haven't gotten my head around your first statement, never mind all these other plans. You will have to go over it again, much slower this time and anyway, it's late. I am on early in the morning. It's time to go to bed." She rose from the couch and he caught her hand.

"Alright, you go up. I'll be there in a minute," she leaned over and kissed him gently on the forehead. He held onto her hand and standing up, drew her into his arms, kissing her tenderly then deepening his kisses until he pulled her towards the stairs.

Chapter 15

Sandra sat drumming her beautifully manicured fingernails, painted a vivid red, on the kitchen table, Enrico standing behind her, massaging her shoulders. Molly sat watching them, disliking Enrico more with every second. What is it with this man, she wondered? Doing her best not to grimace, she dragged her eyes away, shaking an unpleasant image from her mind.

Mum must be twenty years older than him at least; surely, he's just after her money. She let out a long sigh as she fiddled with the crumbs on the table. They waited for the estate agent to take another look over the farm and give them an 'honest' opinion as to the value of the farm and cottage. Alistair had taken time away from the office to be with her and Bertie was handling the phones and enquiries for him. Alice was taking a walk with Jessica in her pram.

It was a stunning day; the rain had gone and the blue sky was dotted with filmy strands of cloud. The door clicked open and in walked the agent, her heels clattering across the stone-flagged floor. She gave a wan smile around the room that only moved her lips, revealing her acute stress level. She was immaculately dressed in a neat little suit; a bit too short, could it even be designer, pondered Molly, surveying her up and down. Her blonde hair was held back at the sides but fell softly over her shoulders. She gave off an air of confidence and knowledge, encouraging you to have trust in her, even if you were inclined not to. Molly glanced down at her tired jeans and comfy sweater and felt rather scruffy.

"Well," she said rather shakily as she sat at the table, "I have given the property another thorough appraisal and it is a magnificent property set in such a lovely valley here in the heart of the Purbeck hills."

"Yes, yes, we know all that," chipped in Sandra, "just get on with it. I want to know what will sell it and for how much, that's all."

"Mother!" declared Molly, "...please Mum. Just give her chance to speak," then turning to the agent, "would you like a coffee? I'm just putting the kettle on." Molly turned to retrieve the kettle, feeling embarrassed at her mother's outburst. Sandra never had much patience; her father was often on the receiving end of her wrath and it seemed that sunny Spain had not changed a thing.

"Yes, please," the agent said to Molly, then to Sandra, "I'm sorry, Mrs Craven, but I was just trying to sum up as it were so that I can give you all a fuller picture. This is rather a different situation to normal with two properties being involved and therein, lies the main problem."

"What do you mean?" said Sandra rather haughtily, "what problem? As far as I can see we have a farm and the land and a cottage. Simple.' She pulled her coat around herself.

"Darling, do not upset yourself, you know that puts knots in your shoulders," he kissed the top of her head, "just relax, it will soon be sorted out and we can go home." Molly raised her eyebrows in disbelief, for once she was grateful to this man. Her mother actually did as he said and allowed him to soothe her once more. Molly placed the coffee in front of the agent who was, by now, visibly shaking. She picked up her pen and opened her file. Taking a sip of coffee, she cleared her throat.

"As you know, we have been marketing the two dwellings separately and the main feedback we have received is that people are not happy with the shared access and the lack of outside space with the cottage. So, I would like to suggest that the property be marketed as a whole and that would give a potential purchaser the opportunity to have a home and income," she paused, glancing around the room, "however, that means we need to take another look at the asking price. The farm is in need of some updating. I know that it is an old building, but today's market is looking for ensuites, modern kitchens and central heating or a knockdown price so that they can modernise the property to their own liking." She paused again and for a moment, the room had fallen silent.

"That makes sense, I can see what you are saying," said Alistair.

"Who asked you?" piped up Sandra, "this has nothing to do with you." Molly leapt to his defence. Enrico smirked, but said nothing.

"Mother, please, Alistair is just trying to help and he is my husband. Whatever has happened to you? If you would just give her a chance, I'm sure we will find out her recommendations." Alistair squeezed her hand and Molly turned to face the agent, "Please, continue." The poor woman cleared her throat yet again and drank deeply from her coffee, before coughing. Taking a deep breath, she continued.

"So, as I see it, you have two choices; you can do all the updating yourselves, which would include a good driveway and repairs to the boundary walls and fences, or you can consider lowering the price and selling it all as it is," she took another deep breath. "I have come up with an estimate for all the works and would suggest around £100,000 spent could add that figure and considerably more to the value of the property, thus making a very sound investment." She leaned back, putting her pen down, delivering a firm stance, which Molly deduced as 'your decision'.

"So, just like that, you expect me to lose £50,000, or worse, spend £50,000, which I don't have by the way and even then, there are no guarantees. Am I right?" At least Sandra was speaking more calmly and even positively for once and Molly chipped in

"Mother is right. We don't have that kind of money to spend in the hope of selling for more in a year or two," then turning to Sandra, "I think we need to seriously consider her advice and we still need to involve Stella before making a final decision. However, I am coming around to reducing the price and let someone else do it up." She looked at her mother who did have a fifty percent share and she needed to be happy more than anyone.

"Yes, reluctantly, I agree, but no changes until we have consulted my other daughter. Thank you for coming." Sandra stood to shake hands with the agent, "We'll get back to you as soon as we can and thank you." Molly dropped her shoulders with relief, as her mother had been civil and more gracious than

Molly had expected. The agent nipped out rather quickly and who could blame her? *She must be quaking after that experience,* thought Molly, with a smirk sliding onto her face. Sandra sat down heavily.

"Coffee, please, dear," she said to Molly, pushing her mug in her direction. Molly bristled, but decided not to make a scene and took the mug. What had happened to her mother to make her so… so sharp? She poured the coffee and pushed it back towards her, saying nothing. "Well, I suppose we have no choice, although I had hoped it would be all sorted out by now," she slumped a little and Molly felt sorry for her for a split second till she remembered that the money was probably going straight to Enrico. "Can you call Stella and let her know. I'm sure that she will agree and then let's hope it now sells. I can't take much more of this flitting backwards and forwards all the time. I'd rather be in Spain," she let out an enormous sigh.

Molly was speechless, wondering if when the farm was sold if her mother ever intended to visit them again! She was saddened by this, her shoulders drooping in anguish. Alistair must have seen her reaction, as he stood behind her, slipping his arm around her waist and kissing her neck making her smile and relax. They all fell silent. Molly watching her mother over the top of her own coffee and Enrico never seemed to stop massaging her shoulders, it was becoming annoying, but if the farm was sold, hopefully, they would not need to see him again. Sandra left after forcefully delivering her feelings once more to Molly who began to see how her father must have felt all those years. Thoughts of her father brought tears to her eyes and she unashamedly let them fall, her sadness for her father mingled with sadness over her mother too. She turned to Alistair who held her tightly in his arms, resting her head on his shoulder.

"I wish my mother would be more… more motherly," she sobbed into his shirt. He stroked her hair, keeping her close. "She's never really been affectionate, but since dad died, she seems to be even colder and more self-centred," she sniffed. "I need to call Stella, let her know what's happened and your mum will be back soon with Jessica," she reluctantly pulled away from him and picked up her phone just as Alice opened the door, lifting the pushchair in behind her.

Chapter 16

Alistair drove back to his office to relieve Bertie, his mind all over the place, not least Sandra and Enrico and the effect they were having on Molly, which only served to make him angry.

He walked in to find Bertie with his feet up on the desk, hands clasped behind his head, big grin on his face. Alistair was relieved to see his old mate looking happy.

"Spill," he grinned at Bertie as he threw his bag onto the floor behind the door, "I know that look, what have you done or should I not ask?" Bertie swung his feet down.

"Ask away, no, I'm going to tell you, but before that, I will make the coffee. I want you comfortable for this," he jumped up and clattered with the kettle, finding his favourite dark chocolate hobnobs in a tin too. Alistair settled himself behind his desk and Bertie pulled up a chair, waving a whisky bottle in front of Alistair.

"Nothing changes," laughed Alistair, "I am pleased to note but just a tiny tot though."

He held up his mug and Bertie did the honours. "Come on, I'm dying to know what you've been up to."

"Right, two things; one work, one personal, which do you want first?" he took a bite from his hobnob, stringing it out for as long as possible, a cheeky grin plastered across his face.

"Work, I can at least hope you did some," he laughed, eyeing Bertie suspiciously. They had worked well together and he did miss his mate and Alistair wondered if he could entice him back. They seemed to have lost touch recently and here was Bertie showing a glimpse of his old self and Alistair was enjoying it. "Come on then, the suspense is killing me," he chuckled.

"Booked you an appointment to meet a new client," Bertie paused for effect, "he's making a lot of money in the timber industry and wants to make some investments but doesn't know where to start."

"That's great, Bertie, thanks... and the personal?" He sat up much more attentive, feeling pleased.

"Now, that's interesting. I thought that I would try and find out more about our friend, Enrico," he pulled out another biscuit, trying to smother a grin.

"Hmm... I can tell that I am going to love this. Come on, Bertie, I haven't seen you like this for a long time." Alistair sat forward in anticipation, dunking a biscuit, keeping his eyes on Bertie.

"Seems he is not quite who he has led us to think he is," he paused for maximum effect, making Alistair sit up and stare, "so, I started with the information we knew and what I managed to get out of him a few weeks ago. That drew a blank, so I made a call to a mate of mine up in the Met and that turned out to be much more interesting."

"Tell me more. I can't wait to wipe that smug smile off his face," Alistair grinned, now really interested. It would give him great pleasure to send him packing. Alistair had always suspected something, but without any proof there was nothing he could do.

"Well, it turns out that Enrico is actually Eric Jamieson and get this, he's from Birmingham." Bertie paused, allowing this revelation to sink in and Alistair let out a long low whistle.

"Bloody hell, I mean I knew there was something dodgy about him, but this is good news. What else could your mate tell you? No, please," Alistair let out a sudden gulp of panic. "Don't tell me he's an escaped murderer or..." he shuffled to the edge of his chair, raking his fingers through his hair, "is Sandra in danger... what...?" He leaned forward, open mouthed at Bertie, the sudden shock overtaking him, flooding him with fear for Molly and their precious baby, Jessica, too.

"No, nothing like that so you can stop worrying, however, he did fleece a woman up in the Midlands and the police would like to speak to him, but nothing criminal. He sounds like a bit of a fraudster, but nothing more dangerous." Alistair heaved a sigh of relief, as much as he found Sandra overbearing and sometimes, he felt like throwing her out, she was Molly's mother and he didn't want to see her lose everything to this man.

"So, how are we going to expose him without alerting him to what we know? This is going to be tricky; I feel like I want to dash over there, confront him and drag him out by the scruff of the neck, kicking him back to Spain. I have a feeling that Sandra won't believe it and that might make her more determined to stand by him." He rubbed his chin and pulling on his bottom lip, he began to try and set out a plan. "Obviously, I need to tell Molly and we can't risk exposing him too soon. How much do the police want to talk to him, any idea?"

"No, but I can find out. Why? Are you thinking of some sort of sting operation?"

Bertie was getting excited at the thought and Alistair, feeling triumphant, let out a laugh.

"You could say that, but now we need to make sure they don't go back to Spain. Not yet, anyway," he grinned. "This calls for a celebration, any more whisky, Bertie?" Alistair was feeling better than in a long time everything was falling into place and with Enrico out of the way, he wondered if Sandra would still want to sell the farm or worse, move back to the UK… he groaned. He had visions of her taking charge of everyone's lives, giving out instructions and automatically expecting to be in control. He gave a shudder as visions of Sandra with her long red talons grew more vivid. He shook himself, returning to the here and now.

"You okay, Alistair? You have turned a funny colour," Bertie had a lopsided grin plastered across his face, clearly realising what his revelations had conjured up for Alistair.

"Sorry, just had an awful picture of Sandra in Army uniform being a right sergeant major," he nearly choked on the horror of his own vision. Bertie started to laugh and laughed so much he had to dab his eyes. Alistair joined in, trying to wash away the sight of Sandra looking like Miss Agatha Trunchbull in Matilda. "Tell you what… I need to get back to reality before I change my mind. I have so enjoyed today, Bertie. Come on, let's go for lunch at the pub before you go home." They left the office still laughing, with Alistair more determined to get rid of this Enrico character than ever. He slapped Bertie on the shoulder, yes, he had missed his old mate.

Chapter 17

Molly wandered across the farmyard and down to the allotment, turning her iPhone over and over in her hand. She had left Alistair with his mother who was delighted at being allowed to take Jessica out on her own. Alistair had quickly explained the meeting between Sandra, the estate agents and Molly to Alice. She made all the right noises as Molly excused herself and exited the kitchen. She sat on the bench, surveying all the hard work that Bertie had put in.

There were neat rows of potatoes, carrots, runner bean canes and onions. The blueberry bushes were covered in tiny flowers, bees busy flitting from one to the other. She looked around, nostalgically remembering the time they had worked on it together. What a lot had happened in the last year and now here she was, contacting Stella, making decisions that could change things forever. Molly leaned back on the bench, closing her eyes, letting the sun warm her skin. She heard a cuckoo and her eyes snapped open in search of this bird – she had heard one with its distinctive call many times, but so far, failed to spot. No luck this time. She pressed the number for Stella.

"Hi. I was wondering when you would call. Mother has already filled me in, but can I hear your version of events, as I am sure that they will be more accurate." She gave a chuckle.

Molly proceeded to recount the meeting and advice from the agent to Stella, saying, "We don't really have a choice, as no one wants to start doing all the work required and maybe, it's time to let someone else fall in love with the farm." She heaved a sigh and swiped a tear from her cheek.

"I know you have loved the farm more than I ever did, but I have to agree with dropping the price and letting go. Goodness only knows the cash injection would be very useful at the moment and it would finalise everything after Dad and this debacle with Mum and Enrico."

"I know, but I can't help feeling sad about it. I'll call Mum and tell her, as she is desperate to get her hands on the money. I just hope that she's not planning to hand it over to Enrico. I couldn't bear that. It's her money though and I am doing my best to accept that what she does with it is her business, as she is fond of telling us." There was a moment of silence before Molly continued, "Sorry, Stella, for being a bit too sentimental and please tell me, changing the subject, how the new venture is going."

Molly clicked her iPhone off, sweeping her gaze over the fields to the sea. The view never failed to make her feel uplifted. She could see what looked like a cruise ship on the horizon, raising her hand to shield her eyes to get a better view. Molly wished for a pair of binoculars, for the umpteenth time making a mental note to put some in the shed.

"There you are, my dear," Alice broke into her reverie and Molly turned, throwing a smile in her direction. "I need to chat with you regarding the Church fete." Glad for the distraction, Molly budged up on the bench, making room for Alice. Alice was carrying two mugs of steaming coffee and Molly was grateful for the thought as she took the mug.

"Thank you. How can I help you, Alice?" Alice launched into the complexities of running a Church fete, leaving Molly still wondering why she wanted to speak to her about it unless she was hinting at Molly taking over, which was never going to happen.

"So, what I need to know is if you have finalised your stand with that lovely Hugh and if you are entering any of our competitions, dear? We haven't had many entrants so far and I am rather hoping that you could help out, you know, put in a few entries and maybe encourage others to do so too," Alice sat beaming at Molly and Molly couldn't help but smile back, knowing she would give in, but she held out a little longer.

"What did you have in mind, Alice? I can't remember all the categories, but I'm sure that I can do something." She sipped her coffee, half-watching a blackbird from the corner of her eye. The blackbird was busy tossing leaves out of the way as he searched for worms, making Molly smile. She pulled herself back to listen to Alice.

"Well, of course, there is the cake baking competition, always hotly contested by most of the ladies in the village, but you could enter the painting, photography, flower arranging, crafts which includes knitting, crochet, embroidery and so on. Then there's…"

"Ooh, slow down, Alice, I might have time to bake a cake, but I'm hopeless at all the other things. I will put a poster up for you and how about I get the 'lovely' Hugh to organise a dog show, would that help? I also wondered about a display of vintage cars. George still has his old 1935 Austin Chalfont, Bertie has an old Jag, we still have dad's Morris traveller and I have my Land Rover. I'm sure that other people must have vintage vehicles, what about Lady Isobel?" Alice was delighted at this idea and they walked back towards the farm arm in arm, chatting about the hope for sunny day.

"There's something else you could do for me, dear. If you don't mind," broached Alice.

"Ooh, what's that, Alice?" Molly was immediately suspicious, thinking that this was really what Alice had wanted from her all along.

"We are looking for a new vicar, as you probably know, and well, the two candidates will be at the fete. The Bishop thought that it would be good for them both to have a look at us more closely and of course, for us to get to know them more personally, before a decision is made." Molly was relieved, as she had visions of Alice wanting her to join some committee or other, eating into her precious time.

"That sounds easy enough, Alice, I'm sure that I can manage that for you. Just introduce me and I will report back later." She grinned with relief.

"Thank you, dear. I knew that I could rely on you. Between you and me, I rather like Suzanne Martin. I found Timothy Wagstaff a bit weak and his wife is not very supportive. Oh, well, see what you think."

"Okay, will do." Molly knew how Alice would always try to influence you without being direct and she was certainly an expert at hiding it, letting you think that you made your own decision, she grinned fondly. They walked back across the farmyard to find Alistair standing at the door with Jessica in his arms.

"Sorry, darling, but I need to get back to the office, let Bertie off the hook," he handed over Jessica and kissed her lightly, hugged his Mum and drove off.

"I must be going too, dear. George will be waiting for his lunch." Alice disappeared down the lane and Molly turned to Jessica, hugging her.

"So, just you and me now, gorgeous, let's go and see Hugh." Jessica made cooing and gurgling noises, attempting to talk to her mummy and Molly kissed her head and hugged her closely. She drove to the practise to find Hugh with a queue. There was Mrs Drummond with her cat; he was a rescue of indeterminate age. She was stroking him and sobbing. Miss McPherson and her dog, 'Charlie'. He was a cocker spaniel who always seemed to be getting into scrapes. There were two other customers who Molly had not met before. She quickly changed to help him out. Jessica had fallen asleep in her seat so Molly placed her in the office, gently closing the door.

"Hi, Hugh," she said, bustling into the surgery. "I'll take Mrs Drummond and Miss McPherson if you can deal with the two new clients." She bustled into the waiting room without waiting for a reply, calling Mrs Drummond in first.

"Hello," she smiled, "what seems to be the trouble?" She asked Mrs Drummond, reaching out to take Sooty from her.

"Hello, Molly. I don't really know; he is off his food and doesn't seem to want to go out. A bit like me," she chuckled. Molly examined him all over, fearing that it was just old age, but she knew how attached Mrs Drummond was to him and pondered the best approach.

"There doesn't seem to be anything wrong that I can find. We could run some tests to see if there is anything more sinister, but I do believe that he is just getting old," she squeezed her arm as Mrs Drummond pulled out a tissue and began to sob once more.

"Is there anything you can do, Molly? I don't know what I would do without him," she wiped her eyes and blew her nose loudly.

"I can go ahead and do tests? Or you can take him home and try to tempt him with his favourite food." Molly knew that it was

140

only a matter of time and that tests would probably be a waste of money for poor Mrs Drummond, who had very little to begin with. "No charge today, Mrs Drummond, but if you should decide on tests, I can let you know the cost."

"Thank you, dear," she scooped up Sooty and shuffled out, carrying her precious friend.

"Hello, Miss McPherson, let's have a look at Charlie. What has he been up to now?"

She held the door open and Miss McPherson tripped in. She was a bit eccentric, with her arm full of bangles, bright coloured flowing skirts often covered in exotic flowers, clogs and huge sunglasses pushed up onto her head. Molly smiled to herself as she could see that her blonde hair was not her natural colour as dark chocolate roots were quite visible.

"I think he's been in a fight again; his paw is bleeding." She whispered so that no one would hear.

"Right, let's take a look," Molly held onto him as he struggled and cleaned up his paw.

"Looks like he has caught it on something, maybe barbed wire. Anyway, we will soon have it sorted, I will put a stitch in it and he will be as good as new."

"I was hoping that Hugh would see Charlie, he's rather cute, don't you think?" she said coyly.

"Err, yes, I suppose," said Molly, absentmindedly. She was concentrating on Charlie as Miss McPherson leaned in with another question.

"Is he married?" Molly missed the implication as she began to neatly place a stitch in Charlie's paw.

"No, not as far as I know anyway," then it dawned on Molly as she looked her straight in the eye. She had always thought of her as being much older than herself, but looking closely now, she had lovely clear skin and could even be younger. Miss McPherson jangled her bangles as she pushed her hair back, looking quite agitated. Molly threw her a big smile.

"We are having a stall at the village fete and Hugh will be there. Are you planning to visit?"

"Oh yes, never miss it, I might even bake a cake," she beamed, warming to the idea.

"Great, I'll see you there then. Try to stop Charlie from chewing his paw and any more problems, please come back. Oh, and keep him away from barbed wire," she called to her disappearing back. Molly washed her hands and popped into the office just as Jessica was stirring from her slumbers, stretching her little pudgy arms in the air. Hugh followed her in.

"Thanks. That cleared the queue. We are getting busier, which is great. I wanted to talk to you about progress on the partnership and about the fete," said Hugh as he furrowed his brow hands on hips, looking kind of 'cute', thought Molly with a grin.

"It just so happens that I have the paperwork with me," Molly pulled out an envelope with a flourish, placing it on to the desk. Hugh picked it up and pulled out the papers, settling into her chair in order to examine the documents. "I will make us a coffee and we can talk. I wondered what you thought about organising a dog show at the village fete."

"Great and great," he looked up at Molly, his lips curving into a smile, twinkling his eyes rather sexily. Molly studied him for a second longer to try and see what Miss McPherson saw. He had soft blue eyes, he was tall and muscular. Perhaps he worked out. He had rather long hair, quite fair, it gently curled onto his collar, giving him a raffish air. He was clean-shaven and had the smell of aftershave, not a smell she recognised.

"Great," she replied, disappearing off into the kitchen, returning minutes later with a mug of coffee for Hugh. "I've just realised that I know very little about you and as you're going to be my new partner, perhaps you could fill me in a little?" She pushed the packet of biscuits towards him, glancing into the waiting room. It was empty. Hugh sat forward, helping himself to a couple tapping the crumbs onto the desk.

"Not much to tell, really, you know, most of it already," he crunched into his digestive, catching the crumbs that fell onto his white coat.

"Okay, what about a bit more personally, family or maybe a girlfriend, that sort of thing," she bent down to pick up Jessica and cuddled her, kissing her head.

"Aar, my Dad died suddenly a few years ago and my Mum still lives in Richmond. I have a brother who moved to the States and is a successful accountant, married, with a couple of kids. I was engaged once, but she dumped me at the altar…" he fell silent. Molly was shocked. She threw him an 'I don't believe it' look and pulling up a chair, sat down.

"What? Literally at the altar, you were standing there and she didn't show up? Wow, that's awful. I'm so sorry, Hugh, I had no idea." Molly gasped at this shocking turn of events.

"Well, it's still painful, but, no, she showed up alright. She looked beautiful…" he was staring into space, as if recalling the whole thing and Molly just waited quietly. "She walked up the aisle, stunning she was and then, when they got to the part about 'if either of you know any just cause' etc. and she looked across at Tom, my Best man…"

"It's alright, Hugh, I get it. You don't have to tell me anymore," she patted his arm. He looked across at her with a weak smile.

"Probably did me a favour anyway. I would never have come to Trentmouth and I love it here, now a partnership. So, put me off women, I have to say and I have stayed single ever since. Not planning to go there again."

"We are not all the same, you know and I'm sure you'll find someone one day. Someone who truly loves you and you love them."

"Yeah, maybe, but I wouldn't count on it." There was a buzz from the waiting room.

"Sounds like we have another customer, can we catch up later and talk about this dog show idea?"

"Sure, see you later." Hugh disappeared and Molly, still shocked by his revelation, turned her thoughts to Miss McPherson.

Chapter 18

The day of the church fete dawned. It was a glorious June day, not a wisp of cloud, just stunning blue sky and warm sunshine. Molly and Hugh were busy setting up their stall. Hugh had achieved quite an array of freebies, plus leaflets for all kinds of pets, from poodles to parakeets. They had borrowed the swizzle stand out of Lucy's mum's shop and it was now filled with attractive toys and gifts. He had even found a very clever woman who made waterproof coats for pooches. They were all sizes and colours, from pink to tartan.

"I wish I'd thought of that," said Molly casually scrutinising the quality of the coats, "these are really good. I can't see Rex wearing one, but some dogs hardly go out so would probably shiver with the cold." Hugh gave a chuckle, holding up a particularly pretty, pastel green one, edged with lace and scattered with yellow sunflowers.

"No, I can't imagine Rex in this lovely outfit either, but lots of people do protect their dogs in coats and why not add some colour and fun." He carefully put the coat back and picked up the bunting, ready to fix to the front of the stand. It was looking attractive and Molly constructed the pen that would hold the chickens with their chicks later.

"I think that I will have a wander, meet some of the other stall holders and look for Alice. See if I can get us a cup of coffee," said Molly, picking up her backpack, placing it over her shoulder. She set off intending to circle the field and end up in the competition marquee, but she heard someone calling her name.

"Molly… over here," she could see Alice frantically waving her arm, heading in her direction.

"Morning, Alice… what a beautiful day, I'm so pleased for you, it should bring the people in."

"Yes, we are lucky and we have a bumper lot of entrants for all the categories. Have you had chance to look in the marquee yet?"

"No, I was just making my way there now, why?" Molly glanced in the direction of the marquee just as a woman came out walking towards them. She looked as though she knew her way around a gymkhana, dressed in jeans, white shirt, body warmer and what looked like Dubarry boots. Her hair was neatly up in a chignon, pearls at her slender neck and she was smiling broadly at them.

"Molly, I want you to meet Lady Isobel. She is one of the judges and we were wondering if you could do some judging too?" Lady Isobel put her hand out to Molly, she shook it, saying.

"Hello, I'm Molly Craven, actually Molly Warren now, from the veterinary practice in Trentmouth. I don't think we've met before."

"Hello, Molly, no, but I've heard lots about you from Alice." Molly felt a flush of pink rising up her neck, wondering what Alice could have told her, probably everything. "I do hope you will join me in the judging, Molly, and I would like to talk to you later, as I am thinking of getting a couple of Alpacas and need some advice." Molly stared for a second, this was just wonderful news, but she couldn't tell her right now that she knew nothing about Alpacas and why on earth did Lady Isabel want some?

"I don't know what use I will be at judging; I might be able to help with home produce, but I don't really know anything about flower arranging and crafts. I have entered a cake myself, so that must disqualify me anyway." She shook her head in defence.

"Don't worry, Molly," said Lady Isobel, "I don't know much either, it's just fun and you can donate your cake to the raffle or the WI in the tea tent if you wish."

"I can see that I am cornered, so, yes, I will be a judge, but not the dog show, as I know them all too well and could never choose," they all laughed. Molly quickly sent a text to Hugh, asking him to research Alpacas as soon as he had a minute, then continued her wander around the now gaily decorated garden. There were all manner of stalls, from wood carving, beadwork, knitted items and homemade lotions and potions. Hearing the familiar jangle of bracelets, Molly spotted Miss McPherson setting up a honey stall.

"I didn't know you kept bees, Miss McPherson, how wonderful," enthused Molly, "you must let me buy some honey later."

"Thank you, and please, call me Felicity. Actually, it's my old dad who keeps the bees, not me, I just sell it for him. He has difficulty walking these days, but he won't give up the bees, part of the family he says," she smiled shyly. Molly hadn't realised that Miss McPherson, Felicity, still lived at home and pondered that she knew very little about her or even what she did for a living, resolving to come back later for a chat. Molly retrieved her cake from the competition marquee and took it along to the WI tent where she could hear the tea urn hissing and bubbling, hoping to get some coffee.

"I've brought you a cake," said Molly to the lady in a white apron with the WI logo neatly embroidered on it and the name Maggie underneath.

"Thank you very much. What kind is it, so that I can write a label for it," she admired Molly's cake, slowly turning it around. Molly grinned to herself. If that had been Stella's cake, it would have brought gasps of delight and people would be looking for cake forks. It probably wouldn't last long enough for the opening ceremony!

"It's poppy seed, actually. I thought that I would try something different. I had intended to enter the cake competition, but as I have been asked to be a judge, I thought that you might like it instead."

"Poppy seed, bah, can't abide it," came a voice from the table next to the array of cakes and scones, "seeds get stuck under my palate." Molly stared at this grumpy old lady and wondered what she was doing there; the fete didn't open till this afternoon.

"Now, Doris, don't be like that. It's very kind of Molly to donate a cake, I'm sure that it will be delicious," replied Maggie.

"Should be scones with jam and cream. It was always scones in my day, none of these other fancy cakes." She shuffled in her chair, arms folded, heaving up her ample bosom.

"Sorry about that Molly. The urn has just boiled, would you like a coffee?" Molly instantly liked Maggie, but couldn't place her: she would have to do some detective work.

"Thank you. Could I have two, please? I've left my colleague putting up the bunting and I should get back. I'm happy to pay," she said, quickly throwing a sideways glance at Doris who appeared to be still grumbling to no one in particular.

"No need to pay, you're a worker and a donor," she handed over the coffees and Molly retreated into relative safety outside. She walked back to Hugh who was wiping his brow. He looked up at her with creases across his forehead.

"Alpacas..." he looked at Molly, accepting the coffee. "What's that all about?" he took a slurp, "No biscuits or cake?" Molly laughed.

"Lady Isobel is thinking of getting some. I don't know why, but she wants to chat to me later. Well, us, I mean. What do you know about them? They are a bit specialist and I don't really know that much, I'm afraid."

"Love them," said Hugh, "Back in Yorkshire, they are very popular. Their wool is quite sought-after, makes gorgeous socks I understand, lovely and warm in winter," he grinned as Molly's eyes shot up in amazement. "So, no worries and it will be great for business, does she have horses too?"

"I don't know, but judging by the way she was dressed, I would probably say, yes."

They finished setting out their stall and Hugh disappeared to collect hens, chicks and a few ducks. Molly went back to the farm to check on Alistair and Jessica, feeling that she should get more involved with the community. It's not that she didn't pick up lots of gossip in the surgery, but she surprised herself how little she knew of the day-to-day happenings, never mind who was who. She felt a need to give back in some way and donating her cake was the first step. Jessica would need a child minder soon and then pre-school... Molly let out a heavy sigh. She pulled into the farmyard, remembering that Alice wanted her to chat to the two new prospects for vicar. *What do I know?* she thought as she jumped down and wandered up to the house.

Alistair came out to meet her, grinning. "There's been an offer on the farm," he took her in his arms, kissing her lightly. "I've put the kettle on, you look all done in." He guided her indoors. Rex ran over, woofing and making a fuss, when he was happy that all was well, he returned to his basket, turning round and round before flopping down, yawning from the effort.

"It has been more exhausting than I thought possible. I haven't got long; we need to be back there before the opening. So, tell me about this offer." She sat down on the couch, gratefully putting her feet up.

"You don't look very pleased, about the offer, I mean, it's low, but I suppose we have to start somewhere. The agent is going to speak to Sandra, rather her than me. I can just hear her saying no." He made her a mug of tea and a cheese and pickle sandwich.

"Come on, eat up and you can tell me all about it. Jessica and I have had a lovely morning. She'll be waking up soon, and I can take care of her. You relax for five minutes." The phone rang. "I'll get that," said Alistair. Molly could hear him saying, "Well, okay, I'll let her know and... thanks." She guessed who it was from the comment.

"That was the agent. Sandra said 'not in a thousand years'," they both laughed, "... anyway, she is willing to compromise a little, so that's something."

"I suppose so, I can't think about it at the moment. I have so much on my mind and now Alice wants me to be a judge this afternoon for all the various categories," she shuffled around on the old sofa, tucking her feet up as she went. "You wouldn't take my place, would you, I'm sure your Mum wouldn't mind?" Alistair handed over her tea and sandwich before sitting beside her.

"Afraid not, darling, not my bag at all and besides, you will do it so well," he caressed her arm, "I will look after Jessica, it will be fun and Bertie and Lucy are coming too." She threw him a miserable look.

"What is it, are you okay?" he asked anxiously. Molly let her head drop back as she let out a deep breath.

"I am okay, honestly, it's just that I have had a funny morning and I feel a bit up-side down and then the news of an offer. I just need to get my head around it all... and I nearly forgot, Alice wants to introduce me to the two candidates for vicar!" she exclaimed in a high-pitched voice, "...what do I know? We don't even go to Church."

"Ahh... I was going to mention that..." he paused, looking sheepish.

"What do you mean? What were you going to mention?" she sat up, staring at him aghast, panic now trickling through her.

"Mum was asking about us having Jessica christened and I sort of said that we would," he held his breath, "…what do you think?" Molly sank back with relief.

"Is that all…" a giggle escaped her, releasing all the days' stress. She giggled again.

Alistair began to laugh too and before long, Molly had tears rolling down her cheeks. Alistair kissed her forehead.

"I do love you; you know that, don't you?" he kissed her again. "Jessica is still asleep. Come on…" he picked up her plate, placing it onto the table. Molly followed him as he led her upstairs.

***

The sound of Jessica making happy noises broke into Molly's sleepy head. She stretched and smiled to herself, wondering what day it was and what time it was. A moment later, she threw the clothes back and shook Alistair as she leapt out of bed.

"Alistair, wake up, look at the time. I must go. You look after Jess and I will see you later," she placed a quick kiss on his lips, grabbing her clothes she headed for the door, turning, she smiled.

"I love you too," with that, she ran down the stairs, downed a glass of water and left for the church fete. She dashed over to their stand as Hugh looked up. He was in the pen, feeding the hens and their chicks.

"Am I glad to see you; I was beginning to wonder if you were alright. You look flushed, everything okay?" Hugh stood hands on hips, his eyebrows furrowed as he gazed at her. Molly felt herself flush even more, but had no time to be embarrassed. She glanced round quickly as the garden was filling up with happy crowds, wandering around the gaily decorated stalls.

"Yes, I am sorry, Hugh, you go and get something to eat. I'll take over here, the opening must be soon…" she glanced at her watch just as Alice came bustling over. She was now dressed in a flimsy pink and mauve outfit, with a matching pink jacket, a single string of pearls and kitten heels in another shade of pink. Molly smiled to herself, biting her lip to stop the smile from spreading to a full-blown giggle. She looked like an eighties' throwback on her way to a wedding.

"Molly, thank goodness. I just rang Alistair to make sure everything was okay. I was beginning to wonder what had happened to you," she hardly stopped to take in a breath before starting to drag Molly over to the marquee, "we must do the judging before the fete opens and put the winners' medals in place." Molly pulled her up short, remembering poor Hugh.

"I have to get Hugh first. We can't leave the livestock unattended. Just give me a minute, Alice, and I will be there. Your outfit looks nice by the way," she dropped a small smile, hoping that it looked sincere and disappeared to find Hugh. Once in the marquee, Molly felt overwhelmed with the variety and amount of entries into the various categories. It was clear that it was a herculean task that lay before them. "No wonder you wanted help with the judging, Alice. I am astounded by the quality and the huge number of entries. I had no idea."

They set to work, first the flower arranging, before moving on and finally finishing with the children's entries. All the medal certificates were set in place. It felt like the Chelsea flower show, she mused, realising that she had thoroughly enjoyed the experience. Lady Isobel did the honours and officially opened the fete. Molly gazed around the garden; it had never looked better. Bertie had worked hard and the stalls were bedecked with colourful bunting, balloons and all manner of streamers. The air was full of happy chatter. Crowds flocked into the marquee; people eagerly searching for their entries, there were delighted screams from winners, mixed with shouts of glee. Molly couldn't help but stand and smile. She felt her arm grabbed once more and turning, Alice was already pulling her towards the WI tent.

"Cup of tea, Molly, we sit down now and rest. Enjoy the view, the hard work is over."

Molly let herself be carried along, Lady Isobel chatting away in the background, praising everyone's efforts and talking to people.

"Oh, I must go and help Hugh. He has done most of the work so far. Sorry, Alice, I will catch you up later," Molly tried to extract her arm, but Alice held on tight.

"No, dear, don't worry. Alistair is helping him and Lucy has Jessica. There is someone I want you to meet."

Chapter 19

Stepping out of the sunshine, Molly found the WI tent dim and it took a moment for her eyes to adjust. They walked over to find Maggie still serving tea. She waved in acknowledgement, indicating for them to sit down and she would bring over the tea. There was a round table set with a pretty red gingham cloth and a vase of flowers, a label propped up stating 'VIP', there were three chairs. Molly plopped herself down gratefully as she scanned the room. Doris was still residing in her corner, dressed all in black. She wore a black hat with a little bit of lace curling down over her forehead. Molly couldn't help but smirk as she saw her thick black wrinkled stockings and neat little black boots poking out from under her skirts. She looked for the entire world like Queen Victoria, but much scarier.

"Here we are," said Maggie, placing a tray onto the table. Molly recognised Alice's best chintz china, napkins, a plate of fruit scones, a dish of strawberry jam and another heaped high with thick Dorset clotted cream. She looked up at Maggie, forcing a grateful smile.

"Bang goes my diet," she exclaimed, hoping to extract some sympathy, but Maggie only laughed.

"No calories in there," she chuckled as she laid up the table, "...just lots of delicious homemade goodness." She picked up the tray and turned to leave then turning back, she put her head on one side, saying, "You should think about joining us." Molly stared for a second and gave Maggie a quizzical look, pondering how best to reply.

"Oh, I don't think I'm the right sort of person for the WI. I... I always thought that it was for older ladies, although," she added very quickly, "...I would have thought that you were far too young."

Maggie threw her head back, laughing, "No, not the WI. I only help out as a favour to Izzie. No, I'm talking about the Purbeck Ladies Club."

"The Purbeck Ladies Club, I've never heard of that one. Tell me more and who's Izzie?" Molly felt quite embarrassed that so much went on around her that she knew nothing about. It's funny how you can live in the same place all your life and know nothing. She felt anguished at the thought, looking up at this attractive young woman who was about her own age. She had dark nut-brown hair tied up into a ponytail and large almond-shaped, chocolate brown eyes.

"Izzie is my Aunt, Lady Isobel. She's great. Anyway, I must go, I'll be in touch about the PLC, okay?" she hesitated a second.

"Yes… yes, fine and thanks for the tea." Maggie smiled, which filled her whole face and left Molly feeling that a whirlwind had just passed through, blowing away cloying cobwebs that Molly hadn't noticed were holding her. She poured her tea, looking around for Alice. She spotted her trying to escape from Doris. There were a couple with two children with her and Doris was smiling sagely and nodding. Lady Isobel was talking to a woman that Molly couldn't quite see, except that she had on pale blue crop trousers and peep toe white sandals decorated with a spray of flowers repeated on her clutch bag. They were enjoying a laugh together and Molly couldn't decide if they were friends, as she appeared to be much younger than Lady Isobel. Molly sipped her tea and absentmindedly, cut into a scone laying on a spoonful of the jam and a smear of clotted cream. The mystery woman was really rather slim and her honey gold hair tumbled down her back; Molly was intrigued.

"I'm so sorry, Molly, to abandon you like that, but I was caught by Doris," Alice pulled out a chair and sat down, pouring a cup of tea. The cup clattered in its saucer and Molly realised that Alice was trembling slightly.

"Are you alright, Alice. You have turned rather pale. Do you want me to find George?"

"No, dear, it's that bi… I mean, damn woman. She can be very annoying, sticking her nose in and interfering. Just because she has been here all her life does not mean that she knows best," she harrumphed. "I could, I could… never mind what I could do.

I need a cup of tea," she picked up her cup, taking a deep draught. Molly suppressed a smile.

"Tell me, who is that talking to Lady Isobel? I don't think I know her," she asked, distracting Alice from her menacing thoughts. Alice turned and immediately, her demeanour changed, a smile spread across her face and she dashed across to them and dragged them to their table.

"Molly, let me introduce you to Suzanne Martin. She is one of the two prospective candidates for vicar," she proudly announced. Molly was astounded. Vicars have never looked like this before; they were usually dour old men, smelling of cigarettes and alcohol, who everyone avoided. Church somewhere cold and uninviting with no life in it, no one ventured through the door except for weddings and funerals. Molly shook herself slightly, realising that her mouth had dropped open.

"Hello, Suzanne," Molly took the hand offered to her and shook it, "take a seat."

"Thanks, Molly. Alice has told me a lot about you. I know you are married to her son, Alistair, and have a baby daughter, Jessica." Molly passed her a cup of tea as Alice and Lady Isobel disappeared in search of another table.

"Yes, and I know nothing about you," they both chuckled. Molly set about finding out as much as she could about this young woman who wanted to make a career within the Church. This was a pretty alien concept to Molly and she was fascinated to talk to her. They could have chatted all afternoon, but Molly needed to get back to Hugh and Alice had other people she wanted to introduce Suzanne to. Lady Isobel was with the couple again and their children. She headed over to Molly just as she stood up to leave.

"Molly, let me introduce you to Timothy Wagstaff. He is also a candidate for the post of vicar, this is Mrs Wagstaff and their children, Toby and Sophia."

"Oh, hello, pleased to meet you. I'm the local vet. Are you enjoying the afternoon?"

"Mum, I'm bored, can we go yet?" chipped in Toby, pulling at his mother's arm and jiggling about.

"Yeah, Mum, we want to go and get a burger," added Sophia.

"Now, children, you know what we agreed," said Timothy. Toby had pushed Sophia who pushed him back, knocking him into his Mother.'

"Come on, Timothy, the children are restless, we should go before they cause any trouble," then turning to Molly, "nice to meet you, but we must be going."

"Sorry," said Timothy, "another time perhaps." This was clearly a statement and not a question, as they disappeared, the two children still pushing at each other with their father bringing up the rear. He looked defeated, his head down, meekly following on behind. Molly felt sorry for him and shrank at the thought of Timothy Wagstaff and crew arriving in Trentmouth. Molly made her way back towards their stand where a small crowd had gathered. She could see lots of children leaning over the fence, watching the baby chicks and a few parents talking to Hugh. She looked around for Alistair, feeling the need for a hug; the thought of Jessica growing up into a monster like Sophia made her grimace. She caught site of Lucy and Bertie pushing the buggy. Jessica must be fast asleep. Molly immediately let her shoulders drop as she fell into more familiar territory and speeded up. She kissed both Lucy and Bertie before peering in at Jessica.

"Hi, how are you both? It seems ages since we had a proper night together and I have so much to tell you, Lucy, and I want to know what you been up to, too. I feel that I have neglected you terribly." It felt good to be back on safe territory once more. All this, being a judge malarkey, had been fun, but not something she wanted to repeat anytime soon.

"That would be great. I have lots to tell you too. What are you doing later? You could come over and have some supper with us if you're not too tired," said Lucy. Molly considered for a moment. It had been a tiring day, but one she had, surprisingly, thoroughly enjoyed.

"Tell you what, you come to us then, I can put Jess to bed and relax." She countered.

"On one condition," Lucy gave a smile with a twinkle in her eyes. Molly was puzzled.

"Oh, and what's that? You look very suspicious to me. Come on, tell me now, I can't wait till tonight. Let me guess," she glanced at Lucy who gave a shake of her head, warning Molly not to go there. "Hmm, I can't guess, so you will have to tell me."

"I was only going to say that we will bring the food. You have had an exhausting day and I'm sure that you don't want to start cooking. Agreed?"

"Agreed," laughed Molly, "I have certainly had an interesting day and remind me to tell you about the PLC tonight. I wonder where Alistair is." Molly looked around for him; at over six feet tall, he would be hard to miss. Lucy and Bertie continued their perambulation around the garden heading towards the refreshment tent.

"You look busy," Molly had found Hugh having just finished talking to a couple.

"Phew, it has been non-stop. I can't believe how much interest there has been. I'm sure that we have picked up a few new customers and the baby chicks have generated a lot of attention."

"Oh, good. I'm sorry to have deserted you so much, you must be hungry. Do you want a break? I can take over for a while." Before he could answer, Suzanne appeared. "Suzanne, hello again, are you enjoying our little fete?"

"It's wonderful," she enthused, "I can see that a lot of hard work has gone into it and it certainly is a success." She turned to Hugh, "You must be Alistair," She held out her hand and Hugh looked as if he had been struck dumb and Molly smirked, rescuing him.

"This is Hugh, my business partner," that had clearly given Hugh time to shake himself back to earth and he held out his hand.

"Nice to meet you, do you live in Trentmouth?" he looked like a startled rabbit caught in the headlights.

"No," she beamed, "… but I do have a dog, he's a Labrador, I had to leave him at home today."

"That's a shame. We have a dog show this afternoon. Oh, help Molly, I'll be late. I must go. Sorry, Suzanne, duty calls, but I hope to see you again soon." He leapt over the stand and shot across to where the owners with their pets were gathering. Suzanne turned to Molly.

"Hugh seems nice, have you worked together long?" she quizzed.

155

"We have only just formed a partnership, actually, and if you do move to Trentmouth, I hope that you will bring your dog into the surgery. What's his name by the way?"

"Axis, he's my best friend. I suppose everyone says that, but he really is. I think that I will watch the dog show and then I must be going. It's been lovely to meet you. I must find Alice and thank her too. Say 'goodbye' to Hugh for me. Bye then." She raised her hand as she disappeared into the throng gathering around Hugh.

Chapter 20

That evening, Molly laid in the bath, luxuriating in its hot depths, bubbles up to the top in danger of spilling over. She felt herself nodding off as she groaned contentedly. Alistair had brought her a glass of sparkling white wine, fed and bathed Jessica and now she was free to pamper herself for an hour before Lucy and Bertie arrived. She reminisced over her day and what a day it had been, and tomorrow, Alice and George were hosting a celebration of their Ruby Wedding and Molly had offered to help. She felt very thankful at this moment that her offer had been refused. They were getting in professional caterers and Stella had made them a cake. Alice wanted everyone to have a relaxing day and to enjoy themselves not be fretting over food or anything else, to Molly's eternal gratitude. She reluctantly climbed out of the bath, wrapping a turban around her head and padded over to the mirror. Alistair crept in behind her brandishing the bottle of wine.

"Hmm, you smell divine," he kissed her shoulder followed by kisses up her neck and he nibbled her ear, "fancy coming to bed? I could devour you," he slid his arm around her waist.

"As tempting as that is, no, Lucy and Bertie will be here soon and I need to get ready," she pushed him gently away. He gazed at her with forlorn, puppy dog eyes. "It won't work," she teased, "so go away, but you can leave the bottle," she chuckled as Alistair slipped out of the bathroom. It had been an extraordinary day, Molly mused, as she reminisced over all the happenings she had witnessed. She felt most peculiar, as if a veil had been lifted from her being, but at the same time, everything was the same. She had seen another facet to Alice with her organisation skills and her knowledge. It was disconcerting having only thought of Alice as her husband's interfering mother. She had met a new friend in Maggie; she shuddered at the thought of Timothy

Wagstaff and co, but then, that was nothing to do with her after all.

She couldn't help a grin spreading across her face as she put her makeup on, finishing with a dab of Dune. Just in time, as she heard the commotion downstairs. Bertie crashed in through the door, calling out, having forgotten Jessica would be fast asleep and she could hear Lucy shushing him as she opened the stair door.

"Wow," Lucy exclaimed, "you look great, positively glowing. Come on, I want to hear everything you certainly hinted earlier that you had lots to tell me." Molly and Lucy began to set up the table and sort out the food that they had brought, telling Lucy all the events of the day.

"I'm sorry I didn't meet Suzanne. She sounds a character, but I did see the other family. I thought that the children were ill mannered; they never stopped arguing and shoving each other. I thought that I had never seen them before. The whole event was a great success though and thanks for the commendation on my lemon drizzle cake. Obviously, I should have won gold, but I realise that you have to be impartial," she pouted, then grinned. They sat down to eat and Alistair kept the wine flowing.

"I nearly forgot to tell you," Molly paused for effect, grabbing everyone's attention, "we've had an offer on the farm." All eyes were fixed on Molly. Bertie raised his eyebrows, staring at her. "It was very low and Mother refused it, of course, but at least she is willing to give a bit more, as she is getting very desperate now." She tucked into another forkful and conversation resumed.

"Are Sandra and Enrico coming over again soon?" quizzed Bertie. He looked at Molly and waited. Lucy quickly reached across and squeezed his forearm.

"What's going on?" Molly looked from one to the other; suspicion and surprise mixing her thoughts up.

"Bertie, old chap, come and help me choose a bottle of whisky. I have an exceptional single malt I would like your opinion on," he stood and Bertie followed him. Molly turned to Lucy.

"Come on, I want to know what that was all about. Alistair obviously knows," she tapped her fingers on the table, watching Lucy squirm.

"Sorry, Molly, I can't, not yet anyway," she dabbed her mouth with a napkin, but Molly wasn't prepared to leave it at that.

"You're not... you know?" a grin spreading across her face, "...because if you are, that's wonderful."

"No. It's nothing like that, but I promise we will tell you as soon as we can. It's just that Bertie and I need to talk things over more yet, that's all." Lucy had flushed red from her collar up her neck and Molly resolved not to push her further. The boys returned laughing about something and Alistair carried a bottle of his favourite malt and two glasses. They returned to their previous chatter with the boys getting more than a little tipsy as the evening wore on.

"I think that you should stay over tonight, as neither of you are fit to drive," suggested Molly.

"Thanks, Molly," said Bertie and Lucy together, "...but we must be up early though and get home or we won't be ready in time for Alice and George's big do."

***

Driving home the next morning, Lucy pulled down the visor, checking her makeup and pulled her hair through her fingers, gazing into the mirror as Bertie drove in silence.

"You had me worried last night, Bertie. I thought that you were going to say something about the farm before we had spoken about it properly," Lucy boxed him gently with her fist.

"I know, sorry, it's just that I saw the possibility of us being able to afford it and got carried away and Alistair thought that I was going to say something else and dragged me off to look at his whisky collection," he threw her a lopsided grin, "...and I'm still nursing a bit of a headache now."

"Don't expect any sympathy. When you two open a bottle of whisky... let's just say you're fit for nothing," she chuckled, "however, we do need a proper chat, but not today, we mustn't be late. I can hear a police siren, I don't know where from, pull over, Bertie." She scanned the road in both directions as the sound grew louder and then she saw the blue lights as the vehicle flashed by. Bertie pulled out again into the traffic as they crawled slowly towards Wareham. "The police are setting up a diversion,

159

looks like an accident on the crossroads. You said that Alistair thought you were going to say something else, what was that?" she queried, "You didn't say."

"Just to do with work. Alistair has a new client. I set up an appointment for him and it looks like a good one, but Alistair doesn't want Molly to know yet, until things are finalised. Don't say anything to Molly, will you... please?" he glanced at Lucy.

"No, of course not, silly, I wouldn't spoil Alistair's surprise. I am still tired after last night though, but am looking forward to today and I have been thinking about the farm. I am just worried about my place." They pulled up onto the drive to find another vehicle there.

"Dad, oh no, I hope mum is alright." Lucy jumped out of the car and dashed to find her Dad dozing. She thought the worst for a split second but he opened his eyes, turning to look at her.

He climbed out of his van.

"Lucy, I'm sorry, luv, but it's your Mum." He cast his eyes down, looking forlorn and lost. Lucy took his arm, pulling him gently towards the house. "I'm at my wit's end I just don't know how to look after her anymore."

"Come on in, Dad, I'll put the kettle on and you can tell me all about it," she led him into the kitchen, grabbing mugs and milk. "Where's Mum now? You haven't left her on her own, have you?" Lucy felt concerned as her Mum's dementia seemed to be getting rapidly worse and she might wander off.

"No, a carer is sitting with her for me. I just don't know what to do anymore," he let out a sob. Bertie bustled in and Lucy threw him a warning shot.

"I'll go and get a shower, Lucy, leave you to it," he shrugged and disappeared upstairs.

Lucy sat down opposite her dad, pushing a cake towards him. He looked dishevelled and needed a shave. His jumper had seen better days, there was a hole in the elbow and the seam was pulling apart. Lucy's heart went out to him. She had never seen him looking so lost.

People with dementia reacted in so many different ways, she knew and she wanted to encourage him, but equally worried about her mum too. Picking her words carefully, she took a deep breath.

"I'll have a chat with social services and see what help we can get Dad. I'm out of my depth here. I know there are specialist Admiral nurses, but that's as far as it goes." He got up to leave, giving her a hug.

"Thanks, Lucy, luv, and we need to sort out the shop soon, if you don't mind taking care of it for me? I just can't be bothered. Oh, and please give our apologies to Alice and George. It was kind of them to invite us, but I couldn't take your Mum; it's too much of a worry. You understand, don't you?" Lucy hugged him back, letting him out and ran upstairs to find Bertie.

She quickly updated him before jumping into the shower herself. Drying her hair, Lucy could see Bertie watching her in the mirror, she smiled coyly. He slipped his arms around her, kissing her shoulder, working his way up her neck, finding her hungry lips. Lucy pulled away.

"Bertie," she cautioned, "I would love to, but we really don't have time," she turned back to the mirror. She felt herself being lifted up, as Bertie carried her in one fell swoop into bed.

"Yes, we do." He nuzzled, whispering in her ear. They were late arriving at George and Alice's party, finding them quickly handing over a card and a bottle of champagne. They had requested no presents but donations instead for stroke research, as Alice had had a stroke the year before.

"So typical of Alice, always thinking of others," she remarked to Bertie as they crossed the lawn to where the food was all laid out. Bertie was starving and she felt rather hungry herself. They found somewhere to sit by the azalea hedge; it was warm and sunny, protected from the breeze that was fluttering around the garden playing with hats and hemlines. Bertie collected two flutes of sparkling wine, sitting down with Lucy, a contented smile filled his face. "Hey, what are you thinking? No, don't tell me. I can guess," she grinned back.

"I never knew it was possible to feel this good. I have honestly never been happier, especially with you. I love you." He leaned over and squeezed her hand. She looked up surprised and thrilled, her stomach did a somersault.

"I love you too."

"Lucy there's something I want to ask you right now, but I'm not sure it is the right place."

"It probably isn't if you are thinking what I think you may be thinking. You will have to ask me later. We mustn't steal the limelight from Alice and George."

"You're right, but I ache inside, wanting you so much. We can talk later." He turned his attention to the plate piled high with food in front of him and Lucy knew how carried away Bertie could get. Ever since they met, he had been full of good ideas, always getting excited about something and she watched him from the corner of her eye, wondering if this was just another idea or a forever one. Her heart clenched tight at the thought of him not being sincere, she couldn't bear to lose him. The garden was full of happy chatter, her thoughts turning to her mum and dad. What a horrible trick to play on someone with dementia and her dad so lost without his guide in life. Lucy realised how close they were without ever noticing before. Her mum had dealt with the finances, shopping, holidays and just about every decision that needed to be made and now she had become locked inside her own little world.

A butterfly landed on the table, dragging her thoughts back to the present, she watched it closely as it opened and closed its wings, so brightly coloured, resting in the sunshine, "I think that's a Red Admiral," said Bertie, his mouth full of wild garlic and goat's cheese quiche.

"They are becoming quite rare as the hedgerows disappear, so do lots of our native species. I was thinking if we are lucky enough to get the farm, I would like to create a wildlife meadow. What do you think?"

"That's a wonderful idea," she threw him a cheeky grin, turning her attention to the food. There was a tapping on a table somewhere across the garden, as George was attempting to get everyone's attention. Lucy watched Alice looking lovingly up at him. Today, she had on a lime green and lemon suit with a cream top underneath and Lucy wasn't quite convinced that it was her colour. She had half expected her to wear something in ruby red. Alice was a bit eccentric and not having daughters to advise her, said a lot. George made a speech thanking everyone for coming and they cut the cake. Stella had made an incredible red velvet cake, topped with a picture in icing of George with his stethoscope around his neck and Alice holding gardening tools –

it was a sensation. They drank more champagne and Stella stepped forward to cut the cake into slices for everyone.

Lucy caught Molly's eye, she waved and headed in their direction.

"What a gorgeous day. Are you enjoying yourselves?" breezed Molly. She was carrying Jessica who had the most divine little pink dress scattered with daises and pink cardigan with daisy shaped buttons on it.

"Yes, wonderful and isn't Jess just a little cutie?" Molly sat down and immediately began to question Lucy about the night before. Bertie jumped up.

"I think that Alistair needs some help, see you girls later," he almost ran across the lawn, escaping any interrogation. The girls laughed.

"You must come over and let us return the favour. We enjoyed last night and I was grateful not to be doing the cooking," enthused Molly, "we will be moving out of the farm soon, as the barn is almost complete."

"Thanks, we would like that, maybe Tuesday or Wednesday, as they are my days off this week, although I am going to have to sort out a few things for dad," she let out a long sigh.

"How about Wednesday and you can tell me all about it. Today has been such a success for Alice. Oh, look, I think that's the Bishop talking to her and she doesn't look very happy."

Chapter 21

Hugh wrote down the third new appointment since the fete, smiling, tapping a pen on his chin.

He turned his attention back to unpacking the boxes from the fete. There was not much left and he made a note to order some more supplies. His mother had been really pleased for him but had wailed that it was a very long way to Dorset from Richmond and she hadn't seen him for months. He laughed to himself as he pictured her distraught look until he suggested that she come for a holiday as soon as he found somewhere to live. Somewhere to live that was a problem. The room he had rented was fine in the short term, but now he would have to find a long-term rental till he could afford to buy. Nearly getting married had cost a fortune, not to mention the cancelled honeymoon, returning all the wedding presents and the humiliation he had felt. He had suffered the embarrassed looks of false sympathy from so-called friends and family. He felt the most sorry for his poor mum who cried for days. He, on the other hand, was numb. He went through the motions of living, not really caring one way or the other. Then he had discovered that Molly Craven in Dorset was looking for a temporary locum and he couldn't get there quick enough.

He looked around the small practise, only one surgery, but that wasn't a problem, as they were building up more farmer clients, a stable and now, maybe Lady Isobel would invest in Alpacas, why? He couldn't imagine, he chuckled. The doorbell jangled and he looked up to see Suzanne from the fete with her Labrador.

"Hi," she beamed. Hugh dropped his pen and just caught himself from staring open-mouthed. She was even more stunning than he had remembered; her blonde curls bouncing round her shoulders.

"Hello, again," he held out his hand and then immediately made a fuss of her dog, "hello, boy, what's your name then?" he ruffled his ears and patted his back.

"Axis, his name is Axis and I thought that I would bring him in for a check-up. He's fine really, but I thought it best for him to have a once over just to be sure, if that's alright, Hugh?" She was tiny. He hadn't remembered that part, only her amazing, long, honey coloured hair that shone in the sun. He pulled himself up to his full six feet.

"Umm, yes, please come through. Nice to see you again. Does this mean that you are moving to Trentmouth?" he opened the door to the surgery, holding it for her to pass through.

She smelt intoxicating and when her arm brushed him ever so slightly, the feeling that shot up his arm nearly knocked him over. He couldn't help himself but feel that he wanted to hug her and touch her and kiss her. He shook himself, quickly remembering why she was there, she was a client. "Come on, boy, let me have a look at you." Axis allowed him to pick him up as he turned his head to look to Suzanne. She ruffled his fur, smiling.

"It's alright, Axis. I'm here, you're safe," she looked up at Hugh, "I don't know if I will be moving to Trentmouth, I do hope so, I'm waiting to hear from the Bishop."

"…the Bishop?" he glanced in her direction as he continued to feel around Axis, checking him over.

"Yes, I've applied to be the vicar here in Trentmouth, that's why I was at the fete trying to meet as many people as possible, see if I like the place and that people like me too, of course. There is another candidate, Reverend Tim. He has much more experience than me, but well I'll soon know, I hope." She paused, looking up at Hugh. Hugh had stopped and was rather staring at her, he was mystified. He couldn't imagine what that meant or even what she was actually talking about. Did he even hear properly? His head jumbled with thoughts that he couldn't sort out. What he did know was that she was the cutest and most disturbing person to ever cross his path.

"You're a vicar?" he felt mortified having had sexy feelings, confused and rather tongue-tied. "Sorry, that sounded all wrong, why shouldn't you be a vicar. It's just a surprise, that's all and well, I wasn't expecting it. Sorry, you know, I think I had better stop talking before I make things worse." Suzanne let out a laugh.

"I often get that reaction. I don't wear my dog collar all the time, it does cause confusion," a red flush crept up her neck rather endearingly, much to Hugh's delight. Hugh continued his examination of Axis, lifting his lip to look at his teeth.

"Hmm… looks like he has a tartar build up problem. Do you clean his teeth for him, Suzanne?" he asked as he opened a cupboard to find a toothbrush and paste.

"No. No, I don't. I didn't realise that I needed to. Is it bad?" Suzanne tried to look into Axis's mouth to try to see the problem, concern on her face. "I'm so sorry, Axis. I have truthfully never come across this situation before, I don't know what to do." She looked up at Hugh, her eyes wide and apologetic, making Hugh smile. Neither did it do anything to ease the pain of desire he felt, only making things worse. He coughed, clearing his throat in an effort to bring himself back to his senses.

"It's no problem, let me show you. It's just like cleaning your own teeth. Come on Axis there's a good boy." He lifted the lips of a struggling Axis and began to scrub his teeth.

Axis tried to pull away from him but then got the taste of the toothpaste and began licking his lips.

"That's it, well done," Hugh patted Axis fondly. "That's all you need to do occasionally to prevent any further build up," Hugh told Suzanne as he continued to congratulate Axis for his good behaviour.

"What sort of toothpaste is it?" enquired Suzanne, picking up the tube.

"Chicken flavoured," grinned Hugh.

"Chicken…!" exclaimed Suzanne, "Ugh, I bet it tastes foul." She pulled a face, turning the corners of her mouth down in distaste.

"Fowl," laughed Hugh. Suzanne looked at him, astonished. "Yes, you know, fowl, as in chicken," he laughed again. Suzanne burst out laughing too.

"Oh, yes, I'm sorry, I didn't realise what I said. How silly of me." By now Hugh had tears in his eyes and pulled out a handkerchief to dab them. He glanced at his watch.

"It's nearly lunchtime. Can I make you a coffee and maybe we can sit outside on the bench and chat?" Hugh lifted Axis down, handing the toothbrush and remaining paste to Suzanne.

"I would love to. Isn't there a café here in Trentmouth, if you can spare the time?"

"No, sadly not. We could certainly do with one. The village shop has closed too, due to a fire some months ago. However, no shortage of coffee and biscuits here," he smiled. He watched her innocent face and felt desperate to know her story. He just couldn't imagine her as a vicar. Fascinated, he wanted to know everything about her. "Excuse me a minute and I will put the kettle on. Take a seat outside, I won't be long." A few minutes later, he immerged into the sunshine, carrying a tray with two mugs of coffee, a packet of ginger biscuits and a few dog biscuits.

"Here we are," he laid the tray on the bench between them and sat down, his long legs sprawled out in front of him. It was a glorious day, the sun warm on his face, a smile creasing the corners of his mouth. He turned to Suzanne.

"Tell me what induced you to become a vicar, if you don't mind me asking?" He picked up his coffee, pulling out a couple of biscuits.

"I could ask you the same question about you becoming a vet," she giggled.

"True, but that is boring. I would much rather talk about you," he turned to look at her, searching her face. He had already noted that there were no rings on her fingers, but that didn't mean that much, as there could be a special someone in the background, after all, she was very beautiful. Suzanne's iPhone bleeped and she pulled it out, opening it quickly, mouthing, "the Bishop," to him. She spoke to him intently.

"Yes, of course, that is no trouble at all. Yes, at three this afternoon I'll be there and thank you." She closed her iPhone, turning to look at him. "The Bishop wants me to meet him in his office at three. I had better go, thanks for the coffee." She got up to leave and Hugh jumped up, desperate to know more and not wanting her to leave. He plunged his hands into his pockets, he looked down at his feet and then back up at her.

"Good luck and… will you let me know how you get on… with the job, I mean?" She threw a beaming smile in his direction.

"Of course, I will." She turned to leave.

"… and don't forget to clean his teeth." He called after her. Suzanne turned and waved in his direction. He watched her leave, feeling down, empty. A whirlwind had blown in and blown out again. He watched till she disappeared, then reluctantly returned into the surgery.

His afternoon dragged on, as he just could not get Suzanne Martin out of his mind. It was driving him crazy, turning his plans to keep away from women up-side-down. She might be off limits for all he knew, already had a partner, not planning a relationship or worse, one of those strange celibate orders. He let out a long deep breath, shaking his head. He looked at his watch for the ten thousandth time and it was a whole minute since the last time he looked.

Hugh made a coffee and turned to his laptop, trying to immerse himself in strategy, publicity and Alpacas, anything to take his mind off Suzanne. Finally, it was five and time to close the door, Hugh looked around, checked on his only patient for the night and switched off the lights, turning suddenly as he heard the roaring of a motorbike as it tore up the main street towards him.

"Idiot!" he exclaimed. Hugh turned the closed sign around as the motorbike pulled up by the front door. He watched, intrigued, as the rider dismounted, wondering where the injured pet was stowed, not in the saddlebag, hopefully. Hands on hips, he watched as the rider who was of a slight build and quite small for a bike rider opened the fasteners on the helmet and pulled it off, allowing a mass of golden curls to tumble out. His mouth dropped open, realising that it was Suzanne riding the big black beast. He stared unapologetically, not just taken aback, but in awe. She strode towards him, grinning. Hugh threw open the door.

"By the looks of things, I'd say it was good news. You gave me a shock climbing off that monster." He couldn't help himself, but grin at her. He bit his lip, trying desperately to reign in his delight at seeing her again and so soon. He wanted to fold her in his arms, but instead, held them in check, unsure of what was appropriate.

"You're right, Hugh, I got the job. I'm thrilled and decided to come straight back here to tell you. I have the keys for the vicarage too, would you join me to go and have a look at it."

She held up a huge bunch of keys, rattling them. It was an invitation that he couldn't refuse and he wondered if he might get a chance to quiz her further too, his head now bursting with so many questions. He just wanted to know everything.

"Love to. Are you sure you want me to accompany you? I thought that there might be a Mr Martin or the very least, a partner?" She gave him a sideways glance, a smile playing mischief with her lips. Oh, how it hurt, not to grab her and kiss her; he felt heat rise up his neck.

"That was subtle," she grinned, "...no. No Mr Martin or anyone else, actually. I was riding by and saw you closing up and well, I just thought that you might be up for it. If you have time, that is?" Her eyes twinkled, teasing him.

"Sure. No problem. I don't have a helmet for the bike though." He had never been on a bike and wasn't sure if he wanted to, but then he would be up close and personal to her and could slide his arms around her waist, wouldn't he?

"I'm leaving the bike here, if that's okay with you? It's only two minutes from here, right by the church," she pointed across the road towards the square church tower sticking out above the treetops.

"Yes, of course, great." He turned the key on the surgery door and they set off across the road. "Congratulations, by the way, on the new job. When do you start or is it different in your line of work?"

"Probably the first of next month, but I could move in as soon as I like. I'm not sure yet, as I need to see Alice Warren and the rest of the committee."

They walked slowly up the incline towards the church, passing thatched cottages, gardens teaming with colour and Honeysuckle tumbling over walls. Bees were happily buzzing in and out of flowers and a heady scent vying for attention from a myriad of places all at once. The stream tucked in by the wall was slowly trickling down towards the sea. A family of ducks came quacking up towards them, but finding no food forthcoming, swam away again.

"Here we are and it looks as though I ought to move in now, looking at this," they stopped by a wrought iron gate staring up at the imposing house for a moment. It was built of Purbeck stone, it had wisteria round the front door, a neglected front garden full of weeds and all manner of plants, all struggling to reach the sun. "Oh, dear," exclaimed Suzanne, "I knew the last incumbent was retiring, but I hadn't realised how neglected the place might be."

"I'm sure it won't take too much work to put right, let's go in and see what might be facing us… I mean you." He corrected.

They pushed open the gate and brushed passed the lavender, disturbing a cluster of small honeybees that swarmed up around them before settling back on to the flowers once more. Suzanne tried the keys till she found the right one, she pushed open the door and it jammed against a pile of letters and newspapers. She squeezed into the hallway, removing the heap of post and opening the door wide. There was a slight damp smell, but as the light flooded the hallway, she was relieved that the house was not as neglected as she had imagined. The hallway was wide with a polished parquet floor. At the end of the hall, a wide staircase rose up, with a tall stained-glass window on the half landing flooding the hall with light. Hugh let out a low whistle.

"What a place, you're going to rattle around in here, I think."

"You're right. Thankfully, I have Axis to keep me company," she let out a strangled chuckle, "Most vicarages were large, because years ago, the vicar would be a married man with lots of children and of course, in those days, they also had a cook, a maid and probably a gardener too. Nowadays, it's a different story and well… here I am."

"You could always get a cook, a maid and a gardener, you know," Hugh looked around astonished at the chandelier dominating the hall. There was not much else, the walls were bare and there were holes in the walls where pictures had been removed and the decorating had seen better days.

"Ha, ha," grinned Suzanne. "I might be able to stretch to a gardener occasionally, but I will have to do the rest myself. Let's go and see the other rooms." She pushed open the nearest door – it was like stepping back in time. The enormous windows stretched from floor to ceiling and had wooden shutters on them. There was an Adam style fireplace with ash still in the grate and a tarnished fender. Another parquet floor covered in dust and leaves gave the whole atmosphere rather a Charles Dickens feel. Hugh shivered involuntarily, despite the sun pouring in to the room.

"Wow!" he exclaimed, "Where to start?" Suzanne had been very quiet and Hugh gave her a sideways look, waiting to see her response. She looked as shocked as he felt and he put his arm around her shoulders, giving her a hug. She looked up at him attempting to put a smile on her face but he could see tears sparkling behind her lashes. She stepped away from him, turning towards the door.

"Let's have a look in the other rooms, it just needs a good clean, that's all." He followed her out and across the hall to the kitchen, admiring her optimism. Thankfully, it had modern wooden units, an electric cooker and gaps, presumably, for a fridge and a washing machine. There was a very old kitchen range at one end that must have been there since the house was built, yet more tall windows, a pantry and a black-and-white patterned tiled floor.

"I can do something with this, at least, make it more homely. What do you think Hugh?" colour had come back to her face and she looked happier, having seen the kitchen.

"I think it's wonderful. What an amazing house. I never noticed it before, being tucked away behind that stone wall. It won't take long to make it feel like home and I am willing to help you when I can, of course." He smiled, wondering how much work was really ahead of Suzanne. It was all very well, having a house with your job, but this was a mansion. They found the library, a snug, a boot room, four bedrooms, two bathrooms, both needed replacing, and an attic where the servants' quarters would have been, a falling down orangery and in the garden was a greenhouse and an overgrown vegetable patch.

"Phew," said Suzanne, "…before I do anything, I think a phone call to Alice would be my first step and take it from there. Thank you so much for accompanying me, I couldn't have done this on my own. Let's go, I've seen enough for now." Hugh's phone beeped and he pulled it out. It was a text from Molly, asking him to go up to the farm before he went home.

"I need to go too. Sorry, Suzanne, please keep me informed and I meant it when I said that I am willing to help." He gently squeezed her arm and they left the house. Hugh collected his car and sat watching as Suzanne straddled the bike and roared away, fear and lust following her. He groaned.

Chapter 22

Bertie and Lucy walked hand in hand up through the village towards the farm. They were both quiet, each with their own thoughts. Little white clouds scudded across an otherwise clear blue sky. The sun was making a brave effort at warming the earth and Lucy shuddered.

Bertie slipped his arm around her, pulling her close.

"Are you sure you are happy with this?" asked Bertie for the umpteenth time, "…only I don't want to do it if you have any doubts at all, you know that, don't you?" he quizzed. He knew that it was a big step and Lucy had only just bought her house and finished doing it up.

It looked great with a new kitchen, wood burner in the living room and a boutique hotel style bathroom. All very glamorous, very Lucy and here he was asking her to give it up and move into a draughty old farm. The garden still needed some work and he had promised to lay a patio, he knew only too well that Lucy had finally managed to get her life straight. Was he being fair or even thinking of Lucy instead of himself? He pondered. After a few agonising moments as Bertie held his breath, Lucy let out a gasp.

"Yes. I'm sure. It's just that I have been there before, remember and only just sorted myself out. I know how much it means to you, not that I'm doing this just to please you, I really do think that it is a good idea and I promise I am happy, if cautious." She smiled, gripping his hand tighter. The lane was alive with noise, sheep in the fields anxiously watching their new-born lambs jumping and gambolling around with their new friends. The birds singing and swooping like mad things searching for food for their own broods. There were masses of flowers fighting for room on the verge from dandelions, wild garlic and dog roses all vying for the attention from the bees and butterflies gorging themselves on the nectar.

Bertie couldn't help the feeling of peace swamping him and he glanced at Lucy, seeing a smile slide onto her face as she turned to look at him, saying, "It is a wonderful place, actually the perfect place to settle down and bring up a family." Bertie threw her a startled look. "Oh, sorry, I didn't mean, not that I wouldn't, but it's not what I was meaning... sorry... again."

Lucy stared at her feet. Bertie grinned watching the cute little red spots appearing in her cheeks.

"There's nothing I wouldn't want more than a happy family with you, I just wasn't sure what you wanted. In fact, this is not how I planned it at all, but..." he turned to face her, dropping down on one knee, taking hold of both her hands. "Lucy Hamilton, you would make me the happiest man alive if you consented to be my wife. Will you marry me?" Her face gave away her surprise, tears sprang into the corners of her eyes as a smile creased her face.

"Yes. Oh, yes, I love you so much." Bertie stood up and landed a kiss on her forehead, her eyes and her lips. His kiss deepened as he hugged her close, wanting to devour her, his heart bursting with love.

"I'm sorry, I don't have the ring with me, I can't wait to put it on your finger, but as soon as we get back to Wareham, I..." Lucy jumped in, nestled safe in his arms.

"You mean you have already bought a ring?" her eyes wide in disbelief.

"Yep, ages ago. Since we first met, I wanted to make you mine," he looked sheepish, trying hard not to grin, but he failed miserably, as the biggest grin grew and overtook his face.

"I love you so much, Bertie," she gently laid her head on his chest and he cradled her, caressing her hair, letting the moment seep into his bones and his memory. "Come on," she looked up at him, "...we need to go. Molly will wonder where we are." They continued up the lane and into the farmyard. The ducks quacked and scattered, the hens looked in their direction and continued clucking, scratching the earth. Rex, who had been asleep on the doorstep, shot up his head and leapt into action, barking at this intrusion.

"Hey, boy, Rex, come here, boy," Rex stopped barking and started whining instead, fussing around Bertie who pulled a biscuit from his pocket for him. Rex took it and wandered off with his trophy, back to his spot by the door. Molly was standing in the doorway, Jessica perched on her hip.

"Hi, come on you two, I have just made some lunch and then we can talk. Lovely to see you both," she kissed each in turn, "...you look suspiciously happy," she grinned, handing Jess to Lucy. Over lunch, they made small talk till, finally, Bertie took the plunge.

"Well, actually, we do have a lot to tell you, but first things first," he took a deep breath, "we, that is Lucy and I, want to buy the farm," he paused, looking at Molly for her reaction. She looked surprised, but said nothing, "...now that the price has come down, we can just about afford it. Lucy is going to sell her house and with my savings and a mortgage, we can do it," he paused again as Molly still gave no reaction, "...what do you say, Molly, can we buy the farm, please?" He watched as Molly in slow motion looked from one to the other, tears welling up in her eyes, she stammered.

"I...I would like nothing better. It's a dream come true. You have no idea how I've hated the thought of strangers buying the farm and doing goodness knows what to it. I will have to call Mum and Stella, of course, but you get my vote." They all hugged each other.

"This calls for a celebration. I'm sorry, I don't have champagne, but I do have some sparkling white wine, will that do?"

Molly jumped up to find the glasses as Lucy said, "We have something else to tell you too," Molly came back to the table carrying the wine, handing it to Bertie to open.

"Don't tell me you're pregnant," Lucy blushed. "I'm sorry, did I steal your thunder?"

Bertie shot a look at Lucy, his eyes wide.

"No, and no, I'm not pregnant, Molly. However, Bertie proposed and I said 'yes'." They both screamed and jumped up and down excitedly. Bertie scratched his head, wondering if this was some strange female ritual that men don't usually see, he mused.

"Let me see your ring," Molly enthused, grabbing her left hand.

"We haven't got that far yet. Bertie proposed just now, on the way here."

175

"How romantic," she sighed, "can I arrange a party here for you on Friday night. We can make it a double celebration, you buying the farm and getting engaged. Please, say yes, it would be fitting to hold it here." Molly looked from one to the other and Bertie and Lucy both nodded in agreement. "That's settled then. Oh, I am so excited for you both." She hugged them once more and the two girls sat down to discuss the forthcoming party. Bertie felt completely left out, but he shrugged, understanding that he was a mere man after all. He collected Rex's lead from the hook by the door and called out.

"I'll just take Rex out for a bit, shall I? See you later." He saw a wave and a muffled affirmation and taking that as his cue, men not required, he set off, pausing at the allotment first. He sat surveying his handiwork, but also conscious that it would soon be all his and Lucy's, but the work would be his. He turned his face up to the sun and let the warmth seep through him. He turned to Rex who was staring at him, wagging his tail, wanting to go. "Rex, old boy, this really truly is the life."

Chapter 23

Alice had laid out drinks and nibbles on the terrace, waiting for the Parish committee. They were going to have their meeting first before Suzanne arrived. Alice was singing. George appeared, paper and unfinished crossword in hand, his glasses pushed up onto his forehead.

"George, dear, are you coming to join us?" Alice looked up, expectantly. She plumped up the cushions yet again, standing back to survey the scene. She was happy, so happy, in fact, ever since the Bishop had telephoned to say that, "he was appointing Suzanne even though she was inexperienced, but knowing that Alice and her team would be very supportive to a new girl, so to speak, show her the ropes etcetera," and that had Alice puffing out her chest ever since. Lady Isobel appeared around the side of the house; Alice beamed as they exchanged an air kiss. "So glad you are here, Isobel, give us a chance to chat before the others arrive. Come and sit down." George harrumphed clambering to his feet. He smiled and kissed Isobel on her cheek, excusing himself, he dashed quickly indoors.

"Isn't it exciting that Suzanne is going to become our Parish Priest?" she grinned, "something new for us all. However, we have Doris to deal with first, I do hope she won't be difficult." Alice poured two glasses of her homemade lemonade, passing one to Isobel.

"I have a feeling that that road is going to be bumpy. She has been a faithful member here all her life. I would have thought that she would want to stay, come what may. But you know as well as I that she can be very difficult and I still don't know which way she will go, it's too close to call." They heard the front door bell. Alice jumped up, but George was already ushering everyone through to the terrace. Greetings over, they settled down to discuss the success of the church fete; everyone agreed that it was the best ever. Then the moment Alice had been dreading, arrived.

"Now, we turn to item two on our agenda and that is the appointment of Reverend Suzanne Martin as our new Minister. I'm sure that we will all give her our full support, helping her to settle in as quickly as possible." Alice paused, Ted, David, Maureen and Isobel all nodded, making positive noises.

Doris, however, as expected, scraped her chair back and stood up, "I told you before, we don't want women here. I will not be in a church where a slip of a girl thinks that she is a Minister for God. I warned you that I would leave and I have no choice but to do so. Good day to you." Doris turned to leave. Isobel stood up.

"Now Doris you don't think that you are being too hasty, do you? Why not give her a chance? She's young, yes, but everyone needs to start somewhere and if the Bishop has faith in her, don't you think that we should too?" Mutterings of 'hear hear' could be heard and Alice twisted her handkerchief round and round, hardly daring to breathe, all eyes on Doris. Doris hesitated for a moment, looking at each of them in turn.

"No. I've said my peace. I can see that I am outnumbered, but don't say I didn't warn you about the perils of having a woman in charge." She picked up her bag and began to shuffle towards the door, everyone started talking, trying to get her to change her mind, but Doris only put her head down and left. Silence descended momentarily as everyone looked at each other.

"We all knew that Doris may carry out her threat and that's her decision," Alice rallied, "…and it's our job now to welcome Suzanne and give her all the support she needs." The doorbell rang, "Ah, that must be Suzanne. George, can you let her in, dear, please." The meeting continued on a much happier note, with preparations being made for Suzanne's Induction service and a thousand and one other tasks that lay ahead of them all. Suzanne took notes and kept referring to her diary, putting in events already scheduled, even the Christmas party.

Finally, Suzanne took a deep breath.

"Firstly, can I thank you all for showing such faith and trust in me and welcoming me to the village," she paused, looking at Alice, who wondered what she was about to say next, "I have had a look around the Vicarage and well, it needs a lot of cleaning and I would like to start as soon as possible and I was wondering if there was a possibility of any help before my furniture arrives… please?" Alice looked her over, realising that she was going to have to help this young woman a lot more than she had anticipated, wondering if she really did have any idea what was involved in running a Parish. Alice threw her a tentative smile.

"Of course, we will all help and there are many in your flock who will be only too pleased to help too. How about we make a start this Saturday, shall we say ten and see how it goes and George and I would be only too pleased to have you stay with us until the vicarage is ready for you to move in to, won't we, George?" Agreement was reached and promises were made to bring tools, cleaning materials and food for lunch, the meeting was closed.

***

"I do hope that we are doing the right thing accepting Suzanne. She hasn't got a clue about running a Parish like ours, but we just couldn't have had Tim. Ooh, his children," she shuddered at the memory, "and his wife would have been no help at all. What do you think, George?" George shook his paper closed, took off his spectacles and looked her straight in the eye. He picked up her hand.

"You must stop worrying, my dear, I am sure that young Suzanne will be perfect, just give her a chance. She's probably afraid of stepping on your toes and she's bound to look to you for guidance till she finds her feet." Alice beamed at him, knowing he was right. She remembered how she had felt herself on her first day at work. It was only helping out at the village shop, but she had been terrified of doing something wrong and running a Parish is much more challenging. She picked up the teapot and topped up George's tea.

"Maybe I'll write up some notes for her myself and we can have a chat when she stays here for a few days. What do you think, darling?" Alice collected the plates together and the crumbs left from their mid-morning toasted teacakes with homemade strawberry jam.

"Excellent idea, but don't swamp her too much. She needs to get to know people and make her own decisions." He shook out his paper once more, picking up a pen, "…now, where were we?" Alice, sensing an end to the conversation, piled up the tray and disappeared into the kitchen. She loaded the dishwasher, she couldn't help but worry she so much wanted a female and yet, had not thought about one so young. Trentmouth was a small hamlet with very little to attract anyone with experience and so few in the congregation. Her shoulders sagged at the thought of having to do even more within the church to help Suzanne, misgivings weighing her down. The fete had been a marvellous success due, in no small part, to Molly. She leaned on the sink, staring out of the window, without seeing her garden, only the weeds in her mind. Molly! What a brilliant thought. Alice grabbed the phone, excitedly pressing her number.

"Molly, dear, are you busy? I was wondering if you could come over this afternoon, I want to talk to you?" Alice's mind suddenly buzzing with ideas, she could hardly wait for Molly to arrive.

"I can come up around four if that helps? What's it all about, Alice?" But Alice was too excited to enlighten her further, she merely confirmed the plan and put the phone down.

Alice resolved not to include George for now. She would see what Molly thought. Four o'clock couldn't come quick enough. George would be out at his walking football practise. He was really enjoying it, she mused. He had not been interested before in football. He was a cricket man deep inside. He had lost some weight and his stomach was flatter, so she didn't complain about his frequent absences; it was rather nice to have some time on her own. Alice had become used to sitting reading, pottering in the garden or creating in the kitchen. She had considered joining the local U3A; it was very popular and you could join a group, doing almost anything from learning a language, pottery, water colour painting, yoga and creative writing. Alice fancied them all, she chuckled. The doorbell rang, making Alice jump inside, she dashed to the door, welcoming Molly and Jessica.

"Come on through, Molly, dear, we can sit on the terrace. I have made some lemonade, can Jessica have some, do you think?" Alice ushered her through. The terrace was cool, as the sun was now in the west, leaving delicious shadows to relax in.

"Just a little, Alice, she has never had any before and she will be due her teatime feed soon," Molly sat down and Alice poured the lemonade and passed Molly a scone with jam and cream.

Molly laughed, "No wonder George has to do so much exercise, Alice, there must be a trillion calories in this and how come you are so slim anyway?" Molly tucked into her scone piled with cream, a little bit smudged onto her lip, she licked it off. Alice passed her a napkin.

"Thank you, Alice, this is delicious, so come on, what is your secret?"

"I don't really have one. I suppose I'm always busy doing the garden and there is no shortage of things to do, either here or at the church. Actually, that's what I want to talk to you about."

"...the church?" said Molly, picking up another scone, "I don't see how I can help you there, Alice, unless you are talking about having Jessica christened. Alistair and I haven't had time to think about it yet."

"That is number two on my list," Alice twitched her lips, as truthfully she had forgotten about that, logging it for later, she smiled, "Actually, dear, I want to talk to you about Suzanne, our new vicar."

"Oh, how can I help you there, Alice? I met her at the fete. She's lovely and she has been into the surgery and seen Hugh, but I can't imagine what use I will be to you," she put her plate down, having dabbed her lips, "...that was scrumptious, Alice, but I had better not eat anymore and I notice you managed to eat only one scone with no cream!" Alice looked up over the top of her glasses at Molly, a smile just making itself visible. Molly poured a little lemonade into a bottle for Jessica. She took a slurp and immediately pulled a funny face, looking up at her mummy, a quizzical look on her face. Molly and Alice both chuckled.

"The thing is, Molly, she is young and inexperienced and I am feeling quite anxious about having made a mistake and wanted to know your thoughts on the matter."

"Me! I have no experience either. As far as I can see, she is just what we need around here. She has energy, youth, full of ambition, I would have thought that you would be thrilled at having someone like her in the church. She could attract the younger generation, put some life back in. I expect she's brimming with ideas; you just need to give her a chance." Molly paused for breath, staring at Alice.

"You are quite right, my dear, I have let myself be side-tracked into thinking that the bulk of the work was going to fall onto my shoulders and it was worrying me. We are meeting at the rectory on Saturday to help Suzanne clean the place, that is, the committee and anyone else I can persuade to come and help. Would you and Alistair be free to help? And maybe you could ask Lucy and Bertie too, for me, please? The more people who help, the quicker it will be done and oh, before I forget, Suzanne is going to stay here with us for a few days till the rectory is habitable." Molly was looking at her open mouthed, her eyes on stalks.

Alice pressed on, "I'm sure you will get on with Suzanne very well and you can talk to her about the christening too. Right, that's that, settled, my dear. I think that I will put the kettle on for a cup of tea. George will be home soon." She picked up the tray and busied in the kitchen, making their usual earl grey tea, leaving Molly looking stunned.

Chapter 24

Sandra and Enrico were due to arrive the following day and Molly was gearing herself up to another interrogation from Sandra. Even the weather conspired against her. It was dull and chilly, forcing her to retreat indoors. Her mother always appeared tense and she couldn't seem to do anything without Enrico, she sighed in exasperation. She had reluctantly decided to accept her mother's choice of partner. In reality, it was nothing to do with her, but it always felt distasteful somehow, she shrugged. Molly had informed her mum of the offer from Bertie and Lucy, initially she had thought of keeping that minor detail from her, fearing she would automatically say no, but the anxiety and guilt at the thought of this slight deception had forced her to come clean. Better to tell her over the phone rather than risk a confrontation face to face. Sandra, as expected, had reacted rather scathingly, accusing everyone of manipulating her. She thought that they should hold out for more but, reluctantly, she had accepted Bertie and Lucy's offer, allowing Molly to let go of the breath she had been holding.

She watched Alistair and Bertie disappear down the lane towards the sea. The sun had begun to peep out from behind the clouds and it was about to turn into a glorious day, the sky the purest blue with hardly a wisp of cloud left to spoil it. The birds were out in force, searching for food to feed their young and the cherry tree in the orchard was heavily laden with sugared almond pink flowers, wafting the most delicious scent across to her on the breeze.

They had willingly volunteered to take Rex out for a walk, making Molly feel highly suspicious, as the boys had said they had something to discuss, but wouldn't tell her about it.

She contentedly leaned on the doorframe. They were more than likely planning something innocent, like a barbecue. She turned to Lucy

"… have you any idea what those two are up to?" Lucy was helping her pack as they were moving out of the farm and into their new home today, now that the barn was finished.

This was a new beginning for them both; well, all three of them, their first proper home together, thus allowing Bertie to move back into the farm. Bertie still had a legal tenancy agreement in place and their solicitor, Mr Bradwood, had explained how Bertie could live at the farm before the sale completed. The only possible holdup may be a delay in the sale of Lucy's house.

"Sorry, no idea, but at least they are out of the way," they both grinned, "Bertie has had one or two furtive chats with Alistair, but I'm sure it's nothing for us to worry about." Molly dragged herself away from the door, raking her fingers through her hair, pulling it back and sweeping it up into a ponytail.

"What do you think to us having a barbecue later anyway?" she suggested as she opened the fridge door to see what might be left lurking and still edible. She found some salad, a bowl of cold potatoes, a carton of cream, a box of mushrooms and some doubtful-looking sausages. Checking the freezer, she had bread rolls, two steaks and, "Hurrah," she called out to Lucy – two pieces of salmon. "We have a feast. What do you say?"

"Great idea and I have found not one, but two bottles of red wine and a Prosecco. I'll put that in the fridge. Hang on a minute, what barbecue? I didn't know you had one," Lucy turned to look at Molly, raising her eyebrows.

"I bought one of those instant ones on offer in town at the end of last year, I'm sure it will be fine and if not, I can always put them under the grill, so no worries. Shall we start on that red now, I am feeling rather thirsty and sometimes a cup of tea just doesn't cut it?" she grinned.

"Your wish is my command," said Lucy, reaching for the corkscrew, making an exaggerated bow. The packing finished, Molly surveyed the kitchen, her eyes fell on the welsh dresser.

"It seems a shame to sell this old dresser. It has been here all of my life and probably is as old as the house. Would you like it,

Lucy? Please don't feel obligated to say 'yes', I can get rid of it if you prefer and I'm sure that Mum nor Stella will want it."

"We would love to have it; it just looks right here somehow," she picked up a curled and faded photograph, handing it to Molly. "Who is this?" she asked. Molly looked at the picture, staring at two young girls sitting on a tractor, with a scruffy looking man trying to steer.

"That's dad and Stella must have been about five or six and I would have been about three," she touched the picture, letting her finger trace the outline of her dad's smiling face, tears stung her eyes, "…he was a good dad when he was allowed to have us to himself. Mum always said that the farm was dangerous to two young girls, but Dad used to laugh. He let us collect the eggs, feed the chickens and when Mum wasn't looking, he took us into the milking shed to show us where our milk came from. Those were the days and yet, all I can really remember is Dad being out all day and Mum scolding us for something or another. I have a feeling that Dad didn't really want to move to Spain, but he was one for a quiet life to please Mum." The door clicked open and the boys bustled in, chatting and laughing. Molly pushed the photo into her pocket and sniffed. "Just in time, we were thinking of having a barbecue."

Molly heard Jessica making noises over the intercom, "Oh, and there's Jess."

***

Molly checked her watch for the umpteenth time. Sandra and Enrico had caught an early flight. By mid-morning, they should be at the farm. Bertie had the coffee on and Lucy had changed her shift. The hospital maternity wing never seemed to be as busy on a Saturday, the reason for this having always alluded them. Molly had stopped off at the supermarket to pick up chocolate croissants and a few Danish pastries, hoping that that would calm everyone's nerves. She was extremely agitated and poor Jessica was fractious too; she instinctively knew something was wrong. Even the warm sun could not help ease the sense of foreboding and yet, there was no reason for it. It should be one of the happiest days for all concerned, but somehow, her mother always put a downer on things. They decided to sit in the garden for coffee. A fly came buzzing over them and Molly absentmindedly wafted it away.

"Come on everyone," she gasped exasperatedly, "…lighten up. If we expect the worst, we'll get the worst. Let's talk about the party on Friday. Have you drawn up a guest list and a food list yet, Lucy? No, leave the food to me. I'll be happy to sort that. I just need to know how many people you are thinking of." She looked across at Lucy who had been quiet all morning.

"I'm sorry, Molly. I just feel that we need to get this over with, first with Sandra, I mean. She could still scupper all our plans. Once that is done, I think that I will be able to breathe again and get my head in gear." Lucy shot a look at Bertie and he just smiled, reassuringly touching her fingertips.

"Yeh, I feel the same. Your mother is quite a character and used to getting her own way. I feel daunted too, which is bizarre," he threw his hands up in mock horror, "these cakes are good though." He reached out, helping himself to another, making everyone chuckle. Rex started to bark.

"Oops, that must be them," Alistair stood up, "I'll let them in, you stay here, nice and relaxed, okay?" He disappeared, returning a few minutes later, followed by Sandra and Enrico in her wake. She looked more like an aging film star than her Mum. She had on a wide brimmed hat, wraparound sunglasses, wedge sandals and a pretty lemon coloured sundress, topped off with a bamboo coloured shrug over her shoulders. The outfit set off her tan. She looked very well and contented. Molly stood up.

"Mum, you look well," she kissed her cheek. "Enrico," she nodded. "Come and sit down and I will make some more coffee."

"I hope it's the proper thing and not your usual dishwater, darling. Bertie, Lucy, nice to see you." Molly disappeared into the kitchen, wondering how her mother could reduce her almost to tears with one sentence. She had nothing but spite and putdowns in her mouth. Could she never say anything complimentary? Never mind, loving and caring. "No," she told herself, "so ignore her and let's get on with the real reason they are here." She could hear the buzz of chatter from the garden and quickly shot upstairs to check on Jessica. She was fast asleep, arms in the air, looking divine. Molly wanted to pick her up and cuddle her, but settled for a quick kiss instead. Alistair crept in behind her, slid his arm around her waist, nuzzling her neck.

"I thought you might be in need of a hug," he whispered. Molly turned around in his arms slipping her hands around his neck. They kissed and tiptoed back downstairs.

"I love you so much, Alistair. You always know how to deal with things. I am just turned to jelly when Mum shows up." She finished making the coffee and took more pastries out of the box.

"That's why I wanted a quick word. I need to warn you that things could get a bit heated, but don't be alarmed, go with the flow and I will explain all later." He kissed her forehead and picked up the tray.

"What do you mean 'things could get a bit heated'. What's going on, Alistair?" he turned, throwing her a quick grin.

"All will be revealed. Now, come on, let's not keep our guests waiting." Molly followed him back into the garden, rather anxious at what Alistair had just said. She placed a forced smile on her face as her thoughts raged about what on earth Alistair meant?

"I was just asking Bertie here, how they could afford such an expensive property," said Sandra, a wry smile trying to escape her lips. Molly's heart sank, she shook her head in despair.

"That's not a question for you to ask, Mum. They can afford it and Mr Bradwood is dealing with the conveyance and he is happy with their financial position. Lucy has already put her house up for sale and that is what we are waiting for now." She stopped to draw breath.

"Well, I am not prepared to wait, goodness knows, how many months waiting for you to sell your house, Lucy. I will give you six weeks, but then that's it, the farm will go back onto the market," everyone started to speak at once, all trying to get their point across. Sandra held up her hand for silence. "Those are my terms and that's that. Now, let's have coffee. Where's that granddaughter of mine? I hope you are not keeping her from me, Molly."

Lucy looked forlornly at Bertie. He gripped her hand, trying to reassure her without speaking. Molly saw the exchange and was shocked, aghast at how cruel her mother had become. She corrected herself with the realisation that she had always been the same. *My poor father,* thought Molly. She flopped down into a chair, not wanting to even look at her mother.

"Jessica is still asleep; you can see her later," she thrashed round in her mind, wondering what to talk about now and found herself wishing they would leave. Enrico was doing his usual fussing thing, making her skin crawl. Lucy and Bertie were standing in the middle of the garden deep in conversation. Bertie slipped his arm round Lucy's shoulders, pulling her to him. Molly's heart went out to them. She threw a look at Alistair, hoping that he would use this moment to spring whatever surprise he had in mind. The atmosphere had turned ice cold, making her shiver despite the lovely sunny day. Alistair got up, calling to Bertie.

"Actually," he said, looking at Sandra and Enrico, "Bertie and I have been doing some research and there is this Eric Jamieson, from Birmingham, who the police would like to talk to about defrauding some woman out of a lot of money a few years ago," the whole group sat in complete silence. Molly's mouth dropped open as she looked from Alistair to Enrico to her mother, "...he looks a lot like you, Enrico."

"This is outrageous, how dare you?" screamed Sandra. "Snooping and prying into people's private lives, you have no right." Jumping up, she grabbed her bag, turning to Enrico.

Molly froze as too many thoughts came crashing into her head, she shook herself, feeling like she was merely watching a film in slow motion. Alistair was looking rather smug as Bertie placed a congratulatory slap on his back.

"No, my darling, please sit down. I will explain," Enrico had reverted to his English accent. He looked down at his feet then seated himself, picking up Sandra's hand. "Let me tell you the whole story."

"This is going to be good," said Alistair, placing his hands behind his head and pushing back his seat onto two legs, an unmistakeable grin plastered over his face.

"Molly, do you think that I could have another coffee, please and I promise to tell you, all of you, the truth?" Molly rose, picking up the empty coffee pot, still shocked into silence, disappearing on auto into the house. Lucy followed her.

"Did you know anything about this, Molly?" she hissed.

"Not a thing. It is as much a surprise to me as it is to you. I knew that something wasn't right with that rat," she spat, "... but I never expected this. He is just out to fleece Mum, get as much as possible, disappear and then take in another poor unsuspecting woman. I think she has had a lucky escape."

"Yes, you're right. I can think of other words to call him but rat will do if that's not an insult to rats," they both chuckled. Coffee made, they returned to the garden without saying a word.

"Well, let's hear it," exclaimed Alistair, still grinning with satisfaction as he looked round from one to the other.

"Yes… part of what you say is true," Enrico looked resigned to his fate as he glanced at everyone.

"I knew it and you were going to rip Sandra off too, weren't you?" Alistair couldn't help but make him squirm even more.

Enrico ignored that snide remark and continued, "I had a successful building firm and took on a job in the Midlands for a Mrs Scott. Everything went well in the beginning, until we discovered some subsidence. Mrs Scott accused us of deliberately causing the damage to get more money out of her, which wasn't true, by the way. She had paid out a lot of money upfront, as I needed it to buy the materials and pay contractors. You know how it is. Anyway, she started being abusive, saying that the work was shoddy, we didn't know what we were doing and on and on. I lost some of my subcontractors, as they couldn't stand her continual interference. Anyway, in the end I walked off the job. I am not proud of what I did, but there was no way I could continue under the circumstances."

"You see," said Sandra, "You are always quick to think the worst, upsetting innocent people," she picked up her coffee, "have you anything stronger to pop in here, Molly? I need it."

"I have some whisky, Sandra, will that do the trick?" Bertie asked as he pushed back his chair to retrieve his precious single malt.

"I admit that I never finished the job and neither did I return her money. I felt I was owed it under the circumstances and I got on the next flight to Spain," he fell quiet, looking down at his hands. Molly almost felt sorry for him. "So, what happens next?" he asked, sweeping a look around the group.

"It's not up to us, mate," declared Alistair, "but don't you think that you should go to the police and clear this mess up, no matter what the consequences?"

"You've had a lucky escape, Mum, you could have lost everything to Enrico... I mean, Eric." Molly went to hug her mum but she pulled back.

"For your information, Molly, I already knew the whole story. If he goes to prison, I will never forgive you or any of you and what I said earlier, still stands." She stood to leave.

"Come on Enrico, we're leaving and Molly, you can get hold of me via Bradwood." She picked up her hat, sweeping out without another word.

They all sat in stony silence, looking from one to the other. Molly let out an enormous deep breath that she had been holding, turning to Lucy and Bertie. "I'm so sorry for my mother's behaviour. She had no right to talk to you like that. I don't know what she will do next. I must admit that I don't recognise her anymore." Molly burst into tears with great heaving sobs as the tears rolled down her cheeks. Alistair jumped up to comfort his wife, holding her to him as she let all the hurt and frustration out.

***

Lucy signalled to Bertie, pulling him to one side they wandered around to the rear of the house in silence and over to the allotment to sit on the familiar bench. They flopped down heavily onto the seat, Bertie slipping his arm around her as Lucy let her head drop onto his shoulder. She couldn't believe what had just happened, her house was up for sale, she was engaged to the most wonderful man in the world, they had had everything mapped out and now... now what?

"Talk to me," said Bertie, "I can almost hear those little cogs whirring in your brain," he kissed the top of her head, "whatever happens doesn't matter as long as we are together," he kissed her head again and Lucy lifted her face up to him, searching for his lips with hers. She loved him so much. Finally, they drew apart and Lucy managed a weak smile.

"I thought that you could see all your dreams ending and I wasn't sure what, if anything, we could do about it. Please, tell me what you are thinking? I can't bear it and poor Molly; she must be devastated to have a mother like that." She looked into his eyes, her forehead wrinkled in concern, having no answers of her own. He caressed her forehead with his thumb.

"Honestly, it's a minor setback. Let Sandra put the house back up for sale if she wants to. Whatever we do will be perfect. I have you and you are more precious to me than where we live. It will just be a different adventure, that's all, not the end of the world," he tilted her chin up towards him and kissed her again. Lucy snuggled up to him, letting her thoughts wander to her own parents. Her mum was increasingly forgetful, disappearing into a world of her own and her father had been to see the Doctor, as he just could not shake off his morose feelings and increasing isolation. Pictures of the shop slipped into her consciousness and she thought again for the thousandth time what was she going to do about it? The shop had been empty now for weeks and she really ought to do something, clear it out if nothing else. Then a thought struck her and she sat up, a smile chasing her blue face away.

"How about we turn mum's old shop into an organic café? We can still live at mine and you won't need to buy the farm at all," she gasped breathlessly, "...you can use your money to do the refurbishment and we can get started straight away. I admit that it needs a lot of work, but I know you can do it," she squeezed his biceps, "hmm, lovely pair you have too," she giggled, "I can help you, what do you think? Tell me." She looked deep into his eyes as he sat stunned for a moment before a smile began to crinkle at his lips.

"Well, let me think," he tapped his lips with his fingers, "I like, no, love the idea of turning the shop into a café but there is nowhere to grow my fruit and vegetables," he pondered.

"Yes, but you could buy from other growers or even have an allotment in Wareham," she enthused.

"Okay, okay, let's go and have a proper look at the shop tomorrow and not a word to Molly at the moment... right?" he kissed her nose.

"Right..."

Chapter 25

Bertie hammered the sign into the ground in front of the shop announcing a sale of all fire damaged stock. He stood hands on hips, staring at the façade. It was a much later red brick extension to the cottage with a tiled roof and looked like it was an afterthought. If he could afford it, he would have it white rendered and thatched so that it looked as if it had always been there... maybe one day. He had pulled out as much stock as possible onto the garden at the front and there was room to get around the inside without falling over. His eye caught Lucy, duster in hand, trying to clean off some of the goods, not that they were worth much, but better than just taking everything to the recycling centre. He picked up his hammer and headed back inside. He halted by the door, it was dark and gloomy after the bright sun outside, not good for a café. He had not been sure about Lucy's plan and as yet, still no buyer for her house, so they had decided to leave things as they were. He scanned the ceiling, all black and water damaged, maybe an atrium would be a good idea – forget the thatch, celebrate the difference to Honeysuckle cottage. He rubbed the stubble on his chin between thumb and forefinger, deep in thought.

"... Coffee?" asked Lucy as she leaned into him. He automatically pulled her in breathing deep of her skin, she bathed in some rose concoction and it smelled wonderful. He laid a gentle kiss on her lips.

"... Yes, please, any biscuits? I have an urge for ginger nuts," he grinned.

"... Really. Let me see," she looked around her, "...this is a shop or was, see what I can find." She pulled away from him to take a look and feeling instantly lonely, like someone had removed half of himself, he watched her walk back into the shop. He felt so happy and content more than ever before in his life, so very lucky to have found Lucy. How his life had changed in the last year, if someone had told him, he could not have believed it. If he had written a plan, it would not have been as good as this, he pondered. He watched as Lucy looked again at her engagement ring, lifting her hand, head on one side as it sparkled in the sun. She looked happy too and a little bit of weight had crept onto her, giving her a shapely, curvy body. He patted his own stomach; he had added a few pounds too, as Mrs W was happy to remind him, taking the credit herself for feeding him up. He laughed at the thought of Mrs W, what a character, she had sussed long before she was told that Jessica could not be his, but the look on her face when Alistair gave her the good news was priceless.

"Where are you? You have disappeared into the past, by the look on your face," she handed him a coffee, "let's sit outside before the hoards descend on us." Bertie followed and they sat on the seat by the door.

"Oh, just thinking about Mrs W and her funny ways," he confessed.

"… Really? Well I've been thinking too," announced Lucy as she handed him the ginger nuts.

"Whoa, no warning, that's pretty scary." She punched him gently on the arm. "Come on then, tell me, what have you been thinking?"

"Well…" she turned to look at her hand, twisting the diamonds yet again. "I was thinking that we should set a wedding date, what do you think? I mean, Mum isn't going to get better and I really would like her to enjoy it while she can," she drew breath, turning to look him in the eyes. He couldn't stop a smile from filling his whole face.

"Nothing would make me happier. I love you so much and can't wait to call you my wife," a gulp caught in his throat as he tried to swallow. He wanted to jump up and down with glee, but settled for a squeeze.

"You sure, I don't want to push you or anything," she looked up at him, those big eyes that he couldn't resist. He placed a finger to his lips as if deep in thought.

"Hmmm, how about tomorrow? I'm free," he chuckled, "name the day, I'm serious. We don't need to wait. What did you have in mind? Come on, tell me your plans," words tumbling out of his mouth, happiness oozing from every pore.

"Well, how about the autumn, September or October and I would really like to get married in the Parish church, bit more traditional. I loved Molly's wedding on the beach, but I'm thinking of Mum and Dad." Bertie just grinned at her, knowing that this was clearly her dream although she was trying to say it was for her parents. He would agree to anything, he knew, picking up her hand, kissing her fingertips.

"That sounds wonderful. I couldn't think of a better place or time. Oops, looks like we have customers. Better get to work." They had a very busy morning. The whole of Trentmouth seemed to arrive at once, looking for a bargain or just being nosy. The stock was disappearing rapidly much to their relief, even dented tins, scorched buckets and crumpled packets were picked over and purchased. At lunchtime, Molly arrived with a picnic hamper full of goodies.

"Molly…" exclaimed the amazed Bertie, "…you're a star. I can't wait to tuck into one of your famous picnics." She laughed as she planted a kiss on his cheek and hugged Lucy, handing over Jessica.

"I thought you might be hungry. How's it going? Looks like a lot of stuff has been sold," she set the basket down, taking a wriggling Jessica back. "You two start, I have brought Jessica's lunch too. She loves her savoury dinners, but not so keen on the puddings." They all sat down outside by the front door. The sun had moved around, giving them some welcome shade. The garden had been trampled to death, first by firemen, now by all the eager buyers.

Bertie pointed to the brave flowers trying to push up towards the sun.

"This garden must have been lovely once I'll have to see what I can rescue," he popped the remains of his sandwich into his mouth, searching for what else might be lurking in the basket, helping himself to a packet of crisps and an apple.

"So… what's next?" queried Molly. Both Bertie and Lucy looked aghast at each other as if Molly had overheard their conversation. Bertie quickly jumped in.

"With the shop, do you mean?" as he crunched into his apple, licking his lips as a drop of juice escaped, threatening to trickle down his chin. He wiped his mouth, taking another bite.

Molly popped a spoonful of food into Jessica's mouth, glancing at them.

"Of course, why, is there something else I should know about?" she threw them a knowing smile, curiosity written all over her. Lucy blushed.

"Actually, we were just discussing setting a wedding date." Molly leapt to her feet, screaming with joy and hugging Lucy and kissing Bertie on the cheek.

"When, where? Tell me all about it, I can't wait. This is so exciting. I'll ask Stella to make you a cake, our treat, naturally," she gushed.

"Thanks, Molly, that's awfully kind of you, but hold on a minute, we haven't decided anything yet. When we have, you will be the first to know, I promise." Bertie picked up Lucy's hand. Smiling, he turned to Molly.

"…regarding the shop, we have a few ideas, but nothing settled yet there either. Is there any cake in that basket, by the way?"

"Typical," laughed Molly as she pulled out a ready sliced lemon drizzle cake, "here you are." They finished their lunch and Molly disappeared to visit Alice. A trickle of people came in and out of the shop during the afternoon, as everything must go, Bertie was almost giving away the last few remaining bits and pieces. As they closed up the shop, Lucy's dad, Donald, came in.

"It's sad to see it all end like this, but…" he raised his hands' palms uppermost and dropped them again, "I suppose everything must change. What are we going to do with it now, I wonder?"

"We have an idea, Dad, can we come and talk to you about it?" Lucy slipped her arm through her dad's, turning him towards the door.

"I'll lock up, be with you in a minute," called Bertie as they retreated next door. Bertie knew this was going to be hard for Lucy, he watched as she greeted her mum, kissing her on her cheek. Today, Tricia was lucid and chatty, but other times were much more difficult. It is a wicked disease, robbing people not just of memories, but purpose and the ability to love. He resolved to try to find out everything he could to avoid it happening to

Lucy or himself, if possible. Lucy retreated into the kitchen to make the tea, leaving Bertie to chat to Donald. He looked shattered and weary, although he was a relatively newly retired man who should be looking forward to many years to indulge in his favourite pastimes. Bertie found he was unable to think of what to say, he used to talk about his obsession with steam trains as he volunteered on the Swanage railway and had a passion for vintage radios; now he barely spoke at all. Lucy returned, carrying a tray piled high with cream cakes and a huge pot of tea.

Bertie jumped up to help her.

"It was a good sale, Dad, there's hardly anything left, just mainly rubbish and we can clear that out tomorrow. I have a few hundred pounds for you too. It's much more than we expected and will help out, now that Mum's not working, so…" Donald cut her off.

"Lucy, hold on a minute," he had his hand raised in an attempt to quieten everything down. Lucy fell silent, her eyes wide. "I have done a lot of thinking since… well, since your mum, you know, and well, tell me about your idea and don't worry about your mum and me. I made a promise, 'in sickness and in health', your mum would do the same for me," he tenderly picked up Tricia's hand, smiling at her, turning to Lucy once more, "So, come on, luv, tell me, I mean, us, all about it." Lucy explained their plan for an organic café and Donald asked about planning and alterations needed as he had been a builder before retiring. They would have to install toilets and a compliant kitchen, go on a food hygiene course, loan from the bank; it seemed endless. He asked about news on the sale of Lucy's house and progress with the farm.

Bertie took up the reins, explaining Sandra's ultimatum and how they may not be able to pursue the farm and the shop.

"Right, I understand and the ideal situation would be to buy the farm and run the café and will you keep your job at the hospital, Lucy?" He raised his eyebrows, rubbing his stubbly chin, looking at her concern in his eyes.

"…of course, Dad. I don't want to give up my career if possible. Not yet, anyway," glancing at Bertie, he nodded encouragement, "we have something else to tell you too. Bertie and I are getting married in the autumn, here in Trentmouth."

"Oh, luv, that is wonderful news. I know you will both be very happy." He jumped up, hugging Lucy and shaking hands with Bertie. "Great news, just what we need, isn't it, Tricia?" he said, turning to his wife who was sitting passively, eating a chocolate éclair. Tricia smiled and nodded.

"Look, you two, Lucy is our only child and one day everything will be yours, so I know that Tricia would approve, if she could. I want to pay for all the alterations to the shop, it sounds marvellous and… I think that you should follow your dreams and buy the farm. It is the perfect forever family home." They all hugged, Lucy cried and Bertie was shocked at the loving family he witnessed and soon privileged to be part of.

Chapter 26

It was too quiet. Molly had been working part-time for a few weeks now and loving it.

Jessica was happy at the nursery. She had declined Alice's offer to have her on the grounds that Jessica was a handful, now that she was crawling and of course, George and Alice enjoyed a nap in the afternoons. She stood at the door of the practise, mug of coffee in hand, watching people walking down to the sea. She scanned the empty azure blue sky, not even a cloud today, it was eerily quiet. Hugh joined her, producing a packet of shortbread, dragging a chair out into the sun. Molly plopped down with a sigh, Hugh reappeared dragging another chair and began to dunk several shortbread biscuits into his coffee.

"There's another poor dog in the back of that car. I hope they don't leave it in there when they park up, it's already panting for water." She turned, looking up the road and spotted Maggie striding purposefully in their direction and waving, making a detour to join them.

"What a beautiful day, thought that I would take a walk along the cliffs, get some fresh air. How are you?" Maggie grinned, looking from one to the other. Hugh jumped up.

"Sit here, Maggie, can I make you a coffee?"

"…ooh, please," Hugh retreated into the cool of the office, "…so, why the long face? You look fed up, anything I can do?" Maggie asked cheerily.

"If only, no, thanks for the offer though, it's just that we had a good uptake after the church fete, business really picked up, but it's gone quiet again and I don't know why," Molly took a sip of coffee, hoping she hadn't said too much. Hugh returned, bringing another chair.

"I think that we will have to install a bench soon that might at least bring people over to our side of the road," he chuckled.

"…good idea and how about an ice cream parlour too," retorted Molly sarcastically.

"You know, Molly, that's actually a brilliant idea," Maggie enthused. Molly let out a laugh.

"I don't think so. I know nothing about ice cream and anyway, how would that fit in with us?"

"Yes, but I know all about ice cream. Aunt Isobel and I have been creating ice cream, as she has cows, spare milk and looking for another outlet for it. We are planning to have a go at making cheese too and I'm planning on butter after that."

"Really, I had no idea, but I still can't see how an ice cream parlour would help us."

"You need to speak to Bertie and Lucy. They are opening a farm shop and an organic café in the old general store. Nice thought though." Molly let her head drop back and she closed her eyes. Maggie finished her coffee, thanking them for the heads up on Bertie and Lucy's plan and set off once more.

"I've been thinking too at what else we can do to bring in the customers and I want to tackle our web page. It's looked the same for ages, it's boring, to be honest, so how about we do a daily log talk about the sick animals that we have, give a progress report and advise, maybe a section on 'thinking of owning a pet' with do's and don'ts, that kind of thing."

"Sounds good. It's worth a try, in fact, what about asking the council if we can put up notices regarding the dangers of leaving your dog in the car on a hot day. We could consider offering a day crèche for dogs," Molly said, liking her own idea better and better. "What do you think?" she turned to Hugh; eyebrows raised.

"I'll get on it, as soon as I get a minute," he chuckled. "Actually, I'm still looking for somewhere to rent… any ideas? Only my one room is getting cramped and I've rashly promised my mum that she could come and stay." He looked downcast and Molly thought of the cottage up at the farm standing empty. They had had to do that as the property was up for sale but now that Bertie and Lucy were buying the farm, it might be possible… she turned to Hugh.

"Look, I have an idea, no promises, leave it with me and I'll see what I can do."

"Great, thanks. You're a lifesaver," he sat up with renewed energy, "I'll get on to the council and start on that website," he picked up a chair and disappeared inside.

"Hmm, okay, I'm just going to make a call and I'll be in," she pulled her iPhone out of her pocket and pressed the number for Stella.

"Hey, stranger, what are you up to?" came Stella's cheery voice, "please don't tell me that mother is kicking off again." She gave a chuckle, "I do admire her guts over this Enrico episode even if I wish she would dump him. Anyway, I'm sure that you don't want to listen to me prattling on, what's up?"

"You make it sound as if I only call when I have a problem and you know it's not true," Molly couldn't help but think that Stella was right and she ought to phone her big sister more often for a proper catch up not only when a dilemma sprang up. Molly proceeded to explain about Hugh and the cottage, followed by the business being quiet and wanted to know how she had made her business so successful."

"Wow, you don't want to know much, do you? And all in one call," Stella took a deep breath, "First things first, I have no objection to you letting Hugh have the cottage, but check with Bradwood and, of course, Bertie as they may have other plans for the cottage, as I presume Hugh would want it more long term."

"Good idea, however, the way things are, we may not have a business. We thought that things were picking up, but it is so quiet, hardly enough work for one…" she paused, tracing a pattern in the dirt amongst the pebbles with the toe of her shoe, "…so what led to your success, Stella?"

"You know the answer, really. I began by just making a few cakes for friends, which led to me starting up full time, but I soon realised that I couldn't make a living just baking for friends. That led me to wedding cakes to bridal shops, photographers, florists, even car hire, wedding planners, venues, anything connected to wedding cakes. I had a professional web page, social media, and interviews on the local radio, magazine pieces and then I produced a book, quickly followed by requests for demonstrations and cookery courses, which reminds me, I have to go in a minute, as I have three ladies arriving from Exeter soon for my next class. You just have to look closely at what you already do. See what more you can do for existing customers. I don't know, could you work with the RSPB or Dorset Wildlife trust in some way? I have to go, sorry, Molly, but ring me soon, you know, just for an old-fashioned chat!"

Molly loved Stella; she was inspirational without knowing it. She collected her empty mug, picked up her chair following Hugh back inside.

Chapter 27

Alice arranged a midsummer get together for her nearest and dearest, plus a few extras. It had taken a bit of organising what with holidays and pre-arranged meetings, so many interferences to her plans, but here they were, finally, on a glorious August day, almost ready for her guests.

Alice laid out the long trestle table that she had borrowed from the church hall on the terrace, covering it with her best white sheets, as her table clothes were too small. It was to be an informal lunch, salads, pasties, and smoked salmon, roast ham followed by strawberries, ice cream, fruit tart, jugs of thick Dorset cream and a gorgeous chocolate cake, courtesy of Stella.

Not that there was a celebration, just Alice wanting to make a fuss and a little matchmaking on the side, she grinned. Collecting her secateurs, she headed for the rose garden. The old-fashioned roses were resplendent and heady with scent. She cut enough to fill her rose bowl, returning to the kitchen.

"There you are, darling, I've just made coffee, thought you might like one before our visitors arrive," he tipped two spoons of sugar into his own mug, gaining a 'tut' from Alice.

She pulled a face at him, but said nothing, putting the roses onto the middle of the table.

"Let's sit outside for a few minutes then I must change into that dress I bought for our cruise," she settled back, closing her eyes contentedly. She could hear George tapping his fingers, knowing the familiar actions before telling her something was bothering him or springing a surprise on her. She waited. Sure enough, the tapping stopped and George took a deep breath.

"Alice, my love, should I serve sherry to our guests first or just the wine? What do you think?" he paused.

"Whatever you like, George, I'll leave it to you. Now tell me, what's really on your mind," she looked at him sideways and grinned. George raised his eyebrows as he shot his head round to look at her. He reached across and squeezed her hand.

"That's what I love about you, darling, you know me too well sometimes," he sighed

"…but you're right yet again, there is something on my mind and, well, I've been thinking about it for some time now," he hesitated, clasping and unclasping his hands.

"Yeesss, spit it out, George, I promise not to bite," she let out a chuckle, her eyes twinkling at him.

"It's just that…" he paused, "…well, let's put it like this. Alistair is settled and very happy, so we don't have to worry about him anymore and, well, after our health scares and I'm over seventy now," he took a sharp intake of breath.

"George… what is it?" she put her coffee down, giving him her full attention, "you're scaring me. Is there anything wrong?"

"No. No, nothing like that, it's just, well, I have always wanted an awfully big adventure and the time is right for us to take six months and go travelling to Australia, New Zealand, see the Great barrier reef, the opera house, oh, so much I want to see and do," he sounded more excited by the minute and Alice sat open-mouthed. "We can cruise there, if you want, hire a motorhome, I don't know, whatever takes our fancy, what do you think? It will be such fun."

He picked up her hand and looked at her, his pale blue eyes shining at her, imploring her to say 'yes'.

"… but what about the house and garden. We couldn't leave it for six months. The holiday sounds wonderful, but six months!" she exclaimed, visions of an overgrown garden, the roof leaking, burglars ransacking the place… she gave an involuntary shudder, gulping down her fears. George let out a guffaw.

"I do love you… so much, Alice, but, please, do not worry about a thing. Leave it all to me," he leaned in, placing a whisper of a kiss on her lips. Alice knew deep inside that it was futile to resist, George would get his way, and this would take some thinking and planning.

Thankfully, they were not planning to go next week. Next week! Alarm bells rang in her head, she quickly turned to George.

"You're not planning on going next week? Or even this year, are you?" a flash of fear began to spread across her face. George chuckled.

"No, my darling, I had next year in mind. There's too much going on this year. We are very lucky, you and I… I know we lost Christopher and he will always be with us, but… look at our life, our lovely friends, family close by, even our social life is full, too full sometimes, but then, I wouldn't change a thing," he leaned in for another kiss, "tell you what, as we have a few minutes before anyone arrives, let's have a sherry." With that, he jumped up to pour out two glasses of sherry. Alice rested her head, closing her eyes she could hear a bee buzzing nearby, the sun warm on her face, she let a smile slide into position as her thoughts flew to Australia.

***

"I can't help thinking that your mother is up to something. She's never done anything like this before… and they have just had that 'do' for their anniversary." Molly was busy filling a bag with things for Jessica, milk, lunch, teething medicine, two changes of clothes, nappies, wet wipes, even her potty. "She needs more than us. Oh, I nearly forgot her cuddle blanket and teddy. What do you think, Alistair, about Alice, I mean?" exclaimed Molly.

"Oh, I'm sure you're wrong, darling. She has me married off, so what more trouble can she cause?" his face twitched as he looked at her. Molly gave his arm a gentle nudge as she let out a huff.

"Well, I'm not too sure about that. You know she has invited Hugh, Maggie and the new vicar, Suzanne, as well and I think that she is trying to partner Hugh off with someone…"

"Not this time, I'm sure. Anyway, let's go. I'm starving." They drove the few short miles up to the Warrens' in relative silence, Molly still pondering Alice's motives for this sudden get together. She could be wrong, after all, she knew Hugh's story and didn't think he was looking to go down that route again anytime soon and anyway, Maggie, yes, Maggie could be the target, as she felt convinced that Suzanne was here to persuade them to have a christening. She let out a sigh as the sound of the gravel drive brought her back to the here and now. Jessica was asleep. Molly squeezed Alistair's thigh lovingly. She was content. He turned to look at her.

"Hey, I might just turn around and go back home if you do that," he grinned, pulling up and parking at the front of the house.

"I wouldn't say 'no'," Molly reluctantly moved her hand, they stole a kiss just as Jessica grumbled at being woken up. They gathered all the bags and Molly transferred Jessica into her pram where she promptly fell asleep once more. The garden was already filling up.

She waved at Bertie and Lucy chatting to Maggie and Lady Isobel. She could see the ever-thoughtful host, George, serving drinks. She spotted Stella with her brood and headed in their direction. Alice caught her eye and Molly diverted across to her. They air kissed.

"Molly, dear, we must have a chat later. How's our lovely granddaughter?" she asked, peering into the pram. "Oh, bless her, fast asleep. Do you want to put her indoors, dear, away from the heat, as lunch is ready?" Alice disappeared, leaving Molly to lift the pram into the house. Jessica looked divine in her pretty pink and white dress; her chubby legs sprawled out, hands in the air, not a care in the world. Molly lovingly caressed her head, gently feeling her tufts of gold shining hair. She smiled.

"There you are, darling…" Alistair slid his arm around her waist, pulling her to him, he nibbled her ear, "sorry to drag you away, but as I expected, we have been instructed to talk to Suzanne about a christening…" he looked forlorn, resigned to his fate.

"I'm sure it won't be that bad and it could even be fun," Molly grinned, "chance to dress up."

"Hmm, I think Mum has more important ideas than that, to her, that is. Come on…" he took her hand and led her back out into the sunshine. Chatter and giggling encompassed the garden. Molly couldn't help feeling her heart swell. Alice knew how to put on a show and this was magical.

Satiated and relaxed, Bertie and Lucy were wandering around the garden and Molly could see him pointing to various plants, Hugh and Maggie had tagged along. A knowing smile pulled at the corners of her mouth as she watched; *maybe romance is in the air,* she mused. She lifted her hand to shield her eyes from the bright sunshine, searching out her nieces playing croquet with Stella, laughing and giggling. Molly realised that she hadn't felt this relaxed in a long time, the birds were singing and although she couldn't see the stream, she watched the ducks jumping in and out, splashing, oblivious to everyone in the garden.

"Hello," a voice broke into her reverie, bringing her back, "…may I sit down?" Molly looked up to see the smiling face of Suzanne. *O… oh, this is it,* thought Molly, slipping her feet down to the floor and sitting up.

"Of course, how is everything going, now that you've moved in?" Molly was genuinely curious. She liked Suzanne; she was young and brave to take on Alice and her motley crew. It can't be easy moving to Trentmouth on your own, knowing no one, she shuddered at the thought and having to start from scratch. Her admiration grew for this young woman and Molly was amazed at finding she liked her. They chatted about the huge house that had been neglected and all the cobwebs so thick that you could knit a jumper with them.

Suzanne admitted that she was finding it hard to adjust, but with her induction coming up, she was also very nervous. The congregation was small and the Bishop had high hopes for her to improve the numbers, bring some life back into the church and the community.

"No pressure then," laughed Molly.

"No. Hmm, actually, I wanted to speak to you about a christening for Jessica. Alice mentioned it, but you haven't, so am I right in thinking that you may not be interested and it is just Alice pushing you?" Cleverly put on the spot, Molly twiddled her hair, pondering on a truthful reply that wouldn't upset anyone. She spied Alistair and signalled for him to join them. He shrugged his shoulders then indicated that he would collect a bottle of wine first.

Nodding to him, she turned her attention back to Suzanne.

"Alistair is coming to join us then we can talk about it. Tell me about your induction. I'm afraid I know nothing about church rituals and as I'm sure you've realised, we don't attend either, although Alice has tried many times to encourage us." Suzanne's face lit up as she proceeded to explain the intricacies of the coming ceremony, her fears of failing in her first post and taking on the committee with her own ideas. Alistair arrived with a bottle of chilled Chardonnay, topping up everyone's glasses followed by Stella with slices of chocolate cake, assisted by Abigail and little Tabitha handing out cake forks and colourful napkins.

Molly patted her stomach, asking for a small piece, as she wasn't sure she could manage any cake at all.

"The trouble is they have all been here for so many years," exclaimed Suzanne, "everyone keeps giving me cake too, if I'm not too careful I won't fit into my new gown," she chuckled. "Sorry, I'm babbling and I don't mean to burden you with my nonsense. It's just that if you did not have a christening in mind for Jessica, please don't feel pressured. I won't be offended." She drained her glass and Alistair quickly topped it up again. Molly looked at Alistair, raising her eyebrows for an answer.

"We do want to have her christened, it's just that we are not churchgoers, so are we being hypocritical?" Molly pleaded, dreading the response for why she didn't really know, as there was no reason to feel guilty, but somehow, she did, perhaps because she liked Suzanne and didn't want to upset her. Suzanne gave them a huge smile that made her eyes sparkle with joy.

"You are at least honest," she grinned, "the church welcomes anyone and everyone into its family. You are not committing to join the church, just to bring up your daughter to learn right from wrong and respect other people. After my induction, come and see me. We can set a date and I will run through it with you. Is that alright with you?" Molly did like Suzanne more than she realised. She had a lovely way with her and would probably make a very good vicar, she mused.

"Right, that's sorted, I need to go and find Dad. He wanted a word about something."

Alistair excused himself and disappeared. Molly wanted to know more about Suzanne and decided to take a chance, hoping that she wouldn't take offence, thinking she was asking questions that were too personal.

"Are your family coming for the ceremony, Suzanne? They must be very proud of you." Her smile faded as she cast her eyes down, clearly struggling about something, "I'm sorry, I shouldn't pry. Forget I asked."

"No, I am the one who should apologise," Molly could see Suzanne gulp several times and she wished she hadn't been so nosey, not that that was the intention.

"My brother, Freddie, is coming, but my... my parents were killed in a car crash several years ago," Suzanne bit her lip and pulled out a tissue, clearly distressed. Molly jumped up, placing an arm around her shoulders.

"I'm so sorry, Suzanne, can I make you a coffee or something?" Molly was mortified. She scanned the garden, but couldn't see Alistair. She wanted to go to the kitchen, but equally was afraid of leaving Suzanne alone. Just at that moment, Hugh walked up the path towards them.

"Hey, what's wrong? Suzanne, what's happened?" He sat down beside her. Molly threw him a grateful glance. He wasn't quite the Samaritan she was looking for, but...

"I'm going to make Suzanne a coffee. Do you mind sitting here for a minute?"

"Of course not," he picked up Suzanne's hand and Molly left, wondering if her radar was still working correctly.

Chapter 28

Molly buttered toast for Jessica, making 'soldiers' for her dippy egg. Alistair finished his muesli and was trying to get a spoonful of porridge into Jessica's mouth without success. Her teeth were clamped firmly shut.

"This is hopeless, how on earth do you get food inside her?" he dropped the spoon back into her dish with a sigh. Molly took out a jar of honey from the pantry.

"…patience…" trying to get the lid off the honey, passing it across to Alistair. "Let me show you. Jessica look what mummy has for you, yummy," she placed a spot of honey onto the spoon with the porridge and Jessica opened her mouth wide. Molly turned to Alistair, her eyebrows raised, a cheeky grin on her face.

"Okay, you're the expert. I'm off to the office," he grabbed his jacket, leaning in for a kiss just as the landline rang. They both looked at each other and shrugged.

"Just feed Jess her egg. I'll get it, it might be an emergency from Hugh," she picked up the phone, pushing her hair off her face, getting in to work mode.

"Hello, Molly Warren here, how can I help you?" Molly slumped down onto a chair and Alistair, teaspoon in mid-air, stared at her. She mouthed 'Mum' and he nodded, returning to Jessica happily sucking on a piece of toast.

"Yes, Mum… yes, well if you want to… no, we don't mind. It's up to you. Alright then, bye," she put the phone down, her mood sinking into her shoes. "How does she do it? One minute I'm so happy, the next, with just a few words from my mother and I feel destroyed."

Molly poured another coffee, shoulders slumped. Alistair put his arms around her hugging her close as a strangled sob pushed its way out.

"Hey, come on, you have Jessica and me. You will have to find a way of putting your mother into a box and closing the lid... firmly. She can't hurt you, no matter how she tries, unless you let her. Don't you see that she is basically jealous of you and your love for Jessica? Don't let her manipulate you, can you put a lock and key onto your emotions and say 'keep out' to her? That way, you are in charge. She is still treating you like a kid and you have to say 'stop, no more'." He kissed her hair and rubbed her back.

"I love you so much, you are right, let her have her silly tantrums it's nothing to do with me...anymore." She sobbed.

"I love you too my darling. I have to go, but we can talk about it tonight." Jessica made a noise, making them both turn and reach for her. Jessica chortled and pushed a piece of soggy toast in their direction. Alistair hurriedly grabbed a slice of toast for himself, ladled on some marmalade, heading for the door. He blew them both a kiss, grabbing his keys as he rushed out.

Molly looked around their new home, letting out a long sigh. It's everything she wanted and try as she might, her mother had put a downer on her mood yet again. Apparently, it was all her fault that Enrico had had to go to the police to explain the circumstances of his disappearance, plus the so-called fraud. It transpired he wouldn't be facing jail, as it was more a civil matter and he now had to refund the money that he had not spent on materials or sub-contractors. *Quite right too,* she thought, but if that wasn't enough, she was really getting impatient with the progress of the sale of the farm and of course, that was her fault too. Her iPhone bleeped.

"Lucy... hi... can you come over and rescue me?" she perked up at the thought of seeing her best friend. Arrangements made, Molly changed Jessica, giving her a cuddle and dancing around the kitchen making her giggle. Coffee on, Molly had a quick tidy up, swept her hair into a ponytail just as Lucy arrived. They hugged. Molly missed her friend, their lives taking different directions; she was a part-time mum and Lucy was juggling her career, her parents, the shop and Bertie... Bertie was full on, all the time.

"So, what shift are you on today? I so need to talk to you," Molly poured the coffee and took out a cherry cake, cutting two generous slices, placing one in front of Lucy.

"Day off today, thankfully, I'm exhausted. Mum is hard work and the house... it just goes on and on. Molly... no, please, I'm trying to lose weight. Look at this," she pinched a tiny fold of flesh on her waist, "if I'm not careful, I won't fit into my wedding dress," she laughed.

"Wow, tell me more. Have you bought it without me? I thought that we could have a girls' day out. Maybe take in a spa, have a meal at that new Italian by the quay, you know?" She bit her bottom lip.

"Slow down, firstly, I haven't bought my dress yet, so plenty of time, however," she paused for maximum impact, "...get your diary, as we have spoken to Suzanne and she has pencilled in a couple of dates, we couldn't decide until I spoke to you, as I want you to be my matron of honour." They screamed with excitement, jumping up and down, hugging each other.

Lots of questions, all tumbled out at once, Molly wanting to know everything, her conversation with her mother forgotten. They decided to take a walk down to the seafront. Molly put Jessica into her pram, packing a bag to hopefully cover any eventuality on the way.

"I've had an offer on my house too."

"Wow, Luce, that's brilliant, but I'm guessing it was too low, by your tone," they walked slowly down the narrow road towards the sea, stopping outside her mum's derelict shop. It looked cold, uninviting and lost. The garden was overgrown, only the roses were making a brave effort as they sprawled untamed up the wall and the pear tree with an abandoned nest still clinging to it, displaying its abundance of fruit. They turned back towards the sea once more, Lucy subdued. Molly had no idea what it must be like having a parent with dementia. She thought of her dad, suddenly, missing him. She took a deep breath in.

"So, what happens next? With the house, I mean, and the shop, of course," Molly placed her hand on Lucy's arm, giving her a gentle squeeze.

"Oh, sorry, I was just thinking about Mum. Anyway, I turned the offer down and I have said what I am willing to accept, so we will see. We can't do anything yet about the shop, it's all very complicated. We need an architect and at the moment, we are in negotiation with the insurance company. Although they have agreed to pay for the fire damage, of course, now we want to extend and totally change the shop, we are hoping that they will give us a cheque towards it."

"Hmmm, so what with wedding plans too, what can I do to help?" Lucy's phone began to buzz. She pulled it out, glancing at Molly, mouthing 'estate agent'.

"Hello, Lucy Hamilton, what news do you have for me?" she nodded to Molly, a smile lighting up her eyes, quickly followed by a grin that encompassed her whole face. "Yes, I accept, and thanks," she closed her phone. "Ooh, Molly, I've sold my house. At last, something is going right. I must tell Bertie. Ooh, I'm so excited."

"Come on, let's go back. I'll make us some lunch and we can find out what we need to do now about the farm and I will let Stella and Mum know." They turned back towards the barn just as clouds began to hide the sun, making them shiver and Molly placed a knitted blanket over sleeping Jessica.

"I think that it might rain," she said, scanning the sky, "let's hurry." They sped up the road, laughing as the first large drops began to hit the ground. They made it just as the first flash of lightening lit up the village and thunder rolled across the sky. The noise woke Jessica and she began to cry. Molly cradled her tiny shaking body, rocking and soothing her. The storm rattled on for over an hour and as suddenly as it began, it moved away, leaving a fresh smell in the air, wisps of white cloud and bright sunshine. Molly opened the door to gaze at the garden. It was a courtyard in reality, with a few pots containing geraniums in stunning reds, oranges and hot pinks and squeezed into one corner, stood a black wrought iron table and two chairs, together with a very wet sun umbrella. Molly breathed in deeply, feeling much better. She turned to look at Lucy, with a wriggling baby crawling away from her nappy change as fast as Lucy was trying to catch her, making Molly chortle.

"Finally, things are coming together. You'll have to be quicker than that to catch Jess. She thinks it's a game," together, they wrestled Jessica into some clean clothes and she sat happily clapping her hands, grinning with just two front teeth peeking out.

"So, let's talk wedding plans. Tell me about your dream day," they sat at the little table soaking up the sun and sipping peppermint tea. Lucy looked into the distance, curling up one shoulder, a tiny smile playing on her lips.

"I've always had this dream of arriving at church. It has to be a village church. I'm not into hotel weddings or jumping out of an aeroplane type of girl, in an open carriage drawn by white horses. I would wear a simple white dress, not too feathery or frilly, a flowing train, lots of bridesmaids and a honeymoon in the Seychelles."

"Sounds fantastic, but now reality, please," said Molly with a giggle, "...actually, why don't we open a bottle of chardonnay. I have one nicely chilled in the fridge?" Molly jumped up to retrieve the wine, chuckling to herself about Lucy's ideal wedding. *Everyone has their dreams*, she mused, *until money, time and family intervene*. She returned to find Lucy studying her diary. "What's up, problem with dates?"

"Not exactly, well, yes, in a way. We wanted to return from honeymoon, moving straight into the farm together. I know Bertie is already there, but my house isn't likely to complete till sometime in November, so it might be a winter wedding yet." Molly poured out the wine, aching for her friend.

"Winter weddings can be magical; all red and white, fur trimmed gown, snow, log fires, all cosy and warm..." she drifted off into the 'cosy by the fire bit', with Alistair all snug and warm with two glasses of brandy and a big heap of logs.

"Hmm, sounds wonderful, but I had my heart set on the autumn," she let out a sigh. "I will talk to Bertie and Suzanne and see what's practical. Talking of Suzanne, are you going to her big day?"

"Yes, we are, welcome her to the village and all that. Alistair isn't keen, but he will... for his mother," she rolled her eyes, "...oh, and Hugh is going too, can you believe that?" they both giggled. "I can't imagine the attraction."

Chapter 29

The celebrations to welcome Suzanne, were in full swing in the village hall. Alice had offered her garden but Suzanne had declined, saying that she felt that more people might come if they used the village hall. Alice wandered around, chatting to the regulars, noticing one or two new faces in the crowd. This pleased her no end, making her feel justified in her support of Suzanne. She spied Doris and weaved her way across to her. Doris had clearly seen her coming, as she began to fiddle in her handbag. Alice proffered a smile, receiving a twitch of the lips in reply.

"Hello, Doris. So nice to see you, lovely service, don't you think?" She made her tone as light and friendly as possible, sitting down next to Doris, offering her a sherry. A grunted acknowledgment from Doris made Alice smile inside.

"Just because I'm here, doesn't mean I'm happy about it. I only came because the Bishop asked me to," she snapped. Doris shuffled in her chair, straightening her back, a haughty look of satisfaction on her face. She avoided looking at Alice.

"I'm sure that Suzanne appreciates your support, after all, it is a very important day for her and the parish, of course."

'Harrumph…', her only response. Alice chased a few thoughts around in her head, trying to think of some conversation that wouldn't be contentious. Doris had been a member all her life and it must be strange to her, joining a different church. The vicar there was very nice, but he was old fashioned, never changed a thing and quite frankly, Alice thought that he and his church were rather boring. Suzanne was already stirring things up; just by being there, people were talking about her.

"I think she has a glow of happiness around her and she has a few new ideas for us to consider. She used to work for the BBC, you know, oh, and she has already booked a wedding and a christening, isn't that marvellous?" quizzed Alice.

Another '…harrumph' from Doris as she shuffled in her seat. Alice gave up, drained her glass and made to stand up. Doris placed a bony hand on her arm, holding her back. "I might give her a chance, but no promises mind…" she let go, folded her arms under her ample bosom, once again giving a good impression of Les Dawson, making Alice smirk a little triumphantly.

"I enjoyed our little chat, Doris. I must find George," she slowly edged her way through the crowds, bumping into the Bishop.

"Ah, Alice, I have been looking for you. I wonder if we could have a quiet word?" The Bishop was a plump, jolly man, probably not short of retiring himself. He had a wispy comb over that constantly fell back over his ears. Alice had often threatened to get a pair of scissors and snip it off, it grated her, thinking that it was unnecessary and made him look foolish. His wife was a dear soul, very shy and clearly doted on her husband. They had never had children and Alice, despite her attempts, couldn't find out why, assuming there might be a medical reason and the subject rather upsetting. Clarissa, although invited to many a social event, remained the support behind the throne. She was as thin as her husband was plump and always wore beige. Beige everything, including her shoes and handbag, Alice chuckled. She had neat short grey hair and wore a beret – beige, of course. Alice pushed this picture to the back of her mind as she sat in a corner next to the Bishop. He pulled a handkerchief from his pocket and mopped his brow as he heaved his bulk into a more comfortable position. He half turned towards her as a slight odour of sweat assailed her nostrils. Alice pulled out her own handkerchief, politely coughing, attempting to move away even a few inches.

"How can I help you, Bishop?" she gave a wan smile, hoping her ordeal wouldn't take too long.

"Alice, my dear, please call me Geoffrey, we're not on parade now," he lurched forward again, instinctively, Alice bent backwards.

"Thank you, Geoffrey, it is warm this afternoon. Lovely service. I think that Suzanne is perfect for us." Alice straightened her skirt, scanning the crowd for rescue.

"Ah, that's what I want to talk to you about. Suzanne is young and although I think she will be admirable, I wonder if you could keep an eye on her? Be my eyes and ears, so to speak…" he paused conspiratorially, heaving out a laboured sigh as he shuffled once more.

"Of course, Geoffrey. I'm sure she doesn't need it, but it if makes you feel more confident in your decision, I will do so. We have already had several meetings and making plans for the future, but I'm not going to tell you, as I think that it will spoil the surprise," she smiled demurely, watching his bushy eyebrows rise higher and higher, causing Alice to force down the urge to laugh out loud.

"Yes, yes, of course… leave it in your capable hands, Alice," he pushed himself up and Alice watched him waddle away into the crowd.

***

Suzanne wandered across the hall, resplendent in her new cloak. It had been handmade and embroidered by the ladies of the church. The design on the back of the cloak representing the Isle of Purbeck with a cleverly worked Trentmouth village, boats bobbing in the harbour, thatched cottages and the church. Even the iconic landmark of Durdle door, the ruins of Corfe castle, even a dinosaur peeping out from behind some rocks. It was magnificent and Suzanne loved it; the gold threads shimmering as she moved. Congratulations, handshakes, cards and gifts from all directions. Freddie stood by attentively. He was a tall man of slender build. His hair curled a little onto his collar, just a shade darker blonde than his sister, but with the same startling blue eyes.

"Mum and Dad would have been so proud of you today," he said, placing an arm around her shoulders, giving her a brotherly hug and kissing her forehead, "…you were wonderful and who would have thought that you would choose being a vicar as a career and leave the BBC."

"I didn't choose this career, Freddie, God chose me and so far it has been a whirlwind," she punched him gently on the arm as she let out a laugh.

"Mm, so you say. Anyway, introduce me to a few people, would you, then I can slip away, as I must get back tonight. I have a lot to do."

"Okay. Oh, come with me. I know just the people for you to speak to," Suzanne glided across the room, her cloak flowing behind her, Freddie in her wake.

"Lady Isobel, Maggie and Alice you've already met," she said, turning to Freddie,

"…and this is my brother, Freddie."

"How lovely to meet you," Isobel proffered her hand and Freddie shook it.

"Delighted, I'm sure," he turned to Maggie, "…hello… um… how are you?" Suzanne stifled a giggle. She had never seen her brother so tongue-tied before, she rescued him.

"Freddie is an architect and he's come down from Oxford for the day," by way of an unnecessary explanation, "Maggie is Lady Isobel's niece."

"I'm also the estate manager," she added quickly, "Apart from the house, we have animals, a number of farm tenants and cottages that all need my attention, plus the other staff, but I love it, wouldn't change a thing."

Suzanne hadn't realised that so much went on up at Trentmouth Manor. Lady Isobel gave so much of her time to the church. She looked again at Maggie to see what had caused her brother to act as if he were dumb. She had shoulder length hair, a deep rich chestnut colour with eyes to match; she was tall, easily around five feet eight and now Suzanne looked more closely, she looked a lot like Isobel.

"Have you had anything to eat yet?" asked Alice, cutting into her thoughts. "Suzanne…?"

"Yes. I mean, no, I haven't," Alice slipped her arm through hers, pulling her slightly to one side.

"Come with me," Alice steered her away and over to the buffet, "I think you need a drink and I don't mean tea," said Alice with a grin.

"You're a lifesaver, Alice. I don't usually drink sherry, but… this is an exceptional day." Alice quickly poured out two more sherries, handing one to Suzanne. Alice wobbled slightly and Suzanne caught her arm, helping her to sit down.

"Are you alright, Alice, do you want me to find George? You are a little red faced. I know it's hot in here." Suzanne sat beside Alice, concerned, knowing about her recent illness.

Alice gave a chuckle.

"I'm fine, dear, might be a bit tiddly, but that's all. I had to talk to Doris who was her usual lovely self, then the Bishop was bending my ear… so I think an extra sherry is just what I need right now." Suzanne was relieved, but cast her eye around for some extra support. It was Molly who saw her and passing Jessica to Alistair, wove her way across to them.

"Is everything alright?" she enquired, sitting down next to Alice. Suzanne at a loss, not wanting to offend anyone, looked anxiously at Alice.

"I think so, but I didn't want to leave Alice on her own," by now Alice's eyes appeared to be quite glazed and she was rocking slightly.

"I'll sit with her. I'm sure she's fine, but can you find George please, Suzanne?"

Suzanne jumped up in search of George. George, who had been amusing his granddaughter, followed Suzanne to Alice. He quickly reverted to his 'doctor' mode, checking his patient, pronouncing nothing more than having had too much sherry.

"I'll take her home, Suzanne, nothing a nap won't cure." Crisis averted; Suzanne returned to find her brother still deep in conversation with Maggie.

"Haven't you got to get back to Oxford?" she asked, looking at her watch.

"Oh, no, it can wait. I might stay on an extra day or two… if that's alright with you?" he looked at her sheepishly. Suzanne gulped down a chuckle.

"No problem. I think I can find room for you."

Chapter 30

Lucy pulled on her coat and headed for the car, she felt exhausted. It had been a day full of complications, the mother she had been looking after had gone into labour early and she panicked, as her husband was away working on the oilrigs. There was no one to look after her two-year-old and the ambulance crew had had no choice but to bring the little boy with them. Lucy had to phone social services and well, things just went downhill from then on.

No one wants their child in the hands of social services and the mother became terrified that he would be taken away. So, a nice, calm birth disappeared for everyone involved. If that wasn't enough, another mum came in, thinking she was in labour, but it turned out to be a false alarm. The mum concerned didn't believe Lucy when she explained that she wasn't in labour and could go home, asking for a second opinion. Finally, convinced that she wasn't about to give birth, had reluctantly returned home again.

Lucy switched on the engine, heading for home, thoughts twittering in her head; could she have done anything different or better? What would happen when the new mum returned, actually in labour next time? Would she want someone else to deliver her baby? She tortured herself with 'what ifs' and 'should haves'. By the time she pulled into the farmyard, Lucy had a migraine, down in the dumps wondering if she was even cut out to be a midwife at all. Lucy dragged her bag out of the car, slamming the door and trudged indoors. Bertie was sitting at the kitchen table, laptop open, his head deep into reading something. Lucy burst into tears.

Bertie jumped up, throwing his arms around her.

"Hey, hey, hey, what on earth is wrong? Are you alright? Have you crashed the car?" she pulled away from him.

"Why do men always think that you have crashed the car?" she pulled a tissue from her pocket dabbing her eyes, answering her own question. "…because that's what men always think. No, I haven't crashed the car. I've had a terrible day and I think that I should resign. I'm not cut out for this job," tears bubbling up once more.

"Okay. I'm sorry, but I couldn't think what on earth could make you this upset and I jumped to conclusions, so, sorry… again," he wrapped her in his arms, kissing the top of her head. "Let me put the kettle on and please… can you tell me what has happened?" Lucy nodded, slipping onto a chair at the table. The whole sorry tale came tumbling out as Bertie listened attentively, putting in ums and ohs occasionally. He held her hand until Lucy, drained and tired, stopped talking, forcing a wan smile at him.

"I'm sorry, darling, it's just that lots of things piled on top of me today. I don't know what came over me," she sniffed, wiping her eyes and streaking her face with mascara.

"Well, how do you feel now? All these worries you are chasing will probably never happen, you'll wonder what all the fuss was about."

"I hope you're right," she sipped her tea. "I think I'll have a bath, that always helps.

"What were you looking up anyway?" Lucy turned her attention to the laptop still open on the table.

"Don't worry about that, now go and have a soak. I'll tell you all about it later and…" he trailed a finger down her arm, "I can always wash your back for you…" he stifled a grin.

"I love you Bertie," she leaned in for a kiss before making her way upstairs. Feeling much better, a good soak always seemed to do the trick. Lucy pulled on some sweat pants and a big floppy jumper, forcing her to chill out and breathe again, her muscles relaxed.

Following the smell of something wonderful coming up from the kitchen, Lucy quickly ran down the stairs. "What a gorgeous smell, I can't imagine the delight you are cooking up tonight," she slipped her arms around his waist, hugging him from behind.

"Hey, I like it, but if you're not careful, dinner might have to be delayed," he grinned, leaning in for a kiss.

"I would take you up on that if I wasn't so ravenous," she kissed him again, "come on, let's eat and I want to know all about your day." Lucy grabbed some cutlery, a bottle of red, two glasses and sat down as Bertie placed a bubbling bean and dumpling casserole onto the table. "Hmm, that was delicious," declared Lucy, taking another sip of wine. There was a sudden rap on the door and Rex rolled over as he fell out of his bed, trying to get to the intruder to tear him to pieces. He scuttled across the stone-flagged floor, colliding with Bertie just as he opened the door.

"Hugh! Come on in, mate," he held the door open and Rex, his ambition to get his teeth into someone ruined, nuzzled in for a stroke on his head instead, "everything alright? You look like a man with a problem."

"Hello, Hugh," Lucy said, kissing his cheek.

"Sorry to disturb you, I didn't realise you were about to eat. I must go and make something soon myself; it's been a long day." He stretched and circled his shoulders.

"Sit down and have some casserole with us, Bertie always makes too much." She collected a plate for him and served up the casserole.

"Thanks, you are too kind, but it does smell good." Hugh tucked into his meal and Bertie, throwing a look at Lucy, raising his eyebrows, pulled open the fridge and passed Hugh a beer. Lucy served up three dishes of warm Bakewell tart with a dollop of clotted cream, before returning to the table with a pot of coffee. She glanced at Bertie taking a deep breath, she turned to Hugh.

"How can we help you, Hugh? No problems at the cottage, we hope."

"No, nothing like that, but I do have a problem that I hope you can help me with. It's a bit... delicate and I don't know where to start really..." he looked from one to the other, "... well, this is going to sound pathetic," he pulled himself up tall and immediately slumped back down again. "It's just that... well, I want to ask someone out and I don't know if I can."

"That's easy, mate, you just ask her," Bertie grinned, slapping him on the back, "who's the lucky girl anyway?"

"Bertie..." Lucy shot him a warning look, guessing it was not that simple, otherwise he wouldn't be here taking up their kitchen space. "Why don't you tell us more about this girl, Hugh. I don't know how we can help, but we'll try… more coffee or another beer?"

"Coffee, please, work tomorrow, you know how it is," he lifted up his cup for a refill.

"Yes, I do," Lucy attempted a smile and made more coffee.

"I met her a few months ago at the village fete actually. She had glorious hair that caught in the sun and a smile that… ooh, it just got me," he rubbed his chest, "…right here. I have never met anyone like her, she… I can't stop thinking about her." Lucy pushed a fresh mug of coffee into his hands and Hugh, as if by remote, picked it up, taking a gulp. "She's heavenly and that's the biggest problem."

"What do you mean, mate, how can that be a problem? Sounds like you've got it bad already."

"She's tiny and dainty, I just want to pick her up, look after her, protect her. She's got a motorbike and when I saw her on it the first time, well, I wanted to…" he shot a look at Lucy, "…sorry, Lucy, I didn't mean to, you know." Lucy grinned.

"I presume we are talking about Suzanne? She is rather special, isn't she?" smiled Lucy.

"God, yes, oops, sorry, see what I mean, I just get all in a mess, my mouth gets confused. She came to the practise with her dog, Axis, he's a great dog. We had a laugh, she asked if I could help her with the rectory garden and I looked around the house with her too," he disappeared into his own memory, as if he was watching a private film of the event all over again. "Anyway, she's lovely and then, at her induction service, I felt so proud. I never go to church or anything like that, don't know much about it, to be honest, and I find myself wanting to go just to see her, but then I feel a hypocrite. See what a mess I'm in and worse than that, she's a vicar. I mean, don't they have rules about that sort of thing? I'm out of my depth here."

He looked at them both, appealing for help.

"Phew," Bertie let out a whistle, "…new territory for me, mate, that's a lot of questions. Bit awkward, I'd say."

"No, it's not. I think it's just wonderful," interrupted Lucy, giving Bertie a 'look', "Firstly, take the dog collar away and she is the same as any other female, don't let her career put you off. Just ask her out for coffee, relax, be yourself, get to know her and if she feels the same about you then it will all fall into place by itself. Don't let the church thing get in the way. Try asking her when she is not officially working, that will make it easier. Her dog collar isn't a barrier, it's just her job!" Lucy raised both hands, palms upwards. Hugh jumped up and hugged her.

"Lucy, you're brilliant. Thanks," he kissed her cheek, "…I must go, thanks, again."

"Glad to be of service."

Hugh grabbed his jacket and swept out, leaving Lucy and Bertie to stare at each other, mystified.

"I know how he feels," whispered Bertie as he closed in for a kiss.

"Hold on a minute, you still haven't told me what you were researching on the web earlier," she grinned at him, pulling back teasingly. She knew only too well that this was a 'Bertie' tactic to take her mind off what he was really doing, she mused.

"It can wait, but this can't," he swept her off her feet, heading for the stairs.

Chapter 31

Lucy and Bertie sat in front of Suzanne, Bertie shuffling nervously on his chair. He pushed a finger around his shirt collar, pulling at his tie that Lucy had insisted he wear. Suzanne scribbled in her diary, she put her pen down.

"Well, that's the date confirmed for your wedding day. Do you have any further questions?" she paused as Lucy and Bertie looked at each other. Bertie looked down at his hands, remaining quiet and Lucy could see from his face that the colour had drained away and he was twisting his fingers round and round. A trickle of fear rolled down her spine. This should be a happy day and here Bertie looked as if he would rather be anywhere else.

"I'm sure that I will think of lots later, but right now, we are just happy to set the date. Aren't we, Bertie... Bertie?" Bertie sat staring, looking shell shocked, he coughed to clear his throat, all eyes on him.

"Yes, of course, whatever you want," he coughed again, still struggling with his collar.

"Whatever *I* want," Lucy fought not to raise her voice, "Its' what we both want, isn't it?" she turned to Suzanne, her eyes betraying her. "Thank you so much, Suzanne, we'll be in touch." They stood up to leave. Suzanne paused, sucking in her breath, laying a hand on Lucy's arm.

"If you need to talk to me, I am available anytime." Lucy forced a wan smile as tears threatened to sting her eyes.

"Thanks, but we are fine, honestly." They left in silence, climbing into Lucy's car, they headed for home. Lucy drove the few short miles, her mind spinning, her hands hot and sweaty. She thought of a thousand things to say, but cancelled them all as the look on Bertie's face had answered all her questions. It was the why that bothered her. Bertie remained silent.

She was relieved that she had to go to work soon and wouldn't have time to talk about what she knew was the outcome. The wedding would be off, but she had sold her house and they were living together. She prayed silently that this whole thing was not a repeat of the fiasco with Lionel. What is wrong with me? She asked herself. She pulled into the farmyard. Bertie was still silently looking at his hands, having pulled his tie off and was now twisting it awkwardly as if he was trying to say something. The last thing she wanted right now was confrontation, so she took a deep breath, scared of his reply, putting off the inevitable, she turned to him.

"I've got to get changed for work, see you later," she jumped out of the car, heading for the door, head down, tears now flowing freely down her face.

"Lucy, wait…" she heard Bertie call behind her, but she ran on into the house and up the stairs, locking herself into the bathroom. Lucy hesitated in sending a text to Molly, even though she desperately wanted to talk to her, they had always supported each other no matter what, but this time, she decided just to fix a date for coffee. She applied fresh make-up, put on her uniform and made her way down the stairs. Bertie was waiting.

"Don't go yet, I need to talk to you," he looked pleadingly, but Lucy was having none of it. She was not going to risk messing up her make-up again. She grabbed her bag.

"Sorry, can't stop. Don't wait up…" she forced a quivering smile onto her lips and shot out of the door, leaving Bertie stranded. Driving to Poole, Lucy tried to think of her mum in waiting at the hospital; any subject other than Bertie backing out of the wedding.

She comforted herself with the knowledge that at least she knew now, but how embarrassing to tell everyone that the wedding is off. A sob escaped her and she quickly chastised herself, endeavouring to get back on track. She turned on the radio to drown out the twittering in her head, that nasty, negative voice that wouldn't shut up, laughing at her.

Make Your Own Kind of Music by Mamas and Papas was playing on the radio.

"Too bloody right," Lucy yelled back, "…but how?" She pulled into the car park and checked her watch. She was early, so she headed for the canteen and a strong black coffee, humming the song that she now couldn't get out of her head. The shift, for a change, passed without incident and in the small hours, very tired, Lucy made her way home. Thankfully, the outside light was on, but otherwise, all was peaceful. She crept quietly into the kitchen, kicked off her shoes and put the kettle on. There was a note on the table. Her hands trembling, Lucy picked it up, thoughts racing round her head. Had Bertie gone? Was this a note to say goodbye?

Lucy, my love, please wake me up when you come in. I want to talk to you to explain. I love you, Bertie xx.

She dropped the note down onto the table as a tear ran down her face. She rubbed at it crossly as if it were taunting her. Tea made, Lucy took her mug and trudged up to the bathroom. Finally, she got into bed.

"I'm still awake," whispered Bertie as he turned over to look at her, "I couldn't sleep till I could talk to you." He sounded sad, concern in his voice. Lucy wasn't sure she wanted to hear it, she was just so tired, and every bit of her body and her mind ached.

"It's okay," said Lucy, "nothing to explain. You've changed your mind, I get it, and you don't want us to get married. Now, can I please go to sleep? I am exhausted." Bertie shot up in bed.

"No. You're wrong, I do want us to get married. I love you so much, it's just that it hit me that there will be none of my family at our wedding," he paused and Lucy wasn't sure if she detected a sob, "… Mum gone. Dad, who knows where, my sister in Australia… I didn't think that it would bother me, but it does, it feels… weird." He fell quiet, dropping his eyes, picking at a bit of fluff on the duvet.

"Are you sure?" Lucy was stunned, "you're not just saying this because I thought that you had changed your mind… and… and you didn't want us to get married after all." Tears began to flow and Lucy couldn't stop them, she grabbed a tissue as her face crumpled, blowing her nose. Bertie threw his arms around her, pulling her to him.

"Oh, my darling, Lucy, you have no idea how much it means to me that you said 'yes' to be my wife. I am the proudest man on earth. I want nothing more than us to be together forever." He kissed her head, her eyes, her lips, caressing her and holding her close. Lucy sobbed, relief and exhaustion creeping over her, she fell asleep.

Over breakfast the next morning, Bertie had his laptop open, excitedly pointing at the screen, a spoonful of porridge aloft and honey dripping onto the table. "Come and look at this, Lucy, it's what I was looking at yesterday," he scooped up the remainder of his porridge, shovelling it into his mouth, pushing his dish to one side. "Did you know that there are dozens of flowers that you can eat? They would be great to add to my organic lunch dishes," he clicked onto the RHS site, "you can eat geraniums, roses, calendula, nasturtiums, pansy, lavender, the list just goes on and they are so beautiful. Just look at the stunning colours. There are reds, yellows, even blue flowers and I could grow them myself, wouldn't that be great?"

Lucy scraped some strawberry jam onto her toast and leant over his shoulder, a loving smile covered her face, she could feel how excited he was, yesterday forgotten.

"I've never eaten flowers before, but they do look good. Are you sure you will have time to grow them as well as everything else you want to do? I mean, you could just order some online when you need them, of course." Lucy poured out the coffee.

"That's it, what a good idea. I'll order them now and we can try them out, see what we like and then I'll know what to grow." He ordered a mixed box for next day delivery and turned to Lucy, his hand stroking the stubble on his chin. "I must look up some recipes to include flowers, try it out on you tomorrow night. What do you think?" He sounded excited and Lucy pushed all other questions to the back of her mind as she kissed his forehead.

"Great idea, why don't we invite Molly and Alistair too? I haven't had a good old gossip for ages and it would be the perfect opportunity for you to ask Alistair to be your best man," she leaned in for a kiss as Bertie grabbed her, pulling her onto his lap showering her with kisses. Lucy came up for air.

"Come on, we have things to do. I'm meeting Molly and Jessica for coffee," she reluctantly jumped up and began to load the dishwasher, Bertie quietly watching her.

"What?" she giggled.

"I have been doing some research and I want to know what you think to me making the café not just organic, but vegetarian and vegan. I want to put Trentmouth on the map. There's nothing else like it in Purbeck or even Dorset, as far as I can tell." He studied her face and Lucy stared at him for a long moment before she hugged him.

"That is a brilliant idea. Yes, I'm all for it. I don't want to spoil things, but we don't even have an architect yet. I know the council are happy in theory, but we need to make some plans, get things moving."

***

Lucy almost danced up the path to meet Molly at the garden centre; she was so ecstatically happy. She wanted to do some research of her own with regard to edible flowers, not wanting to poison anyone and had a notebook in her pocket and her head bursting to talk to Molly. They sat in the garden with two large cappuccinos, soaking up the still warm sun.

Talk inevitably turned to wedding plans and the lack of a suitable venue for the wedding breakfast.

"It's just that we wanted a quiet, simple wedding with Mum as she is," sighed Lucy. "I'm just grateful that she still has lots of good days and hope that our wedding will be one of them."

"I'm sure it will, you'll see," Molly squeezed her arm, "When do you want to go wedding dress shopping? We haven't long and you need to be making some decisions," Molly enthused.

"Actually, I have some holiday due, so I have booked a week off from Thursday. How are you fixed for Friday?" she sipped her coffee, watching Molly over the edge of her cup.

"Yes, I can do that. I'll ask Alice if she can look after Jessica. We can make a day of it."

"No…" Lucy shot her a quick look, "…bring Jessica, she's going to need a bridesmaid's dress the same colour as yours, as you are my matron of honour," they squealed and hugged each other, drawing startled looks from the other people in the garden. Both girls burst out laughing.

"Oh, hello, we wondered who was making all that noise. May we join you?" They both looked up to see Lady Isobel together with Maggie, carrying a tray of coffee. Lucy and Molly were surprised and delighted to have their company. Molly disappeared collecting two more coffees and four raspberry jam doughnuts. She had developed a taste for them recently and just could not turn one down. They sat chatting about the forthcoming wedding, including the lack of a suitable venue for just thirty people. Lady Isobel and Maggie looked at each other and smiled.

"Actually, we have been considering Trentmouth Manor as a wedding venue. We already have a chapel in the grounds, we would need a licence, of course, and the possibility of turning one room into a bridal suite. Now we couldn't do all that for your wedding, but would be delighted if you would like to have your reception with us." Lucy, momentarily speechless, welled up, she dabbed her eyes. "I mean, it wouldn't be too fancy, as time is short and bear in mind, we haven't done anything like this before… but if you are willing, we will do our best for you."

"That is just wonderful, I can't believe it, yes… yes, please."

***

The next week flew by in a frenzy of flowers, photographer, the cake ordered, before, finally, Lucy and Molly found themselves sitting in the drawing room at Trentmouth Manor, talking to Maggie and Lady Isobel.

"This would be our first wedding reception and although we hadn't quite seen ourselves as a wedding venue as yet, it would be a good practise to see if that is a future route for us," said Lady Isobel, turning to Maggie, "you're sure about this too, as the work is going to fall on your shoulders?"

"Quite sure, it's really exciting. Now let me get some tea and we can go over the details," Maggie disappeared, leaving Lucy amazed at the effort and concern for her happiness.

She hardly knew Lady Isobel, but here she was opening up her home for her wedding. Her heart swelled and tears were threatening to overcome her as she realised that her dreams were going to come true.

"Thank you so much, Lady Isobel, I am thrilled to bits to have our reception here. Maggie is amazing, isn't she?" Lucy was delighted.

Trentmouth Manor sat in a hollow, sheltered from the worst of the wind and weather. It was an imposing house with a long sweeping drive to the front. The entrance was under cover and was designed for a coach and horses to pull into so that guests could alight out of the rain. She could not think of a better place to be holding their reception. Even if they were guinea pigs, she didn't mind. Parts of the house dated back to the seventeenth century, especially the front entrance and hall, which was magnificent. Beyond that, the house had had many additions, although most of it had been closed up years ago, as staff had dwindled and costs had rocketed. Now, Lady Isobel resided in just a few rooms and had a part-time cook, a cleaner and groom.

"She is and please, call me Izzie. Ah, here's the tea then. I have things to do and will leave you with Maggie."

Chapter 32

Suzanne sat in her study, struggling with her Sunday sermon, turning her pen over and over.

Ideas had deserted her and she stared around the room, hoping for inspiration. She considered who would be sitting in front of her on Sunday morning, wondering how she was going to increase the numbers and still have a message for the stalwarts who have probably heard it all before. She tried to remember what she had been taught in college and not to try to force an idea, but to look around her, listen to what people said and the ideas would flow. "All very good in theory," she told the blank piece of paper in front of her. Added to that, she had her first wedding coming up in a few weeks and a christening this Sunday too. She sat back, staring out of the window, trying to clear some space in her head. She closed her eyes, thinking back to her days at the BBC, hoping she hadn't made a big mistake. She opened them again, still looking for inspiration and watched a crowd of starlings pecking in the grass. One flew off and all the others quickly followed, even though they probably had no idea why. The scene made her laugh, reminding her that birds don't worry about food, they always find some, neither do they worry about where to live, in fact, they just live their lives, in the moment.

Suzanne snatched up her pen, scribbling down the gist of her sermon as inspiration flowed.

The doorbell chimed and Suzanne glanced at her watch, she had been writing solidly for an hour and her appointment at eleven was on time. She dashed to the door.

"Alice, please come in. Let's grab a coffee and we can sit and chat." They air kissed each other and headed for the kitchen where Suzanne already had a tray laid up. Alice held out a carrier bag. "What's this, Alice?"

"Just a few muffins I made to go with our coffee," beamed Alice.

"Alice, you definitely shouldn't have. I can see that living in Trentmouth is not going to improve my waistline, but, thank you, they look delicious. Let's go into the sitting room." Alice followed her where they sat in the large bay window that overlooked the garden.

"Your garden is looking much improved, Suzanne, you must have been very busy."

Alice had taken up a position by the window to survey the garden. Suzanne watched her, wondering what might be coming next.

She took a deep breath, "More by chance really, Alice, I can pull out a few weeds, but Hugh has been mowing the lawns for me. You know what I could really do with is an expert to prune the trees and shrubs, tidy it up more." Suzanne smiled, hoping that Alice might suggest helping her. Alice ate her cake. "I was wondering if you might know someone, Alice. I would be willing to pay for a couple of hours' labour." Suzanne bit into her muffin; they were scrumptious and waited for Alice to have inspiration. She didn't have to wait long.

"Actually, my dear, Bertie does a lot of our garden, although with his new business venture and a wedding, of course, I'm not sure how much time he might be able to give you."

She drained her coffee. "I'm so thirsty, dear, any chance of another?" She smiled sweetly at Suzanne and Suzanne began to realise just how beguiling Mrs Warren was, she had been warned. However, up till now, she had rather relied on her. Maybe it was time to get things changed round and churned up a bit.

Suzanne dutifully made another pot of coffee, saying, "Let's take our coffee into my study, Alice, I want to show you something," she smiled, hiding the bombshell she was about to unleash onto poor Alice. "Please, sit here. Do you know anything about computers?"

"Of course, my dear, I'm not that ancient," she chuckled. "I send emails, browse the net and I do produce our list of services and notices every week," she sat back with a satisfied grin, arms folded. Suzanne's turn to smile, taking a deep breath.

"That is good news, Alice, as I want you to look at the websites of various other churches and for you to see how forward thinking they are. Look here at this one," she pointed to the screen, "... they have all the usual things listed up here, but then, they have an events page. This one is headed young people, music, help needed, invitations, it goes on and on and this church is packed. Look at these photos," Suzanne continued to scroll through pictures and information regarding a number of churches in the area and beyond.

"Well, yes, I can see what others do and we have our church fete every year," she said defensively.

"Oh, Alice, I know that and it was brilliant; a real credit to your organisational skills, but a once a year event is not enough. It brought in some much-needed funds, but we need bums on seats every Sunday. We need to think in what ways we can attract new members and make better use of the church hall, it is a much-underused resource," she let out a long sigh before picking up the mouse again and scrolling through more websites.

"We don't have enough members to be doing anymore, Suzanne. I think we have to accept the way things are." Alice shifted uneasily and Suzanne, detecting that Alice might have the wrong idea, she turned to look at her.

"Alice, I'm not expecting you to organise more events, but we need to start somewhere. Once we get a few new members, they will do things and hopefully, new ideas will invigorate the church."

"Yes, I see what you mean. So, if we had a breakfast meeting or a lunch club for the over 60's, that might attract more people?"

"That's right, Alice, you're getting the idea and it doesn't have to end there. We can maybe have a parent and toddler club and next year, a flower festival. We just need to inject some new thinking and people need to see that we are approachable, friendly, not the old-fashioned image that is often conjured up when people think of church."

"So, where do we start?" Alice was getting excited now and into the spirit of things, "I mean, this sounds all very well, but what can I do?" Alice raised both hands in the air in a hopeless manner. Just the response that Suzanne was looking for, she smiled.

"You, Alice, are going to be my kingpin," Suzanne grinned.

"I am? What do you mean by that?" Alice looked aghast, her hand clutching her chest.

"Well, you know everyone in this village. You can spread the word that things are changing and tell people to 'watch this space', get them excited. Ask people what they would like to see happening in the church hall? You get the idea, I'm sure," Suzanne swivelled on her chair again, clicking at the screen. "…and I am going to set up our first very own website."

"Ooh, this is exciting. I can do this for you and by the way, I will ask Bertie if he can manage to spend some time in your garden." She looked exalted, making Suzanne inwardly smile.

"Changing the subject entirely, if you don't mind, dear, but I know that Bertie and Lucy have kindly invited you to their reception up at Trentmouth Manor. I was wondering, but will you be asking Hugh to be your plus one at all?" Suzanne was shocked at the question, carefully aimed and delivered, but held herself back, remembering that she was warned about Alice and her matchmaking.

"Actually, Alice, my brother, Freddie, will be joining me. He seems to have found a new interest in me and my surroundings," she twinkled, teasing Alice.

"How nice, dear. It's just that I thought that Hugh had been helping you out rather a lot and I do believe he sat in the back of church last Sunday. I wonder why that was," Alice sat unfazed as she looked Suzanne in the eye, taking a sip of coffee.

"I can't imagine, Alice, except that he was sitting next to Molly and Alistair who were here because of the christening coming up," she paused, "…and I do believe that Hugh is to be one of the Godparents." She looked questioningly at Alice, with one eyebrow raised.

"Oh, yes, I had quite forgotten. I'm sure that was it. I think that I need to be going, as I have lots of news to impart to lots of villagers." Alice hurried out, leaving Suzanne mystified.

Grabbing the phone urgently, she pressed Freddie's number.

"Freddie? Sorry to bother you, but will you be my plus one at Bertie and Lucy's wedding, please?"

Chapter 33

The day of the christening dawned. Molly stretched and yawned, peering at the clock. It was early, still not quite light. All was quiet. She turned and watched Alistair who, still asleep, was gently making bubble and pop noises. She smiled at him lovingly. In the stillness of the morning, she laid thinking how very lucky they were, feeling grateful for lovely friends who rallied round. Bertie, she knew would be up, already preparing the buffet for later. Stella had insisted on making a cake, several in fact, Lucy would be laying up the tables and arranging flowers. Even Alice and George had come to the rescue, organising tables and chairs from the village hall and fixing up pink bunting that Alice had made herself. It was going to be a wonderful day – even the sun had promised to shine. She could hear the birds beginning to sing in the garden and as the light filtered through the curtains, Jessica was stirring, cooing to her toys. Molly slipped out of bed, pulling on her dressing gown she made her way to the kitchen, switching on the kettle, pulling cereals out of the cupboard and preparing breakfast for Jessica and tea for herself and Alistair. She made her way back up to the bedroom with a mug of tea, intending to wake Alistair, but he was sitting up, grinning at her.

"Morning, my darling," he whispered, "come and get back into bed for a cuddle." He held the covers open for her. Molly hesitated.

"I can hear Jessica awake and we haven't really got time," she smiled, putting the mugs down.

"There's always time for a cuddle," with that he took hold of her arm whisking her into bed beside him. "I want to hold my wife for a minute before the mayhem of the day takes over," he leaned in for a kiss and Molly automatically snuggled in to return his embrace. He smoothed her hair away from her face, "…you are so beautiful. I love you so much." Before she could reply, he slid her down the bed and he raised himself onto one elbow before kissing her again and making love. Molly stirred at the sound of Jessica crying, for a moment, she couldn't think what was happening or even what day it was, then the memory of the forthcoming day flooded her brain. She shot up in bed, nudging Alistair, tea cold, the sun high in the sky and they were due in church in less than two hours.

Somehow, they made it and Jessica looked adorable in her new daffodil yellow dress covered in daisies with a matching headband, even little white shoes with bows that Alice had made from leftover scraps of the dress material. The event went according to plan, with the church packed with friends, family and well-wishers, including some of George's old patients, people who brought their pets to Molly and newcomers to the village wanting to see what was going on. Reverend Suzanne took advantage of the crowd before her, taking the opportunity to tell people about events coming up and welcoming everyone, inviting them to come again. The garden at the farm looked resplendent and Molly felt guilty at not having helped out as she had promised, blushing as she recalled the reason why.

"You okay, Molly?" asked Lucy, "you look a bit flushed. Come and sit down. I bet you haven't had anything to eat yet, have you?" Molly had to admit that she had been talking to so many people that she hadn't had time to eat and only managed a cup of tea. Jessica was having a nap and so she sank down into a comfy cane chair, gratefully taking the plate of food that Lucy had brought her together with a glass of ice-cold chardonnay. She took a sip, instantly relaxing.

"We will stay and help you clear up, Lucy. It's the least we can do. I'm glad it's all over, actually. Your turn next for all the attention, a couple more weeks and you will be Mrs Sinclair," she tucked into a sandwich, throwing a grin at Lucy. "How are the plans going by the way? Is there anything that I can help you with?" Molly gratefully ate another sandwich.

"I have a final fitting for my dress this week and I would love some company if you can manage it."

"Hmm, yes, love to. What about the reception. I haven't seen Maggie to talk to, for a week or two. I know she was looking forward to preparing their first big 'do'. If all goes well and they launch the manor as a wedding venue, that can only bring a lot of business and visitors to Trentmouth."

"Yes, it could and Bertie and I want to talk to you both about something. Do you fancy staying for supper tonight and we can talk it over?"

"Great, we can catch up on all the gossip. I wonder if Alice would babysit for us."

"What's that, my dear, I thought I heard my name mentioned?" Alice had wandered over to them and sat herself down under the sun umbrella.

"Lucy has invited us to join them for supper and I was wondering if you would be able to babysit for us tonight if you're not busy, that is, Alice?"

"We would love to, Molly, dear. I must find Suzanne. I have been doing a job for her and need to report back. See you later, about seven?"

"Perfect," After a moment, she leaned into Lucy, "…bit mysterious, don't you think? I wonder what Alice is up to now?"

***

Later that evening, Molly and Alistair were on their way back up to the farm. Molly had changed into jeans and a comfy top. She slipped her finger along her waistband, wriggling in her seat.

"I must have eaten far too much earlier or these jeans have shrunk," she sighed as she undid the top button. "I wonder what Bertie has made for us?"

"I'm more interested in what they want to discuss with us, sounds intriguing. Didn't Lucy give you a clue at all?" quizzed Alistair.

"No, she didn't. Sorry. Alice came in halfway through the conversation and that sort of put an end to it," she wriggled some more before letting out a huff, "…that's it. I will have to go on a diet. These trousers are just too tight." Alistair couldn't help but laugh.

"You are gorgeous just the way you are… except maybe 'that extra inch' round your middle," he raised his eyebrows looking at her abdomen as Molly laid a gentle punch on his arm, grinning. Alistair pulled into the familiar farmyard to be greeted by an excited Rex. The hens scattered clucking loudly as Rex raced round and round. Molly looked around her old home, nothing had changed. Even the broken bit of gutter was still hanging off the end of the barn. The door opened and Lucy hugged Molly, pulling her in to the warmth of the kitchen.

Bertie shook hands with Alistair and they perused the contents of the fridge before settling on the local Piddle brew. Lucy picked up a bottle of red, waving it at Molly.

"What do you think to red tonight or would you prefer a white? I have one nicely chilled in the fridge," Lucy pulled open the fridge door.

"Red, I think, please, but I am going to cut back as I need to go on a diet. Do you think I can lose a stone in three weeks? Or I won't be able to get into my dress…" Molly said, pulling at her waistband again.

"A stone!" she tutted, "no chance. Anyway, you don't need to lose weight, just take Jessica out for a few walks, tighten up those tummy muscles."

"Is that your professional opinion, midwife Hamilton?"

"Certainly is, now let's get this open. Bertie has made a luscious caramelised onion and goat's cheese tart and I, for one, am hungry." They sat chatting about the day and laughing at the horrified look on Alice's face when she realised that Jessica was not wearing the long silk gown that both Alistair and Christopher had been christened in, not to mention, herself, when she was a baby. It was a family tradition, she had gasped. Molly had tried to explain that the white silk had yellowed with age and a few moths had had lunch in its creases, not to mention the musty smell. This only gained a harrumph from Alice as George lovingly patted her arm, defending Molly's position. Suzanne had been brilliant, allowing Rex to attend the service and although she drew the line at him being a godparent, he sat quietly watching the whole proceedings, being rewarded with a bone for good behaviour.

"So, come on Bertie, what's this big secret you want to discuss with us," asked Alistair, "we are intrigued," he drained his glass, looking quizzically from one to the other.

"Well…" said Bertie, scraping his chair back, "…first things first. Let me get my bottle of single malt that I have been saving and we will fill you in." Bertie retrieved the bottle and two glasses, he hesitated, "…you two girls want some?" They both shook their heads. Bertie poured two generous slugs and began to tell Alistair and Molly their plans for the café, including his idea for edible flowers. "So, what do you think?" he asked at length, looking from one to the other. Molly jumped in first.

"I think that it's fantastic, what a marvellous idea. My only reservation is that I can't see you doing all that on your own. What about staff? I mean, you couldn't possibly do it all yourself," she looked from one to the other, "…and I was thinking, where do we fit in? Is it all finalised or did you just want to bounce off a few ideas?" Molly threw Alistair a look and before Bertie could reply, she took another deep breath. "I mean, fill us in on the rest of your plans. It all sounds very exciting." Bertie smiled at them.

"Well, yes, we are only planning on a nine to five operation. So, coffee and cakes, light lunches and cream teas certainly to begin with, see how it goes."

"Yes, and I will be helping out when my shifts allow," said Lucy, "our biggest problem at the moment is finding an architect."

"What about funding?" cut in Alistair, "I know you have the insurance money, but that won't cover it."

"My dad is insisting on paying for all the work to be done, which is wonderful. After that, we are on our own."

"Hmm, knowing you, Bertie, I'm sure you have something already worked out. So, come on, what's the rest of the story?" Bertie replenished their glasses, sitting back to expand on their plans. When he finished, Alistair let out a low whistle as he turned his glass round and round. He looked at Molly, his eyes quizzing hers and she nodded to him in reply. Molly could guess what he was thinking and would support what he might say next. Alistair was very shrewd and knew a good business plan when he heard it. He and Bertie had worked together for years and knew each other pretty well.

"Are you, by any chance, looking for a business partner, because if you are, we are in?" a smug smile spread over Bertie's' face as they proceeded to thrash out a deal. Finally, he put out his hand.

"Partners," they both announced, "this calls for a proper drink," he jumped up to collect a bottle of champagne and taking off the cork with a loud bang, bubbles spilled out as they all laughed.

"I've had an idea about an architect," said Molly, "I'm sure that Suzanne told me her brother was an architect. I know he lives in Oxford, but he might be interested. You could give her a call." They clinked glasses, all thoughts as to who was driving home forgotten.

Chapter 34

Molly flopped down in the office, the surgery was full. Her morning had been fraught from the start. Poor Jessica was teething, keeping Molly wide awake most of the night. When she finally nodded off, her alarm rang, giving her quite a fright. Jessica safely delivered to the nursery with instructions regarding her teething, Molly felt more relaxed. It didn't last long.

She surveyed the room, forcing a smile as she took in the mayhem with a sweep of her eyes.

"Molly, oh, please, can you look at Sooty. He's not at all well," Mrs Drummond looked up at Molly, her bloodshot eyes ringed red, there was a drip on the end of her nose ready to fall, making Molly recoil a feeling of nausea rising up to her throat. She handed the tissue box to Mrs Drummond, "Thank you, dear," she sniffed, removing the offending drip.

"Give me a minute, Mrs Drummond. I just need to get myself sorted out and I'll be with you. Okay?" Molly disappeared, heading for the bathroom and switching the kettle on as she passed the kitchen. What seemed like hours later, she sat by the door, coffee in hand.

Hugh, his head resting back on the door frame, eyes closed with the sun on his face, chuckled.

"We wanted more business, so no complaints from me," he let out a sigh, "I noticed you didn't charge old Mrs Drummond again today. We can't keep doing freebies, as much as I understand her age and you not wanting to charge her." Molly stiffened.

"She's been coming in ever since I opened and I know that Sooty is about sixteen or even seventeen. All I did was encourage her to keep him safe and warm. He'll probably be gone by the weekend, so I am not charging her for that," she snapped at him. Hugh opened his eyes and sat up.

"Hey, sorry, I didn't mean to upset you. Are you alright, this isn't like you at all," Hugh stroked her arm as if she were an ill pet herself. Molly attempted a smile as tears welled up, dribbling down her cheek.

"Hey, hey, come on, what is wrong? Are you ill? Please tell me," he pleaded.

Molly took a gulp of her coffee, drying her eyes. Her thoughts brought back her lack of sleep, her aching back and the thought of poor Sooty dying. It was nonsense really; she had put many pets to sleep over the years, so why Sooty was any different – she had no idea. She turned to Hugh seeing the concern on his face.

"I'm fine, honestly, promise," she squeezed his arm, "…but I am really tired. Jessica is teething and kept me awake half the night. I know she's suffering too, poor lamb. I'll be alright after a coffee and a rest. I don't suppose there are any biscuits left by any chance?"

"That's better, you had me worried for a minute. I'm sure we have biscuits left," he put his cup down by the door, getting up in search of sustenance. Molly closed her eyes, gaining a few seconds breather. Hugh came back bearing gifts of not only bourbons, but Jaffa cakes too.

Molly reached out, taking one of each.

"Hmm, that's better already," she picked up her mug, taking a sip, "Hugh… I've been meaning to ask you for days. How things with you and Suzanne are? Have you asked her out yet?" she turned a searching gaze on him. Hugh gulped, nearly choking and spluttered, making Molly smile as attention was cleverly diverted away from her and her problems.

"Well," he said, after recovering his composure, "I have talked to her a few times and taking your advice, kept things simple. I even made her a coffee one day and she sat where you are now, but…" he hesitated.

"You haven't actually asked her out to dinner yet," Molly finished for him.

"Well, no, but I am building up to it. I've been finding out a lot about her though," he turned to face Molly, "did you know what happened to her parents? That must have been devastating."

"Yes, she told me all about it and speaking of parents, when is your mum coming to stay?"

"Oh, well, actually she will be down when it is Bertie and Lucy's wedding and they have kindly included her. She is so excited, been shopping and all that," he rolled his eyes, "I told her to wear what she bought for my wedding, as its new, but she wouldn't hear of it. Said she had to buy something else as that outfit was too expensive! I don't understand women," he threw his hands up in exasperation, shaking his head. Molly chuckled.

"I've been meaning to ask you about your mum. What does she do? I realise, I don't even know her name." Molly crunched into her biscuit, wiping the crumbs from her lap onto the patio.

"Tell you what, as its lunchtime, why don't I collect our sandwiches and I'll fill you in." Hugh stood up.

"Better than that, you lock up and we can go next door and have a proper sit down," she suggested, pushing the last bit of luscious orange and dark chocolate into her mouth.

"Great. Give me a minute and I'll be there." Molly unlocked the barn door; it was warm and snug, she breathed in the peace. It was almost the end of September; the leaves were just beginning to turn. She loved the autumn with its dazzling display of red, gold, crunchy browns, sizzling oranges and berries of every hew. She pulled open the fridge and put out salad and the remains of the leek tart she had made the night before. Hugh knocked on the door and came in carrying his little parcel of sandwiches.

"Come and sit down. I have elderflower cordial if you would like some," she said, reaching up for two glasses.

"Please. I wasn't expecting all this, but I have to say that it is very welcome. I miss my mum and her cooking." Molly looked up in surprise.

"Really, tell me more," they sat down. Molly served up the tart and they settled into lunch; sandwiches forgotten. Hugh seemed pleased to talk about his childhood and clearly loved his mum.

"Her name is Emma and she is the best mum. She has always supported me, even if she didn't always agree with my plans. She never interfered and I think that she is still worried about me down here, wanting to send me food parcels," Molly laughed.

"What is it about Mums and boys?" she shook her head, thinking about her own mum.

Sandra was nothing like Hugh's mum, Emma. "So, what is she doing now?"

"She didn't get many qualifications at school, probably why she is so proud of me now," he paused, staring into the distance for a moment, "…anyway, she just has a job helping out in the Cherry Tree café overlooking the village green back home. She makes sandwiches and scones mainly, waiting on tables and washing up, that sort of thing. She enjoys it, saying she doesn't want to do anything else, but her greatest love is painting. She loves her art, always out walking in the countryside with her watercolours. I've told her she's good enough to sell her paintings, but she thinks that no one else would like them and I only do because she is my mum," he scooped up the remainder of his fruit and ice cream, dropping the spoon into his bowl. "That was delicious, Molly, thank you." Molly couldn't help but smile, he reminded her so much of Bertie.

"I am looking forward to meeting your mum. She sounds lovely and I bet she would get on with Alice, no problem," Molly gave a knowing smile at the thought.

"Oh, I hope so, it would be good for her to make a friend, as she only comes out of her shell in the café where everyone thinks she is a real chatterbox, but that is only a façade."

"When does she arrive?"

"Saturday, I wanted her to settle in and meet a few people before the big day. Right…" he glanced at his watch and pushed his chair back, "I must go and open up again, you stay here for a bit and have a rest. I'll call you if it gets really busy." Hugh returned to the surgery and Molly sat down on the couch and instantly fell fast asleep.

Chapter 35

Molly stood in the arrivals area at Heathrow with Lucy. They had concocted an elaborate plan, telling Alistair and Bertie that they were having a girlie spa day up in London and hitting the shops ready for the big day. The boys thought that it was a good idea and were looking forward to a couple of days free to catch up on the chess tournament they had been playing for ever and Alice was more than delighted to have Jessica all to herself. So, all was set, except that Molly did not feel right. She couldn't understand why she was feeling so tired and had frightened herself when she snapped at Alistair more than once and was actually relieved to have this time away. Being so stressed and uptight when normally she was quite laid back just didn't feel right, wondering if she should have a check-up at the doctor's. She turned to Lucy only to see her scanning the arrivals board, looking a little concerned.

"Looks like we will have a longer wait. Her plane is delayed only by about half an hour. I could do with a coffee, want one?" Lucy turned to Molly, "you look tired, come on, let's sit down." Lucy collected two cappuccinos, plus a couple of Danish pastries and caught up with Molly who had slid into a corner booth near the window, but still in sight of the arrivals board.

"So, tell me all about Vicky. You've met her and I feel out of my depth here," she took a sip of her coffee, a white streak of foam sticking to her top lip. Molly licked it away. "That's just what I needed." She placed her cup down, turning her full attention to Lucy pulling sticky bits from the corner of her Danish.

"Well, Vicky is really nice. She welcomed me with open arms when we turned up in Adelaide. She looks just like Bertie. It's uncanny and when I got in touch with her about coming for the wedding, she was thrilled. It's a pity she has to come on her own, but they just couldn't afford for the whole family to come and what with school and work commitments, at least she is coming." Lucy bit into her Danish, "She does the books for John, who has a successful plumbing and heating business and looks after the children, of course." Molly nodded, tucking the last few crumbs into her mouth, feeling better already.

"So, what else does she do? I'm guessing volunteering at the school, am-dram or an absolute whizz in the kitchen, am I right?" she laughed.

"No, sorry, but you're nearly right. She does do some volunteer work in a local thrift shop; no am-dram, I'm afraid, but she makes her daughters' ballet costumes and most of her own clothes too."

"I knew it," grinned Molly, "…everyone is a super mum except me. I mean, look at Stella and now Vicky. I feel positively lazy," she let out a stilted laugh, "…and what are the children's names again?"

"Natalia and Beatrix and they are so cute. Let me show you some pictures." She pulled out her phone and scrolled through to find some pictures of the family, showing them to Molly. An announcement came over the loud speaker, making them sit up and listen. Vicky's plane was in and they scrambled back to the arrivals gate to look for her. She walked through and Lucy waved to her. Molly's mouth dropped open, realising she should have taken more notice of what Lucy was saying. Instead of the dumpy little housewife that Molly had conjured up in her mind here was a tall, slim, beautiful woman, who did look just like her brother. Molly was introduced and they were soon heading towards the exit with Lucy and Vicky chatting away, catching up on the wedding plans and discussing the arrangements for keeping her existence a secret from Bertie till Saturday.

They drove back to Dorset, with Vicky asking a million questions and Molly too wanting to find out as much as possible, not only about the family, but life in Adelaide too.

They finally pulled onto the drive at the Warrens', Molly having texted George the expected time of arrival to be met by George and Alice eager to meet Vicky, bombarding her with questions, excited at the secret they were involved with. Molly stole upstairs to check on the sleeping Jessica before joining everyone in the snug and a delicious array of crumpets and muffins, including a bottomless pot of tea.

Vicky apologised for yawning, she had not been able to sleep on the plane and was feeling jet lagged. She wanted to call home before trying to get some sleep as well as take a shower. Arrangements were made for the next few days. Molly collected Jessica and they headed for home.

"How on earth we are going to keep Vicky a secret from Bertie?" asked Molly.

"To be honest, I've so much to do before Saturday, I don't think it will be too difficult and Bertie has no reason to visit Alice and George. I did have an idea though," she cocked her head towards Molly.

"Oh, yes! What cunning scheme have you come up with this time?" Molly laughed knowing her friend so well, remembering the time she had organised a surprise weekend in the Cotswolds and it rained the whole time, not to mention the many days out to West Bay and Lyme Regis. She was full of fun and adventure.

"The thing is I have booked us all in for a manicure over at that new retreat. Alice will bring Vicky and we can then all have lunch together," she clapped her hands with glee.

"Brilliant…" chuckled Molly, "…and we can all get together again in the evening, as I have a hen night planned, so no boys and that will help us all to get to know Vicky better."

"Oh, dear, nothing too scary, I hope. I don't want to wake up covered in paint or pink hair or stranded on Round Island in the middle of Poole harbour as other brides have done," she looked aghast.

"No, would I do anything like that to you… although the pink hair does sound interesting," Lucy laid a light thump on her arm. "My biggest problem was getting Vicky to the local pub, as I couldn't risk anyone seeing her and speaking to Bertie, so I have had to change our plans somewhat. Suzanne has invited us all to the rectory. It's big enough and much more private and probably more fun too."

"Molly that's brilliant. Yet again, you are a genius. It will be fun and I couldn't wish for a better hen night."

Chapter 36

Friday morning and Molly, having made an appointment at short notice, sat in the doctor's waiting room with a squirming Jessica. Alice walked in. Molly's face dropped, of all the people she didn't want to see and in she walked.

"Molly, dear, is everything alright? I wasn't expecting to see you in here. I've come for my usual blood test. Shall I look after Jessica for you?" she smiled sweetly at Molly; her arms open to receive the happy baby now excited to see her.

"No. No, thanks, it's Jessica who needs to see the doctor," she lied her cheeks feeling hot, "she's teething. I just wanted to make sure that's all it is. What with this meningitis scare and everything…" Molly stuttered, hoping that that sounded convincing.

"Quite right, dear, one can't be too careful where babies are concerned. Shall I wait for you and we can go for a coffee?" Alice quizzed her head on one side before claiming a cuddle from Jessica who had her arms out to her Granny.

"As lovely as that would be Alice, I can't today, what with the wedding tomorrow, I just do not have the time." That was the last thing her mind, but plausible and Alice accepted it.

"What a pity. Never mind, perhaps we can do it next week?" Alice kissed Jessica and began talking to her in baby language just as the nurse came out, calling her name. Alice handed Jessica back and followed the nurse down the corridor, much to Molly's relief. An hour later, Molly was at home, Jessica was fast asleep, Alistair was still at work and Vicky was sitting in her courtyard with a glass of ice cold Pimm's. Molly took her opportunity for a chat.

"So, I have been dying to ask you, what made you move to Australia and what's it like? I want to know everything," said Molly. Vicky let out a laugh.

"It's a long story really. I'm sure that Bertie will have filled you in on our parents and, well, Bertie and I drifted apart after that and when I met John, he had always wanted to emigrate to Australia and I suppose I thought 'why not'. So, we went with the idea of staying a couple of years, that's all. Then the business took off and I had the children and we settled into a very comfortable lifestyle. There's a different attitude out there, people have the idea that you work to live life to the full, which is not difficult. Sadly, here it seems as though that people live to work and to pay the mortgage. To us, that's mad," she exclaimed. Molly was wistful, thinking how idyllic it sounded. "Then there's the lovely sunshine, the beach on our doorstep. Australia is a huge country and so diverse, we love it and would never come back," she sipped her Pimm's.

"I have to admit; I would love to visit one day. It sounds fantastic and the endless sunshine is enticing too," Molly declared wistfully.

"Please, come and visit, stay with us. We would love to have you." There was a clatter at the front door, making Molly jump and instantly panic that whoever it was might wake Jessica. She excused herself and opened the door to find Bertie stood grinning on the doorstep, with Lucy behind him, her arms raised in the air, mouthing '…sorry'.

"What a surprise, come in, Jessica is asleep. I'm glad you popped in, actually," she said, quickly thinking on her feet, "there is someone I want you to meet."

"Oh," said Bertie, following Molly out to the courtyard garden. She stood to one side and let Bertie pass. Vicky stood up arms outstretched, grinning at her baby brother.

"Vicky," he screamed, "I… I can't believe it," he rushed to her grabbing her and squeezing her tightly, lifting her off her feet, "when did you get here, where are the family? I just can't believe you're here." Molly gestured to Lucy that they go inside and leave them to it.

"You know, I think it's better that Bertie saw Vicky today. Tomorrow in the church might just have been too much for him; he is so overwhelmed," declared Lucy as tears threatened to add to the emotions already welling inside.

"Yes, you're right. Anyway, how come you were over here? Is there something I've forgotten?" Molly quizzed.

"No, not at all. Bertie has been so fidgety and he wanted to see Alistair about his speech and I just couldn't stop him. However, now I'm here, is there anything else to do? Apart from the rehearsal tonight, of course."

"After the rehearsal, do you want to eat here tonight with Vicky, of course, before you go to your mum's and Bertie stays here with us?" asked Molly, "I've invited Suzanne and Freddie too, it will be fun."

"Great. Yes, why not, I have butterflies playing with my butterflies at the moment and I could do with something to take my mind off things."

***

Trentmouth Manor was resplendent, festooned with white and pink ribbon and bunting to match the flowers in Lucy's bouquet. Maggie had arranged for strings of lights to be placed all the way up the drive to guide people to the front of the house. Inside, a trail of pink rose petals led to the dining room, their scent filling the air. Stella had made the cake as promised and it was a stunning creation, not your usual three tiers with a bride and groom on top, but rather a cake shaped like the farm house, with Bertie in wellies tending the allotment and Lucy in uniform as near to a midwife as she could make it. Everyone admired it. She had even put rows of cabbages and carrots, a washing line, even Rex by the farm door. It was a masterpiece, perfect. Speeches over, Alistair could relax and the music began. Maggie had managed to find a local group who played a little jazz and some easy listening music – just what they all needed.

Lucy welled up, she grabbed a tissue, dabbing her eyes, careful not to smudge her makeup. She gazed around the room; it was magnificent. Lady Isabel and Maggie had really gone to town on making this the best day ever. Her mum, although quiet, had enjoyed herself and her dad had never looked happier. Her heart swelled as she watched Bertie thrilled to have his sister here with him. Even Alistair had surprised everyone with tales of their London life.

Bertie absently squeezed her hand, love coursed through her veins, making her long to be alone with him. She squeezed his hand and turning, he whispered.

"I love you, Mrs Sinclair, and I can hardly wait to get you all to myself," he leaned in for a tender kiss, exciting every cell in her body. *It had been a perfect day,* she thought, her face aching from all the smiling.

***

Alistair sat down and turning to Molly, he said, "I have one last task to perform. Lucy wants to throw her bouquet, so I need to gather all the single girls together," he stood to corral the waiting females. Lucy stood in the middle of the dance floor, her back to the gathered throng of giggling girls, all excited to join in the fun. Alistair called.

"Ready? One, two, three," Lucy threw her flowers high in the air and the girls began jumping and screaming to catch it, but it was Maggie who claimed the prize. Everyone clapped and gathered around her. Alistair returned to Molly, looking relieved. Jessica was fast asleep in her pram.

"How she can sleep with all this noise going on, I do not know," he laughed. "What did you want to tell me?" he asked, finally turning his attention to Molly.

"You know I went to the doctor's the other day?" Alistair immediately looked concerned, taking hold of her hand.

"What is it? Please tell me you're not ill," she smiled at his anxious face.

"No, I'm not ill... I am pregnant," Alistair sat staring for a moment, then he jumped up and kissed her and hugged her.

"Molly, I love you so much. I am the happiest man in the world," he said before kissing her again.

The End